UNDER ONE SKY

ZOË FOLBIGG

B
Boldwood

First published in 2018 as *The Distance*. This edition first published in Great Britain in 2025 by Boldwood Books Ltd.

Copyright © Zoë Folbigg, 2018

Cover Design by JD Smith Design Ltd.

Cover Images: Shutterstock

The moral right of Zoë Folbigg to be identified as the author of this work has been asserted in accordance with the Copyright, Designs and Patents Act 1988.

All rights reserved. No part of this book may be reproduced in any form or by any electronic or mechanical means, including information storage and retrieval systems, without written permission from the author, except for the use of brief quotations in a book review. This book is a work of fiction and, except in the case of historical fact, any resemblance to actual persons, living or dead, is purely coincidental.

Every effort has been made to obtain the necessary permissions with reference to copyright material, both illustrative and quoted. We apologise for any omissions in this respect and will be pleased to make the appropriate acknowledgements in any future edition.

A CIP catalogue record for this book is available from the British Library.

Paperback ISBN 978-1-83678-766-2

Large Print ISBN 978-1-83678-767-9

Hardback ISBN 978-1-83678-765-5

Ebook ISBN 978-1-83678-768-6

Kindle ISBN 978-1-83678-769-3

Audio CD ISBN 978-1-83678-760-0

MP3 CD ISBN 978-1-83678-761-7

Digital audio download ISBN 978-1-83678-762-4

This book is printed on certified sustainable paper. Boldwood Books is dedicated to putting sustainability at the heart of our business. For more information please visit https://www.boldwoodbooks.com/about-us/sustainability/

Boldwood Books Ltd, 23 Bowerdean Street, London, SW6 3TN

www.boldwoodbooks.com

To Mark, Felix and Max.
My heart beats to your names.

1

MARCH 2018, TROMSØ, NORWAY

So, ro, lillemann, nå er dagen over... Sleep tight, little one, now the day is over... Cecilie can't stop the blasted lullaby from spinning around her head, twinkling like a hanging mobile doing revolutions above a sleeping baby. *Alle mus i alle land, ligger nå og sover...* The song is rotating calmly and methodically in Cecilie's brain, distracting her from the couple sitting in front of her as they wait for her to take their order. It is also distancing her from The Thing That's Happening Today that she's been dreading for weeks, hoping someone will put a stop to it or change their mind.

The lullaby must have been swirling in Cecilie's head since she sang it in a quiet corner of the library this morning; to mothers with grey crescent moons clinging to their lower lashlines; to fathers, over the moon to be enjoying their parental leave in a much more relaxed way than they think their partners did. Mothers and fathers and gurglers all joined in with Cecilie to sing nursery rhymes in the basement of the library, but now those songs and the sweet and happy voices are taunting her.

So, ro, lillemann...

Cecilie thinks of the large print above the fireplace in the living room at home. The room is an elegant haven of greys, browns and whites, dominated by a long, wooden dining table that stands out against the modern touches of the alternate grey and sable plastic Vitra chairs around it. It's a table where everyone is welcome for heart-to-hearts and hygge at Christmas, although most of the time Cecilie eats breakfast there alone. She likes the grey chairs best and always chooses to sit on one of those while she eats her soda bread smeared with honey and stares out of the window, to the vast and sparse garden beyond. On the white wall above the fireplace hangs a print of a static Alexander Calder mobile that her mother Karin picked up on a trip to London. 'Isn't it wonderful, Cecilie?' she exclaimed, her blue eyes lighting up against the silver of her bobbed hair as Cecilie's brother and his boyfriend lifted the black matte frame onto the mantelpiece with a heave.

'Wonderful,' concurred Morten, the partner of Cecilie's twin brother Espen, as he pushed his glasses up his little snub nose. 'The beauty and intelligence is astounding,' he added. 'I just wish I could see it in motion.'

Karin nodded with vigour; Espen had already left the room.

Cecilie looked at the print dreamily, her pale green eyes gazing up at the black Vertical Fern, while it didn't oscillate as it had in the gallery, or might have done in a breeze. Still, Cecilie imagined herself fluttering up to the largest of its black fronds to see what it would look like to gaze down at her mother and Morten's faces from above. Cecilie had a knack for drifting out of position on a whim or a daydream and seeing the world from above.

Karin, a pragmatist and a politician, found it hard to understand her otherworldly daughter.

'Cecilie?' Karin had urged.

Cecilie crinkled her nose and snapped back into the room with a blink.

'It's wonderful, Mamma,' she agreed, although she couldn't fathom why her mother had bought an inanimate print of something that ought to be in gentle movement. It seemed so unlike her. Karin Wiig was the least static person Cecilie knew.

'Well, yes,' confirmed Karin with authority. 'They were just so stunning, you really ought to go to London and see them in motion before the exhibition ends,' she said with a wave of her hand, although everyone knew she was really only talking to Morten. Even if Espen had still been in the room to hear, he was too wrapped up in his life at the i-Scand hotel on the harbour to bother with the inconvenience of a weekend break, and Cecilie had never travelled to a latitude below Oslo, which was something a diplomat and an adventurer like Karin couldn't understand.

'Why is your sister so happy to stay in one place?' she once asked Espen in despair.

'Perhaps Cecilie's daydreams take her to better places than a flight ever could, Mamma,' Espen had replied.

So, ro, lillemann...

The flash of the frond in her mind awakens Cecilie, and she wriggles her inert feet inside her black Dr Martens boots. The lullaby evaporates and disappears, and Cecilie is back with the couple sitting in front of her, at their usual table.

'Pickle, are you all right?' asks Gjertrud, her kindly weathered face looking up at Cecilie. 'It's just Ole asked you three times for the spiced Arctic cloudberry cake, but you seem a little... in the clouds yourself today, my dear.'

'Oh, I'm so sorry, so much to think about...' Cecilie replies as she writes *cloudberry* onto a pad in a wisp of ink.

Gjertrud wonders how much Cecilie can possibly have to

think about as she studies the waitress's face; her eyebrows arch to her temples, framing pale green eyes that usually flash with the iridescent brightness of a dragonfly's wing – only, today, they are dulled by a film of pondwater. Her blonde hair is pulled into twists of rope, piled at the back of her head, exposing the love heart shape of her face.

Gjertrud's round, purple cheeks flush with the heat of coming indoors when it's cold outside, and she gazes at Cecilie and wonders what goes on inside that dreamy brain of hers. She can't be that busy in her quiet life here in this quiet town. She doesn't even have children like Gjertrud and Ole's daughters did by the time they were Cecilie's age.

Gjertrud and Ole see Cecilie every afternoon for coffee and cake at the Hjornekafé teashop after their post-lunch walk. They always take the table with four chairs against the far wall so they can look out of the large expanse of glass onto the small backstreet of the Arctic harbour town. Each window panel has a little etching in the middle, an illustration of the exterior of the quaint corner cafe, the same illustration as the one on the cover of the menus Cecilie hands out. Gjertrud always chooses a seat so she can sit with her back to the wall, to hold court and see everything going on in the Hjornekafé. Ole sits facing his wife, although he can see cafe life back to front in the rectangles of the mirrors on the wall in front of him. Gjertrud and Ole use the vacant wooden chairs next to them to pile their layers of hats, scarves, gloves, jumpers, crampons and duck-down coats onto while they rest their walking poles in the corner between the wall and the floor-to-ceiling window. Ole always orders a *kaffe* and the *kake* of the day, whichever the never-present cafe owner Mette made most recently. Gjertrud always has a pot of tea 'and nothing else, thank you' – which means she will eat half of Ole's cake, until he protests so much that she concedes to ordering a slice of her own.

'One *kaffe* and spiced Arctic cloudberry cake for you, Ole, and your usual pot of tea, Gjertrud?'

'Yes, just a tea, thank you, my dear.'

'Oh, have your own cake, woman! You will anyway, after eating half of mine.' Ole's grey curls are matted from the woolly hat he recently took off and launched onto the chair next to him. He turns to Cecilie with bemused, irritated eyes as small as currants. 'One and a half pieces of cake for my wife, every day! If she just ordered her own now, she would have a piece for her and I would have a whole piece for me. Why is this notion so difficult to comprehend, heh, Cecilie?'

Cecilie raises a diplomatic eyebrow and doesn't say anything.

'I only want a forkful, Ole. Why do you have to be such a stingy sausage?' Gjertrud's ruddy cheeks rise and she lets out a mischievous chuckle. A bell above the door rings as two young backpackers walk in. Their eyes widen as they see the cakes in the small climate-controlled glass cabinet on the counter, and they take off their mittens excitedly.

Cecilie looks up. Ordinarily, she would be pleased to see young tourists walk in; a chance to improve her English, to learn some more modern words and slang. But today she isn't. She doesn't see the point. Cecilie no longer feels the desire to learn new ways of saying that something is wicked, ace or sick; or to practise her they're, there and theirs any more.

Cecilie nods as she writes down an order she and fellow staff Henrik and Stine know by heart anyway, although today just Cecilie and Henrik work a sleepy afternoon shift. 'Take a seat, I'll be right over,' Cecilie says to the couple at the counter as she tucks her pen behind her ear, and it disappears into a cascade of heavy hair. Somehow, Cecilie can tell that these tourists are

Canadian, even before she sees the maple leaf sewn onto the North Face daypack on the young man's back. She wonders what brought them here; where in the world they have been already. Might they have seen his hometown too?

The Hjornekafé manager, Henrik, has already started making the drinks. He exchanges a look with Cecilie, as they usually do when Gjertrud and Ole have their little tussles, only today Cecilie isn't rolling her eyes and smiling warmly. Today, her face is tense and terse, her eyes dulled, as she makes her way to the cake display cabinet at the end of the counter. The dark and rickety wooden furniture is brightened by the mirrors on the walls in the modest cafe space, and what little is left of the spring daylight streams in through the floor-to-ceiling window façade to the street.

The Canadians marvel at the wrought-iron latticework trimming the ceiling and scrape their chairs back to sit down. The noise of wood dragging on wood tears through Cecilie's brain but is drowned out by another rotation of *So, ro, lillemann*.

Cecilie looks at her watch. It is 3.18 p.m. She silently counts backwards as she raises the thumb and four fingers on her left hand and the thumb and index finger on her right hand. Seven. Always counting back seven. She feels a blow to her abdomen and recedes to take it as she bends down to pick up a tray from under the counter. Cecilie's not sure if she feels hungry, winded or heartsick, but she rises up with the tray, standing to stay strong. She takes out the spiced Arctic cloudberry cake, made by Mette at her home this morning. Bright orange berries burst with pride atop vanilla cream, layered three times on sponge swathed in playful cloudberry-coloured jam. Flecks of nutmeg, cinnamon and cloves pepper the pristine pale crumb. Arctic berries shimmer golden and warm surrounded by spices. The orange hues remind Cecilie of photographs she's seen in books in the library and on the internet, of a place a world away, where buildings are painted ochre and terracotta; where doorways bask in a shade of sunshine she has never seen for herself. Cecilie carves out a square of cake with a knife and places it on a vintage floral plate that doesn't go with the black and white cups Henrik is preparing the drinks in. Nothing matches in this hotchpotch corner of the world, but that doesn't matter. Customers slink in reliably for a quiet slice of cake between hiking to the world's northernmost cathedral or summiting the mountain ledge in the Fjellheisen cable car by day, and chasing the Northern Lights at night.

With heavy feet and a heavy heart, Cecilie plods into the cavernous kitchen out the back to the freezer. She takes out a tub of blackcurrant ice cream and thoughtfully curls a quenelle to accompany the cake. The ice cream at the Hjornekafé is made by Mette's daughter and Cecilie's best friend, Grethe, who owns the ice cream parlour on the high street. Ice cream sells surprisingly well in these parts, and Grethe churns the best.

Henrik, a bookish man with round glasses and floppy brown hair parted in the centre, places the pot of tea, cup of coffee and two glasses of icy tap water next to the cake plate on the tray. Cecilie collects two forks and clinks them down next to the plate, knowing she will be coming back for another slice in a few minutes anyway. She walks around to the front of the counter, gives the Canadian tourists two menus with the small illustration of the Hjornekafé on the front from her shaky hands, and picks up the tray from the counter to take it to Gjertrud and Ole at their end of the cafe. As she walks the short distance to the back wall, Cecilie's mouth dries, her hands shake and the tray feels like the weight of an iceberg as it releases from her pale grip. She looks down and sees it fall in slow motion beneath her to the floor, smashing onto the ground in hot and cold shards.

The vintage cake plate smashes, sending flowers flying, splatted and smeared with varying shades and textures of orange and purple and cream, all over Cecilie's boots. Hot tea and coffee scald Cecilie's legs in her pale blue jeans as she lets out a little gasp of pain and embarrassment. The Thing That's Happening Today, that Cecilie is dreading, is actually happening and there's nothing she can do about it.

At that precise moment, eight thousand nine hundred and nine kilometres away, eyes widen and pupils shrink.

Hector Herrera has woken with a start, to a crash, on the morning of his wedding day.

2

MARCH 2018, XALAPA, MEXICO

'What the fuck... What are you doing, *Gallegita*?' Hector murmurs as he sits up slowly from under the bedsheet. His wide trapezius rises from solid shoulders as he rubs cinnamon-flecked eyes with his palms, moving sleep out and up into dark brown soft curls that kiss his temples and rest gently above his forehead. When Hector is animated, his eyes are wide, flirtatious and impassioned, but in his resting state they are as thoughtful and earnest as a pleading revolutionary's. Right now they are in transition as his fuzzy brain tries to figure out where in the world he is. In the doorway of their bedroom, Hector's tiny bride-to-be drapes herself against the frame, bottle in one hand, champagne flute in the other, and curses the broken glass fizzing at her bleeding feet.

'*Joder!*'

'What was that?' Hector says, no longer alarmed but puzzled by the smash as he reclines against the bare wall behind him. The rough spikes of the whitewashed plaster press into his shoulders, taking the focus off the thumping in his head.

'Not "was". What "is" that, baby,' Pilar purrs mysteriously as she flicks broken glass off the arches of her feet. 'No use crying over spilt cava – we can share this one,' she says, shaking the remaining flute in her hand. Pilar steps over the debris on the terracotta tiles and wipes her sticky toes on the foot of the sheet, smearing Freixenet and blood onto their marital bed. Careful not to spill any more drops, Pilar edges up the mattress and curls her legs around herself primly as she sits facing Hector.

'I didn't think we owned champagne glasses,' Hector says, taking the flute from Pilar's proffered hand.

'Something borrowed.' She winks. Pilar's hooded Moorish eyes, a constant reminder for Hector of her Old World blood, aren't usually this playful, but this morning she is giddy. She takes a cigarette from the red and white Delicados packet on the bedside table and lights it with her free hand.

'Baby, you're a schoolteacher, you'd lose your job!'

'Something borrowed!' she repeats irritably, then laughs as she blows the first cloud of smoke into Hector's face. His eyes narrow in discomfort. He feels too rough to have a drag and so shields himself by raising the glass to his lips and taking a sip of tepid cava. 'I'll take them back!' Pilar snaps when she sees Hector isn't laughing. 'Well, I'll take this one back anyway.' Her defensiveness softens with a husky laugh as she pulls the glass away from Hector and tops it up from the bottle resting on the bed between her thighs.

Hector lifts the cigarette balancing dangerously between her thin lips and concedes to take a puff before resting it on the overflowing ashtray on the bedside table. He slips his hand inside her white-satin dressing gown and strokes her shoulder, his eyes less flirtatious than usual.

'You didn't steal them from Lazaro's, did you?'

Pilar tuts and changes the subject. 'Wanna surprise?' she asks with a mischievous smile.

The robe drowns Pilar's slight frame and her black back-combed hair looks three-days tousled, even though she just spent half an hour doing it while she watched her lover sleep. Pilar loves watching Hector sleep. When he sleeps, his long lashes sweep down over earthy-brown cheeks, kissed with a pink hue from the heat he works up while he's dreaming. His small straight nose that looks like it was carved from clay is perfect and still, and his usually loud mouth is poetically plump and sealed in silence while he breathes rhythmically. Everything is peaceful and harmonious when Hector Herrera is in one of two states: sleeping or sketching in his notepad. There are no exuberant gestures or loud laughter, just serenity. His silence calms Pilar's rage, and with a haughty nose she gazes down at him and wonders how she ended up with a man as beautiful as Hector.

'More surprises? I'm still traumatised by that crash.'

'That was an accident, baby. I planned this one,' she says with a naughty wink as she sips more cava from the glass.

Hector pulls Pilar in closer, waking his dry mouth to place a kiss on hers. His Cupid's bow lips are small but full and Pilar imagines the same mouth when she pictures their son in a far-ahead future. Hector tastes the cava on Pilar's tongue and it takes away the stale remnants of vodka and excess on his. She slips her robe off her shoulder.

'Look!'

Hector gazes at Pilar's chest. Past the dents above her left breast, he sees a blue heart with his name etched across a ribbon in a swirly script. It is too big for such a small space. Hector's eyes widen and he is lost for words among the famine of her sternum.

'You don't like it?'

'A blue heart? For our wedding?'

'Yes. You make me sad,' Pilar says matter-of-factly. 'I thought it could be my "something blue". I thought you'd like it. You don't think it's cool?'

Now Hector understands why Pilar had been so unusually coquettish for the past few days. He thought she might be saving herself for their wedding night, or might feel uncomfortable that her parents and sisters were in town when she wanted to give off the aura of a virginal bride, despite the fact she was straddling him in a bar in front of thirty friends last night after her three prudish sisters had returned to their hotel to get some sleep before the big day.

'You didn't want me to see it,' Hector says, piecing together the jigsaw puzzle around her heart, distracting her from his dislike.

'I was saving myself for you too,' she says, taking another drag of the cigarette from the ceramic ashtray. 'Imagine how great I will taste tonight, *mi amor*.'

The bell on the cathedral clock chimes twice, meaning it is half past the hour. Hector must get up.

Pilar hands the glass back to Hector to finish the warm dregs as she swigs the remnants from the black bottle and puts it on the bedside table. She winces from the hit of bubbles and alcohol and gives Hector a quick double clap to move him along. 'Right, let's get moving,' she commands as Hector stretches his body into his yawn. 'I'm so excited, baby,' she adds with wide eyes.

Hector, usually the giddy one, always the life and soul, the person people gravitate towards, is finding it hard to galvanise himself this particular morning. He doesn't feel excited right now. He just feels sad.

3

On the steps of the Spanish colonial cathedral, Hector's swarthy skin is lit by the building's yellow façade, intensifying his morning-after pallor. From all around him, people are shouting offers of congratulations, cheer and *suerte*. Taxi drivers, the men who drop Hector home in their green and white Beetles when he can barely speak at the end of a night out, beep their horns in solidarity. The women who work in the old department store, where they worked alongside Hector's mother thirty-five years ago and who still clutch him to their hearts sympathetically when he pops in, walk past and blow Hector a kiss. Volunteers who work at the Villa Infantil De Nuestra Señora orphanage hurry along with a wave as they head back to tidy up, while the nuns who run it, and all of the children who live there, are in the cathedral awaiting Hector's arrival. Barmen pass on scooters on their way to open up cantinas Hector frequents for the start of a new day's trade, although they don't expect to see Hector in there later. Most people in the town of Xalapa know Hector Herrera, and if they're not filing into the cathedral right now to support their *compadre*, they're tooting their horns or raising their hands to wish him well.

A more austere party approaches as Hector's soon-to-be mother-in-law, Mari-Carmen, and her other three daughters, Federica, Beatriz and Julieta, walk around the corner and up the steps of the cathedral. Hector greets them with a single kiss each to the left cheek. The youngest two girls, still teenagers, give each other a sideways look. Only last night, in their hotel bedroom, Beatriz and Julieta were wondering how on earth Pilar snagged such a hot husband, so they wrote their names next to Hector's to work out what percentage the strength of their love with him would be in a little letters-and-numbers experiment that wasn't entirely scientific (Beatriz was 72 per cent, Julieta 98 per cent, but she cheated). Hector's grandfather, Alejandro, stands at his shoulder and nods sedately to Mari-Carmen and the young women.

'Mari-Carmen, you look wonderful! The New World air suits you,' says Hector, with a vivacity that attempts to disguise his hangover.

'Don't be ridiculous, Hector.' She scowls with thin, immaculately made-up jowls. 'We're all still jet-lagged, we look awful. Poor Federica's eyes are still puffy.'

Sullen Federica, the eldest of the four Cabrera sisters, rolls swollen eyes in embarrassment; Beatriz and Julieta stifle a giggle.

Alejandro nods; he can't help agreeing.

'I don't know why we couldn't do it in Spain,' Mari-Carmen says gruffly. 'It's tradition to marry in the *bride's* family home; and there are only two of you in your entire family. Eighteen of us have travelled all this way and there are hundreds of friends and family back home who are upset to miss this. She's the first Cabrera to get married.' Mari-Carmen, hat to toe in oyster, shoots Federica an exasperated look, and her puffy eyes shrink even further back. Much to Mari-Carmen's indignation, Federica has never had a suitor, which makes it even more inconvenient that their unruly second daughter found one first, all this way away, in the *Third World*. Her small, eagle-like eyes measure the men standing in ill-fitting suits before her. Hector is taller and broader than his grandfather, who has sunken into his suit through years of labour in the gardens of the Museum of Anthropology on the outskirts of the town.

Only two of you.

Seeing the lines around his mother-in-law's acerbic mouth makes Hector realise, for the first time in his life, that being 'only two of you' might not be such a bad thing. He didn't want the travelling circus from Spain. The *Gallegos* and their ridiculous lisps. This all seemed completely unnecessary to him.

When Pilar told Hector at Christmas that she wanted to get married, and that she would hurt herself if they didn't marry soon, it was the first Hector had heard of it. They had never once discussed marriage in the six years they had been together. So he assumed she wanted a quick and quiet wedding; perhaps on a beach on the Mayan Riviera. Maybe she was ready to consider children, although Hector knew they'd need to make some life changes first. But the eighteen-strong Spanish armada? *No, gracias.* At least Beatriz and Julieta looked happy to be there.

'Well, this is what Pilar wanted, *Mami,* and I'm sure you and I only want the same thing – for your daughter to be happy.' Hector nods his most charming smile and Pilar's three sisters try not to slide down the steps of the cathedral on the crest of their sighs.

Mari-Carmen frowns at Hector, as if she can't understand his slow and well-meant diction, then turns her head in a look of relief to see her sister approaching.

She almost smiled.

'Ah, there's Teresa. Go help her up the steps, Hector, and show her to her seat. This is all too much for her.'

Hector dashes down the cathedral stairs, his head thumping with each double step he jumps, to help the stately woman with a puff of white hair combed into a cloud behind her. Elephantine ankles are squeezed so tightly into beige court shoes, she can barely lift her feet to shuffle up each stone notch.

'Doña Teresa, *encantado*...' says Hector, not in the least bit charmed, but the half bottle of Freixenet followed by the three shots of tequila he and Pilar did before they went their separate ways to the cathedral are helping him see the funny side.

Pilar made no ceremony of putting on her dress in secret. She had no qualms about Hector seeing her on the morning of their wedding or that it might bring bad luck. When her father Leonel came to the apartment door to collect her, broken glass was still shattered on the bedroom floor, but she knew he wouldn't see it. He didn't want to acknowledge that his daughter lived with 'The Mexican', let alone enter their bedroom and see the well-worn sheets.

'*Papi*, come!' Pilar shouted, as if she was an excited teenager, dressed up and ready for prom or her *quinceañera*, not her own wedding. Only the white satin dress and the plastic calla lily in her backcombed black hair were telltale signs.

Leonel Cabrera, an unexpressive man, silenced by a life surrounded by women, didn't know what to say to his daughter. This was a new experience for the both of them.

'You look beautiful, *cariña*,' he said stiltedly, as if he were reading it from the back of his hand.

Pilar and Hector rushed around, trying not to bump into each other but sneaking tequila shots from the kitchen counter behind Leonel's back as he sat on the sofa staring into space.

Then, Pilar, in her white dress and red lipstick, said she was ready.

Leonel looked away uncomfortably as Pilar jumped up and locked her legs around Hector's waist and slipped her tongue in his mouth, her palms pressing into the back of his head. He held her easily but self-consciously, under her father's gaze.

'Don't make me blue,' Pilar whispered romantically. 'Or I'll slit my veins so deep that every last drop of my blood pours down the cathedral steps.' She gave him a loving smile.

'I'll be there,' Hector assured her. Then he unwrapped Pilar's arms and legs from their grip around his neck and waist, kissed his bride goodbye and went to the bathroom to throw up.

4

'I'll show you to your seat inside.'

'I don't know why you didn't marry in Spain,' says Tia Teresa, her voice even gruffer than her sister Mari-Carmen's. With a wobble on a thick ankle, she concedes to take Hector's arm.

Alejandro, smaller than his grandson but as solid as an ox, stabilises Teresa by her other arm.

'I'll take Doña Teresa inside, *mijo*,' his grandfather says quietly. Alejandro is a man of few words, but he is astute and perceptive, and he can see the lingering look of sadness in Hector's eyes.

Alejandro and Teresa pass Sister Miriam as she comes out of the cathedral, searching for Hector from behind tiny spectacles.

'Ah, there you are! The children are all settled and can't wait to see you, Hectorcito,' says the tiny woman in a grey and white habit as she rubs her wrinkled palms together.

'Thank you, Sister,' Hector says warmly, taking her hands in his. Sister Miriam's face wears the first bit of real cheer Hector has seen all morning, and it lifts his sallow shadow a little.

Sister Miriam looks around to check they are alone amid the traffic noise, cheers and chaos of a Xalapa morning.

'You know, Hector, I understand this must be a bittersweet time for you. It must be hard doing this on your own.'

'I'm not on my own, Sister. I have Abuelo, and you, and the children...' Hector squeezes Sister Miriam's hands tighter. 'And now I have a new mum and dad from Spain!' he says, with a roll of his eyes.

Sister Miriam gives a cheeky smile back. She couldn't help but notice the grandiose women with big hats and big hair, and Hector sees the mischievous sparkle behind Sister Miriam's glasses before her eyes become sombre.

'Your mother and father would have been very proud of you, Hector,' she says.

'Thank you,' Hector mumbles, looking down at the floor.

'You have become a fine man. A fine man with lots of friends and people who care about you. Look at how many people are inside there rooting for you. The children haven't slept properly all week, they've been so excited about today.' Sister Miriam releases a hand from his to wipe a faint smear of red lipstick from the collar of Hector's shirt, but it won't come off. 'Thank you for inviting them.'

'They're my family,' Hector says as he looks beyond Sister Miriam's spectacles, then down at his shoes with a smile. He wears brown lace-ups that look as if they are as old as Hector, even though he's only worn them twice.

'And you are theirs,' she says, looking up at him. 'You give them hope, Hector.'

A wave of nausea washes over him again and he feels terrible. He inhales a deep breath and then takes, and kisses, Miriam's remaining hand to release her. Amid the beeping horns and shaky engines, the faint sound of unabashed, uncontrollable child laughter trickles out of the cathedral.

'I had better get back to them...' Sister Miriam smiles warmly, then she turns on her heel. 'Oh, Hector, please don't be a stranger to them after you're married. They've missed you these past months.'

Wretched guilt that was fizzing away in Hector's stomach since he woke now rises like bile in his throat.

'Sorry, Sister, it's been a busy time planning all this.' Hector gestures his hands towards the cathedral. 'I'll come visit next week when we're back from the coast.'

'Do. And bring your paintbrushes. Your mural needs a bit of work. The children can help you this time.'

Hector smiles and remembers the summer spent breaking his back, painting the entire façade and ceiling of Sister Miriam's orphanage; the smell of the thick syrupy cacao Sister Juana made for his rest breaks; the mousy English girl who came out to volunteer and help with the refurbishment but ended up unwittingly changing Hector's life; the unusual eerie silence in the old hacienda as the kids were shipped off to stay at an orphanage in Coatepec for the summer; the tales they told Hector about lazy days at the waterfall when they came back.

It must have been ten years ago already. No, twenty.

Hector smiles to his shoes again, thinking about how, at eighteen, he was painting walls, frescoes, ceilings – his canvas and his imagination had no limits. Now he is a political cartoonist for the local newspaper, *La Voz de Xalapa*, his art limited to a 10cm x 5cm box. He's pressurised into being witty and sardonic about the day's news before the sun goes down and the paper goes to print; before Hector can relax and go out to a cantina, or to find Pilar in a bar.

'Good luck, *compadre*!' yells a thick, deep voice that makes

Hector's heart sink and the contents of his stomach curdle. It's a voice that travels up Hector's spine and climbs inside his brain, and each time he hears it he wishes it were the last. He looks out onto the street but can't see sinister eyes smiling back at him; he can't see the sun beaming off a gold tooth. He scans the park opposite for a bare arm, slashed and scarred, giving a jovial, menacing wave from the tight constraints of a black leather waistcoat. He puts his hand to his brow to look towards the brightness of the day but can't see the figure he's looking for, and hiding from. The voice comes again, accompanied by a frantic wave of an arm. This time, the voice seems softer. Less menacing. Hector exhales a sigh of relief. He sees a newspaper seller standing on the corner, leaning on the exterior wall of a colonial arch of the Palacio de Gobierno, shouting and waving again. '*Suerte!*'

'*Gracias, Chava!*' Hector shouts back, flushed with relief that distracts him from the heaviness of what's ahead. It's Salvador Mendoza, Chava to his friends. Hector remembers everyone's name in Xalapa, from all the women who work in Lazaro's to the tellers at the Post Office, to the boy who gets the coffees for their editor at work, to the guy who sells the newspaper on the street corner. And they all know Hector.

He looks out at the view from the cathedral steps. In the distance, beyond the stalls selling candy floss, churros and plastic toys in the tree-lined terrace of Parque Juárez, he sees the Pico de Orizaba, snow-capped and mighty, looking back at him with a look of disapproval.

Hector glances back down towards his hands and sees the Spanish flag rubberised in a band on his wrist. A gesture of love for Pilar and the culture he's marrying into. Or was it just because her football team was better than his? Hector can't even remember the night he put it on, but the blood-red stripes that encase a golden centre remind him of the *sangre* Pilar promised she would shed for Hector were he to let her down. He puts his hands in his pockets.

'Always the *extranjera*, always the foreign girl, *cabrón*!' is what Hector's friend Ricky said when Hector told him he had met a cool schoolteacher who had come over from Spain. It stuck in his mind so much that he remembers the off-the-cuff comment from six years ago. But Ricky was right. Hector fell in love with foreigners very easily; perhaps it felt safer if things were lost in translation, and it was mostly easy to find a reason to end it when the time came.

There was the quiet English girl at the orphanage that summer, who he's surprised he sometimes thinks about; the long-limbed Australian who was in town for a year learning Spanish at the university; the sincere American who managed to get Hector to visit her in Oregon; her best friend who he fell for on his first – and last – visit there; Pilar all the way from Spain...

At least his romances seemed to finally be getting closer to his culture – he and Pilar did speak the same language after all, even if her *Gallega* lisp made their friends laugh. And Pilar is the only woman to match Hector drink for drink and laugh for laugh, which he marvels about every time he looks at her. But five minutes from the altar and looking back up at Orizaba's disdain, Hector thinks of the one girl he's tried to forget about, but can't, for the past few months – the past five years. The strangest *extranjera* of them all because he can't imagine anything about her snowy life on top of the world, even though he thinks she could have been his soulmate.

If I climbed that mountain, would it bring us closer?

A woman with crisp orange curls hurries up the steps of the cathedral, almost late.

'Ay, what a handsome groom!' she says appreciatively,

holding her hand to her chest before opening her arms out. The woman wears a grey jacket and matching pencil skirt, the uniform from Lazaro's department store from where she's ducked out for an hour to see Lupe's boy wed. 'You know your mother would have been very proud of you today, Hectorcito,' the woman says, embracing him.

Hector feigns a grateful smile. 'Thank you, Cintia. I'm glad you could come, it means a lot.'

'I wouldn't miss this for the world!' Cintia puts a hand on each of Hector's upper arms and breathes out a sigh of admiration. They both know what she's thinking as she lingers over his face – how much Hector looks like his mother. 'Now, come inside, Hector, I thought I was late. She'll be here any minute!'

Hector hugs Cintia tight, accidentally tasting hairspray from a crunchy lock.

'I'm just getting some air, *guapa*, I'll be a little second, you go,' Hector says with a reassuring wave before he puts his hands back in his pockets.

'OK, don't run off now!' Cintia says with a wink as she rushes up the stairs in the hope of getting a decent seat, her tight grey skirt testing the seam that runs down her squashed bottom.

Alejandro walks out of the cathedral, looking for his grandson. His straight hair is white and neat, like a frame around his head.

'Everything OK, *mijo*?' he asks as he puts a hand on Hector's shoulder from the step above.

I miss her.

'Sure thing, Abuelito.'

I will never touch her.

'It's time to go. Pilar will be here any minute.'

'I know.' Hector takes his hands out of his pockets and opens his arms wide up towards his grandfather.

'I'm very proud of you, you know, Hector,' he says, falling into Hector's embrace and patting his back with a liver-spotted hand.

Hector smiles and lifts Alejandro off his step a little and both men laugh, very differently. Hector's is wholehearted; when he laughs, his thick straight brows rise in the middle and he shakes all the way down to his shoulders. His grandfather's laugh is sedate, just a little lift of his eyebrows and the flash of a playful flicker in his eye.

Beeps and cheers in the distance signal Leonel and Pilar approaching in the bridal car.

It is time.

'You know your mother and father would have been very proud of you today,' Alejandro says sombrely.

Hector gives a wry laugh. He wouldn't be sick of hearing it if he thought it were true.

'No, they wouldn't.' He smiles, kindly, as he pats his grandfather on the back to usher them both up the steps.

Hector doesn't really remember his mother or father. He remembers the noise of metal being punched by branches and bracken; he remembers last gasps and young cries of despair. But when Hector tries to remember what his mother and father looked like from memory, he only sees them with blank faces. He filled in the blanks from the few photos of them his grandfather gave him. His favourite is pressed to his heart on the inside pocket of his suit jacket right now. It isn't their wedding photo; it's the photo of a young Victor Herrera, his hair straight and neat like his father's, his arm draped around a woman with beautiful soft waves that tumble around her bare shoulders. Behind her ear sits a pink hibiscus flower, its petals yellow at the edges, the colour bursting out from behind Lupe's black curls, even though the photo is faded. Hector imagines his father had recently picked the flower for his mother and gallantly placed it behind her ear. She gazes, almost flirtatiously, at the camera. Victor's slightly serious face is imbued with pride, and it always struck Hector that the face could have been cut and pasted from a photo from the nineteenth century, not the 1980s. His look is timeless.

As Hector walks the stone steps to the cathedral door, he wonders how Victor and Lupe might have felt on their wedding day. He wishes he could time travel, to escape here, to be a guest at their wedding, in the same cathedral, almost forty years ago. Just to witness a snapshot in their lives, to be able to sketch in the blank faces in real life. To look at his father and gauge what face a groom ought to have on his wedding day. To see movement and laughter and tenderness and contentment, to see more than the wedding photo pinned to the wall above his desk at home, or the photo hugging his chest from the inside pocket of his jacket. To hear their voices. For their stories and their laughter to be so much richer than the anecdotes told by the older ladies who still work in Lazaro's. Hector imagines his mother's laughter as infectious.

As Alejandro and Hector enter the cathedral, a hundred faces turn towards them in excitement. Best men Ricky and Elias stand at the front, seeming relieved by the groom's arrival. Elias gestures to his wristwatch and gives Hector a nagging look. To his right, a curve of chubby hands wave at him in excitement and unison. Hector swallows the rising bile and smiles back at little faces, his eyes creasing playfully at the corners, glad at least that his wedding has brought joy and excitement to the children of the Villa Infantil De Nuestra Señora.

5

MARCH 2018, SUFFOLK, ENGLAND

'Kids! Breakfast! It's getting cold!' bellows an angry voice, meekly, up a flight of stairs. The intention was there but her execution was wobbly, as often is the way with Kate. Her voice lets her down. 'Honestly, George,' she flounders across an octave, 'they're not listening. *You* need to tell them...' she says, trying to get them to be a team again, but her plea is lost among the clatter of breakfast bowls, pans and spoons. A paper-thin film forms over three bowls of porridge, and she waits to see which is first to be devoured without gratitude or appreciation.

'I don't know why I bother talking,' Kate puffs as she clutches a damp tea towel tightly and puts a fist on each hip. 'Or cooking their breakfast. Or packing their bags. The girls are old enough to do it themselves for that matter...'

'Well, what else *would* you do?' A caustic voice cuts Kate down in her tracks.

'George!' she gasps with round, hurt eyes.

George shrugs as he finishes his coffee and clumsily places his mug on the thick wood surface of the island in the middle of the kitchen. Kate knows those bumbling hands will have caused a coffee mark on the worktop, but there are so many piles of paperwork, letters from school, forms to action, that Kate doesn't know where to begin in tidying it up, so she lets the coffee mug go while that comment stings her. She'll clean it up later when everyone has gone to work and school. When they've forgotten about her and what she might be doing.

Kate looks back up at George, searching for support, for kindness. Her husband clearly feels guilty enough to give an explanation.

'Well, I imagine this happens every morning. Just let them experience the displeasure of cold porridge, or going to school hungry. They'll soon learn. Don't let it wind you up so much. If it does, get a job and we'll get a nanny.'

George's flippant tone shocks Kate.

'Why are you still here anyway?' she bites back daringly, punctuating her question mark with a light, wobbly laugh to lift the tension.

'You said I had a bloody dentist appointment at eight thirty. I thought you were taking me before you took the kids to school?'

Kate gasps again and puts the damp tea towel to her mouth. The fact that it doesn't smell of fabric softener any more reminds her that it needs a wash. 'Oh bother. Your check-up.'

'You're taking me in the S-Max, yes?'

Kate flattens her heavy brown fringe and rejigs her mind. 'Yes. There's no point you driving, it'll take you so long to park and walk to the surgery and back to the car. You'll miss the train.'

'Yes. I thought that's what we discussed,' George says matter-of-factly, as if Kate is his PA.

'OK, so I'll drop you and take the kids, then you'll get a taxi from the surgery to the station, yes?' she says, now smoothing the hair in her ponytail.

'Yes, that's what we discussed,' repeats George flatly.

'I've got a WI planning meeting straight after drop-off, otherwise I'd race back to the surgery and take you to the station myself. KIDS!'

A slight boy with a swishy blond fringe pads down the stairs and skulks through the glass double doors to the kitchen, rubbing his eyes. 'Mum, can I scoot to school today?'

'No, we're dropping Dad in the village first, so we're all going by car. Anyway, you haven't been wearing your helmet. You're not scooting to school without a helmet.'

Kate turns her back on the conversation, puts on her pale green marigolds and fills the sink with water and washing-up liquid, the sound drowning out the protest she knows is about to come.

'But that was the garden, Mum! Do I really have to wear a helmet even in the garden?'

George laughs to himself while he ties his tie, and their son, Jack, tries to negotiate.

'You're so cautious, Kate,' George says, undermining her.

Kate turns around sharply, her cow-like brown eyes looking at George again, hurt and confused. She changes the subject.

'Where are your sisters?'

'Dunno,' Jack says with a shrug.

'Well, you eat your porridge before it goes cold. GIRLS!'

'I'm going to clean my teeth,' announces George.

'Send the girls down, will you?'

George scratches his cropped silver hair and jumps up the stairs two at a time. Kate starts to wash up the porridge pan. While she circles the inside of it with the brush, she goes over her revised plan for the day ahead. Drop George outside the dental surgery; take Chloe, Izzy and Jack to school; head to the village hall to meet Christine Leach, Antonia Barrie and Sheila Eldret from the WI to discuss the spring fair...

Who's got the keys to the village hall?

Bake for the PTA coffee morning on Friday...

I'm sure Sheila took the spare key after the last meeting. Pick up the kids from school. Take Izzy to Brownies. Take Chloe to drama. Bring Jack home to do his homework.

Collect the girls. Do tea.

Sausage and cannellini bean one-pot.

Take Chloe to look around the new school she'll be going to in September.

Check the babysitter can still make it.

Kate sighs and pushes her fringe to one side, leaving soap suds on top of it.

Did I book Susannah or Philippa?

Jack laughs but decides not to tell his mum about the bubbles on top of her head, sitting like a wonky tiara on a deflated prom queen. It's worth a laugh from his sisters when they do eventually make it downstairs for breakfast.

Kate rinses the pan and ponders her baking options. She can't do a Victoria sponge again; she did a three-tiered one at the NCT Easter party last week, and half of her NCT friends are also on the PTA.

What about a Sachertorte?

Antonia Barrie made the most beautiful one for last month's WI meeting, as glossy and as polished as Antonia herself.

I'll bake one of those. No one at school will know I copied Antonia Barrie. That's if she even made it herself; one of her staff probably did it. That mirror glaze...

Kate laughs to herself for being so petty, removes her marigolds and places them over the brushed-steel tap. She squeezes her engagement and wedding rings back into alignment and washes her hands. A little diamond solitaire she knows she would never pick out in a line-up clings onto a gold band beneath it, and Kate notices how her rings have never felt so tight. She smooths down her apron over her hips and feels a pang of guilt when she remembers the big bar of Fruit & Nut she managed to finish when she was watching the *Sewing Bee* last night while George was at badminton.

Perhaps I'll dig out my Weight Watchers gumpf.

'Stop nicking my stuff!' shouts a banshee entering the kitchen.

'I didn't! It was just in my room. I don't know how it got there!'

'Mum, tell Izzy to leave my stuff alone – I spent ages looking for my rose-gold skinny scarf and she had it all along!'

'I didn't take it! I don't know how it ended up in my room!'

'Girls, girls,' says Kate through gritted teeth. 'Please sit down and eat your breakfast. We have to drop Dad in the village on the way to school.'

Chloe and Izzy sit alongside Jack at the breakfast bar on one end of the island and Kate, joining them on the stool nearest the sink, decides to forgo breakfast for coffee.

I'll finish up their leftovers when I get home. I'm sure I kept all my Weight Watchers booklets.

Kate gazes at her girls. So angry, so beautiful. She wishes she had been so sassy at their age. Her daughters are eleven and nine, and Jack is seven. A biennial production line of babies Kate managed to birth (all by herself, without drugs she'll have you know), and each baby caused her tummy to become a little bit softer, a little more ravaged by silvery tracks – and caused George to become slightly more repulsed by the goriness of it all, and by her body.

George walks into the kitchen with his suit jacket slung over one hand and his phone in the other. Silence consumes the light, bright family kitchen while the children eat lukewarm porridge and, for a brief moment, Kate feels like she might be in the calm at the centre of a storm. Papers and school photos and bank statements rise in a pile threatening to topple over. Kate takes a sip of coffee and the silence is interrupted by a beep coming from somewhere on the island. She looks for her phone and finds it under Jack's homework folder. A text from George. She looks up at him, puzzled.

> Can't wait for lunch X

'Lunch? Are you not going into London after the dentist?'
George looks confused. And pale. His small blue eyes seem to recede a little into his head. 'What?'
'A text from you about lunch...'
George puts both hands to his thin cheeks in panic, creasing his jacket into the crook of his arm.
Four faces look at him expectantly.
'Lunch!' he says with a strained laugh. 'I'm having lunch with Baz Brocklebank from the Sydney office – we've got a mega deal up our sleeves that is going to wipe the floor with anything Tim and his team will pitch. Did I just send that text to *you*?'
Chloe plugs in her headphones; this conversation is boring. Izzy returns to her porridge, feeling uncomfortable about her dad's ill ease, and Jack studies his father's face.
'You put a kiss on it. A big one.' Kate's mouth is upturned, her face quizzical.
The ends of George's crow's feet become pink and he brings his hands to his face again.
'Did I?'
'Awkward...' says Izzy, nine going on nineteen, as she stares down at her bowl.
'How embarrassing!' bumbles George. 'Thank God I *didn't*

send it to him! Oh well, Baz is OK, he would have laughed it off if I actually had sent him a kiss. But... well... dodged a bullet there...' he mumbles.

Kate studies George's face and he keeps talking.

'We're going to Hutong up The Shard; the octopus is amazing, Kate.'

'You know I hate seafood, George. The risk of tummy bugs from marine toxins is so high.'

'Well, this is worth the risk. I'll have to take you there.' Kate's brown eyes flicker as she searches for reassurance.

'Me too?' asks Izzy, a daddy's girl.

'You too, sweetheart.'

'It's just you sound very chummy with Baz,' Kate says. She can't escape the ill feeling in her hollow stomach.

'Hahahaha, funny,' says Jack. 'I called Mrs Francis "Mum" the other day. I suppose it's a bit like that.'

'Well, I'm just relieved I didn't send it. It would be embarrassing, as cool as Baz is...' George smiles at Jack. His ratty morning demeanour has disappeared.

'OK, kids, clean your teeth, we need to get moving,' George says, looking at his watch.

Kate tries to shake the disquiet she feels by focusing on the shine of a Sachertorte.

Do you heat the cream and add the chocolate or is it the other way around?

6

Kate plonks the keys in the bowl on the little table next to the front door and removes her scarf. It's late March, and there's a distinct feeling of spring, having taken a long time coming, starting to lift the veil of grey from the lawns and the faces of the people in Claresham village.

Kate looks at her reflection in the long mirror. She didn't realise when she joined the WI that she would come away from meetings and get-togethers feeling like the dowdy one. Her small face looks both young yet mumsy, as if she might have looked this age since her teens but has now caught up with herself. Her narrow shoulders, wrapped in a navy long-sleeved jersey top under the hug of a black cardigan, belie her soft stomach and doughy bottom half, squeezed into black boot-leg trousers that she knows won't fit for much longer.

Unless I do something about it.

Her brown hair is tied in a scrunchie, and remnants of washing-up liquid that bounced unmentioned on her fringe this morning now make Kate think she walked through a spider's web somewhere between Claresham Church of England Primary School, having deposited two embarrassed daughters and one cuddly boy into their classrooms, and the village hall.

How embarrassing! They must have noticed.

Kate mats her fringe down to hide traces of webbing and wonders what she would look like with red lipstick on. Would George find her sexy in red lipstick, or would that repel him too? She can't think of an actual event she would wear red lipstick to. Perhaps the PTA summer social, if she can drag George along. He so hates these things and acts like a spoilt child in the weeks running up to them if Kate ever reminds him that it's happening, and that so-and-so will be there. But when he's there he seems to enjoy them and gets stuck in.

Kate takes her phone out of her cardigan pocket and slides it onto the telephone table. She remembers the text received by mistake this morning and feels discomfort in the pit of her hungry stomach.

Can't wait for lunch X

Rewrapping her cardigan around her, Kate decides to leave the empty breakfast bowls for a bit longer, kicks off her shoes, and goes upstairs to their office. A little study at the top of the stairs that overlooks the satisfying neatness of their garden.

It was the neatness of the garden that won them over when they were looking at family homes in Suffolk. Kate and George were renting a one-bedroom flat in Blackheath when Kate fell pregnant with Chloe. George's family were in Dorset and Kate's were in Norfolk, but George relented and said Suffolk was as close as he could be to Kate's sister and parents. They looked around many villages and towns, but Claresham made do, with its nice village green, strand of essential shops and decent schools. The house was a new-build in a cul-de-sac and Kate and George didn't mind that it lacked character – the sixteenth-century cottages that lined the green were far too dark and pokey for a growing family. This greige house on The Finches was perfect: detached, functional, low maintenance. A good family home. The fittings were nice, the garden was spacious enough, if not very verdant, but that would come with time. There was a garage and space on the drive for two vehicles and, most importantly, it was a short car journey away from the train line to Liverpool Street where they both commuted to, working in the offices of Digby Global Investors in the City. Nowadays, Kate rarely goes further than the village.

Can't wait for lunch X

Kate looks out onto the garden and sees a goldfinch on the bird feeder, but it doesn't hearten her as it usually would. Her rumbling tummy makes her feel both fat yet hollow, and the agitation coming from within it gives her an urge to delve. She sits down at the desk and randomly taps a button on the keyboard to awaken the computer.

X.

Lights flicker and the machine twinkles at the attention. Desktop, dock, documents... Kate clicks on the tab that says 'Google calendar' and looks at the colour-coded diaries. George's diary is blue. Kate never cares to look at it; she's usually busy in the default family diary, which is colour-coded yellow, full of Brownies, Beavers, birthday parties, dancing and gymnastics. She looks at today, then clicks on George's blue box.

Dentist 0830. Stand-up with Swiss team 1100. Meeting AIA 1130. Lunch B 1300. Toby appraisal 1530. Chloe school 1930.

Lunch B.
It must be Baz from the Sydney office. Of course; why would

she think anything else? Kate blows a sigh towards the computer and sees her black muted reflection in the screen. Drawn and tired.

Maybe I will try the red lipstick for the PTA summer social. I've got four months to practise applying it.

7

MARCH 2018, TROMSØ, NORWAY

Cecilie stamps the snow off her boots and wipes her feet on the coarse mat.

'Do you have a spare half-hour?' she asks her friend Morten.

'I'm hardly busy,' he replies, pushing frameless spectacles up his nose, then beckoning Cecilie in with a jaunty wave.

Morten has only had one customer all morning, which means the salon is spick and span: not a hair on the floor, every horizontal wooden panel on the wall cleaned to perfection (not that you can tell; they're meant to look artfully distressed), sparkling smear-free mirrors, and the aroma of fresh coffee wafting through from the room at the back. Morten is always happy to see his boyfriend's twin sister, as if she were his own, although Cecilie rarely has cause to go into a hair salon.

'You want a chat or a haircut?' Morten laughs, already heading towards the back kitchen to make another round of coffee, so they can sit down for a gossip.

'A haircut actually.'

Morten stops in his tracks and pivots around conspiratorially.

'Really?' His mouth hangs open, revealing the gap between his two front teeth. 'Are you sure?'

'Sure.'

'Had I better call Espen?'

Cecilie removes her long grey feather-down jacket as if she's about to go into battle and slings it onto a hairdresser's stool.

'He might micromanage everything at the i-Scand, but my brother doesn't have to approve my haircuts. Besides, he's disapproved of these for years,' Cecilie says, tugging on a ragged end of a long blonde dreadlock as she looks into the mirror.

Morten pulls his braces up over his checked shirt, making him look like a friendly garden gnome, as he readies himself for the task at hand.

'Take a seat,' he says, ushering Cecilie into his favourite chair, the one closest to the windows that look out onto the small high street.

Cecilie slinks into the square-shaped seat of the brown leather chair and looks at her face. For someone with such delicate features, with fingers that can pluck a harp like an angel, Cecilie is quite ungainly, and she slumps forward to look at her reflection, her DM boots anchoring her to the well-swept floor. Morten lifts ends of rope before they can entwine themselves into Cecilie's jumper, the seat, the ground.

'It's a big deal, Cecilie. I'd have to get rid of all this length. Your hair would be almost as short as mine,' he says, smoothing his hands across the light brown fluff that caresses his dome.

'Take them off, short is good,' she says determinedly. 'I just want them gone.'

Morten looks at Cecilie's reflection in the mirror and they lock eyes. He wants to ask if it's about The Mexican, but he recognises that obstinacy in those dragonfly green irises. He sees it every time he and Espen have an argument, so he decides not to push his luck. Anyway, it's academic. Cecilie wants a haircut, so he will give her a haircut.

'OK, well I have no bookings until 3 p.m. and Nils is in Oslo for a few days, so the salon is ours. Let me get you that coffee first. Milky, *ja*?' Morten walks to the kitchen and lets out a chuckle. 'Espen won't believe it! Your mother neither.'

But it's neither Espen nor her mother who Cecilie thinks of as she looks in the mirror and stares at her reflection. The mirror frames Cecilie's face perfectly. Blonde twists cascade past cheekbones that rise like the two curves of a love heart and tumble past her chin. Her eyes are several shades lighter than her jumper, a colour unique to Cecilie and Espen, and it's a colour Morten is mesmerised by. 'You must be the only two people on the planet with this eye colour,' he often marvels. Brother and sister blush when Morten says it: thick lashes sweep down in unison as Cecilie and Espen wonder what their father's eyes were like. They can't remember.

Cecilie's otherworldly beauty doesn't need reinforcement, and she rarely bothers but for a flick of eyeliner above feline eyes, parallel to the arch of the dark-blonde brows that reach out to her temples. Looking at her face in the mirror for so long makes Cecilie see herself through the eyes of Hector Herrera, and she rises out of her body, out of her chair, and flutters across the timeline of her life. From above, she sees Hector pacing a room, remembering what he said to her the first time they saw each other's faces. Then she slides a tiny bit further back and looks down on the library, at the time they first found each other.

8
JUNE 2013, DAY ONE

Cecilie wasn't looking to cause trouble for herself the day she met Hector Herrera. She was in the library at 8 a.m., as usual, before chief librarian Fredrik came in at 8.30. The two of them would always chat quietly, genially, and be ready to open for 9 a.m. Cecilie always loved to hang out in the library before anyone else got there. It was such a peaceful time of day. Dark in the winter, light all summer, and the huge glass façade of the modernist four-storey building looked out onto the small grid of the town, the harbour, its bridges, its mountains beyond, the world below. Sometimes in winter Cecilie could see the Northern Lights through the window that rose all the way to the top floor. A green whisper arced overhead, reminding her how isolated she was from the world she read about in the books on the shelves.

That day, Cecilie didn't go to the basement first to sort out the children's activity table. She didn't put out the pencils and paper ready for the school trip, or the soft-back books and tambourines in anticipation of the baby rhyme-time session. That light and bright June morning, Cecilie got herself a milky coffee and went up the open staircase to the rows of computers on the first floor. She turned the machines on with a satisfying switch switch switch of the clean white sockets behind each terminal.

She looked up to the top floor, to the quiet reading and writing areas among the rows of books, but decided not to go up and turn the lights on. She didn't want to draw attention to her private world in the public glass space. Anyway, it was June, and there was sufficient light night and day to not warrant them.

At the second terminal in, on the first row of machines, Cecilie leaned over the desk without sitting, typed in the staff login, and waited for a sand timer flipping over and over on itself to align her to another time. Another latitude she had no idea she would soon long for.

Switch switch switch. She stalked the library, awakening, opening, connecting, before coming back to the second terminal. She sat down at a screen, facing out over the Arctic Circle below her.

Cecilie tied her locks into a thick trunk running down her back and took a sip of milky white coffee, holding her cup with her thumbs threaded through holes in the wrist of her jumper. Cecilie went on her usual journey across the world: NRK for her news fix before the bundle of papers arrived; Facebook to see what friends who had set sail from this port town were up to, as far afield as Oslo, Edinburgh, San Francisco and Quito; then her habitual look on *NME* to see what was going on in her favourite music sphere. At home, Cecilie unwound by playing the harp to an empty house, but picked herself up again to British synth-pop and electronica.

Depeche Mode played Leipzig last night.

Cecilie took a sip and sought out gig reviews, finding herself in a chatroom for other eighties electronica Anglophiles in no time. She thought she might scour the reviews, the forums, the chat, to find out about future concert dates that hadn't yet been announced. She logged in and gave herself a moniker: Arctic Fox. With delicate hands that had dry pads for fingertips, she typed.

Arctic Fox: Anyone know if DM are coming to Scandinavia?

I Feel You: More likely Scandinavia than Mexico @arcticfox! Been too long since they came here.

Cecilie's eyes widened and she marvelled at the world she was connected to. Like-minded music fans thousands of kilometres away.

Arctic Fox: You in Mexico?

I Feel You: Síííííííííí.

Arctic Fox: Wow, what time is it there?

I Feel You: Party time. Where are you? Copenhagen??? They play Copenhagen tomorrow. Stockholm in a few weeks. Go go go!

Arctic Fox: Nope. I'm in neither.

The steam from her coffee cup rose above Cecilie's head towards the roof.

Arctic Fox: I'm in Norway – in a building, a library in fact, inspired by a Mexican architect.

I Feel You: Félix Candela?

Arctic Fox: Yes! You know him?

I Feel You: I studied him. Love that dude's waves.

I Feel You added a smiley face and an emoji of a great wave.

Cecilie looked up to the curve of the thin, white parabolic roof that hugged the glass tiers of the library like a snowdrift. It made her feel cosy and safe and she inhaled another slug of coffee, then put her mug down to type.

Arctic Fox: Small world!

The apples of her cheeks rose as she smiled at the words on her screen.

I Feel You: So, what are you doing in the library, Arctic Fox?

Arctic Fox: I work here. I'm the only one here right now. Opening up.

I Feel You: Well... encantado. Nice to meet you, cool Norwegian librarian girl who likes Depeche Mode.

Cecilie felt the change in tone. She twisted a blonde rope around her right index finger.

Arctic Fox: How do you know I'm a girl?

I Feel You: I dunno... I... I Feel You...

Arctic Fox: Hahahaha.

Cecilie added a smiley face with a wink. She had a definite feeling that I Feel You was a boy, but if she had understood Spanish she would have already known he was.

Encantado.

Someone called 'Dave Gahan's Left Bollock' entered the conversation.

Dave Gahan's Left Bollock: Get a room.

I Feel You: Jajajajaja. Sorry Dave Gahan's Left Bollock! Just being friendly, nada más. Cool name!

Arctic Fox: What is 'left bollock'?

Hector Herrera clicked on a box to message Arctic Fox privately.

I Feel You: Bollocks bollocks bollocks.

Arctic Fox: Yes, but what is bollocks?

Hector's grasp of English swearwords was better than Cecilie's then. He knew what bollocks meant, so he eagerly cut and paste an explanation from the dictionary, hoping Arctic Fox wouldn't leave the conversation.

I Feel You:
bollocks
noun UK /ˈbɒl.əks/ US /ˈbɑː.ləks/ uk
[plural] offensive for testicle

> [U] offensive nonsense:
> That's a load of bollocks.
> Bollocks to that (= that's nonsense)!

Cecilie laughed to see the explanation laid out so clearly before her in black and white.

> Arctic Fox: Ah I get it now! Testiklene in my language.

> I Feel You: We have many words for them in mine. Cojones, huevos, pelotas, aguacates, albondigas... But yes, Dave Gahan's Left Bollock must be a superfan. But never mind the bollocks...

I Feel You added a smiley face with a wink and two hazelnuts, and Cecilie laughed.

> Arctic Fox: Hahaha. Thanks. So where are you partying?

> I Feel You: Xalapa, Mexico. You?

Cecilie quickly googled Xalapa and her eyes widened. It looked so... different to the pale jagged landscape around her, full of whites, greys and blues.

> Arctic Fox: Well, I'm not partying, I'm working. Tromsø, Norway.

> I Feel You: Hang on, lemme google...

Cecilie liked how honest I Feel You was about looking Tromsø up, when she had just searched his homeland surreptitiously. While Cecilie waited for a response, she looked at the clock in the bottom left-hand corner of the screen. It was 8.30 a.m.

Fredrik will be here any minute.

A second later, Cecilie heard the heavy side door to the library open and clink shut, followed by the soft noise of a bike being wheeled in. A jangle of heavy keys clattered down onto the welcome desk.

Like clockwork.

Fredrik, a broodingly handsome mountain of a man with a bushy beard and hair tied into a bun, must have been the most reliable man in the Arctic Circle: always arriving at 8.30 a.m. precisely, always able to call in a book from anywhere in the world for any visitor to the library, always wielding a flask of green tea and a jam jar of Bircher muesli, soaked overnight in almond milk in his fridge at home. Morten had been trying to matchmake Cecilie with Fredrik ever since he and Espen got together, but Fredrik was always reliably – yet annoyingly – entwined with, and loyal to, his yoga-teacher girlfriend, saluting the sun with her day and night at this time of year.

Being pulled away from another world gave Cecilie a feeling of urgency in her tummy. She knew she ought to hurry up.

'*Hei*, Cecilie,' said a soft, deep voice.

'Up here!' she called, standing and walking away from her terminal to start pulling out the stands with magazines and journals on them. She did that every morning: checked her favourite news and music sites in a world beyond the library before she started checking the newspapers and journals inside the building, putting out-of-date ones on a pile for the recycling box, bringing the bale of papers on the desk up to the first floor. Only, that morning, Cecilie had got a little sidetracked and was running behind. She looked back to the screen.

> I Feel You: You still there…?
>
> I Feel You: Arctic Fox…?
>
> I Feel You: Ah, no mames…

Cecilie walked back to the machine and put the well-fingered newspapers down next to the keyboard to free her hands so she could reply.

> Arctic Fox: Hei, still here, I have to get to work now though. Bookworms incoming, 30 minutes!
>
> I Feel You: Tromsø library. I see where you are now. Beautiful. It's like the pavilion at Valencia. Félix Candela designed that one. You been to Valencia?
>
> Arctic Fox: Nei. Never left Norway. Have you been to Spain?

Hector Herrera, sitting among the colourful mess of his colourful apartment in the tallest building in town, thought about his ties to Spain. His girlfriend Pilar, across the room, cross-legged on the sofa as she put on her make-up ready for the night out ahead of them, looked like Spanish royalty with her hooded eyes and haughty nose.

> I Feel You: Nah. I only left Mexico once. Pinches gringos let me into USA.

Hector inhaled his cigarette and suddenly wondered if Arctic Fox was a kid. If she had never left Norway she might be a child, in which case he really ought not to be talking to her at all, let alone doing winking smiley faces. But then the kids Hector knew, the children at the orphanage or the students at Pilar's school, preferred Demi Lovato to Depeche Mode, so he blew that thought away as he exhaled a stream of smoke at his dented laptop with a cracked screen.

'Some idiot nearly knocked me off my bike,' said Fredrik, without attempting to raise his voice so Cecilie might hear him on the first floor as he poured green tea into his favourite mug. Cecilie hadn't quite heard, and she knew she ought to ask Fredrik to repeat himself. Fredrik was a man of few words, so when he spoke, Cecilie liked to listen, although she was bit reluctant to that particular morning.

Arctic Fox: OK I have to go now. Chat later?

I Feel You: Síííííí. You sure?

Arctic Fox: Yes! I Feel You is my very favourite Depeche Mode song. If that's your handle, we must chat more.

I Feel You: It's my favourite song too.

Arctic Fox: What's your real name?

Hector looked over at Pilar, putting a swipe of ruby lipstick across thin lips.

I Feel You: Doesn't matter, does it?

Cecilie's heart-shaped face flushed pink and she wiped her cheek with a newsprint-stained palm. Of course it didn't.

Arctic Fox: Nope. OK I gotta go.

I Feel You: December 13.

Arctic Fox: What?

I Feel You: Depeche Mode are to play Oslo on December 13. Is that near you?

Arctic Fox: Yes! Well, not really, but happy news. That made my day.

You made my day.

I Feel You: Cool. Make sure you get tickets.

Arctic Fox: I will. Hadet!

I Feel You: Hasta luego.

Cecilie had never had a conversation in an online chatroom before, so she felt somewhat daring. She jumped down the stairs two at a time like a clumsy fairy in DM boots and saw Fredrik tending to his bicycle leaned up against the welcome desk.

'Gosh, what happened?'

'Some idiot nearly knocked me off. I buckled my wheel slamming into the kerb away from him.'

Fredrik's vast back leaned over his bike, his furrowed brow looking particularly irked, his manbun ruffled. Cecilie handed him his green tea and said she'd do his jobs too so Fredrik could tend to his bike.

Cecilie spent all that morning in the library, busying herself by tidying, lending, answering, singing... It was only as she left at lunchtime that Fredrik noticed the newsprint on Cecilie's cheek and went to wipe it off with a giant, gentle thumb.

In the Hjornekafé that afternoon, I Feel You was all Cecilie could think about. The colours of the town in which he lived; how he knew what a Candela roof looked like; that 'I Feel You' was his favourite song by *their* favourite band.

Then it occurred to her: she didn't even know if I Feel You was a man. But that was how she pictured him. A man. Of about Hector's actual age. Looking almost exactly as Hector did, in colour and stature, although the facial features were slightly blurred. Cecilie's whimsical way meant she was rather good at dreamily imagining and accepting something far-fetched as a truth. It was something that made her mother worry. That Cecilie wasn't streetwise enough, that she was too dreamy.

'Your name means "blind". You don't question things enough like your brother does. Perhaps that's my fault for giving you this name.'

On the contrary, Cecilie's daydreams made her feel far from blind; she could see things no one else around her could; she could imagine what a stranger looked like and almost get it right. When Cecilie drifted out of a conversation or closed her eyes as she played the harp, she could see more clearly than anyone.

Either way, whether I Feel You was a man or woman, Cecilie couldn't wait to go back online and chat some more.

* * *

The next morning, Cecilie woke to everlasting daylight at 6 a.m. She showered and grabbed a slice of soda bread and smeared it with honey, then slipped out of the family home quietly at 6.30 a.m., so as not to wake Espen. She trudged the kilometre-long footpath of the elegant cantilever bridge that arched over the strait like the spine of a whale, connecting the colourful wood-panelled houses at the foot of the mountain, to the hub of the town on Tromsøya island. As Cecilie crossed the bridge, she thought, as she often did, of her father Kjetil, and his secret that only the bridge knew, and she hurried to get to the library for 7 a.m., to try to catch I Feel You before he went to bed.

* * *

I Feel You: Hey! I'm just on my way out.

Arctic Fox: Oh, how funny!

Cecilie felt silly for not realising people in Mexico went out partying at midnight on a Wednesday, although of course, not all of them did.

I Feel You: That's OK though, I can talk. My girlfriend is doing her nails, so I guess that'll be another hour.

A nail polish emoji popped up, followed by a face crying with laughter, but strangely Cecilie didn't feel like laughing.

He is a boy. He has a girlfriend. Who has pretty nails.

She looked at her own nails, pale and unspectacular other than for the damage done by playing the harp, peeping out from under the cuffs of her long fluffy jumper.

I Feel You: Did you get tickets for Oslo?

In the space of twenty-three hours, Cecilie had worked out an entire backstory for The Mexican and had filled in the blurred details of his face. He had sun-dappled terracotta skin, wide, bronze eyes as passionate as an insurgent and as romantic as a revolutionary. His lips were still and plump as he concentrated on typing, and his shoulders were not tall but strong, curled over the keyboard of his computer. She had no idea that was precisely what I Feel You looked like.

Cecilie hadn't factored in the girlfriend, so she felt a bit embarrassed for having completely conjured a handsome man based on a few minutes' chat in a fan forum – and not thinking he would have a girlfriend.

Silly me.

She hoped now I Feel You was in fact female, and girlfriend meant girlfriend the way Grethe was to Cecilie. They could be long-distance buddies, like the pen pal her mother once procured for her, the daughter of the German chancellor, and forced Cecilie into writing correspondence to in stilted English.

Arctic Fox: Nei, no tickets yet, not on sale for a few weeks. And I'd need to get a flight down to Oslo, so I'll think about it.

I Feel You: You have to see them. I saw them in Mexico City, 2009. Changed my life.

In the quiet of the library, secure that Fredrik wouldn't wheel his bike in for at least another hour, Cecilie wondered what I Feel You's life was like before he saw Depeche Mode and how it had changed since. She suddenly felt unadventurous and naïve. She wanted to connect with this stranger, but knew deep down she wouldn't book tickets and fly two hours to see a band play, even one of her favourites. She would love to have the confidence to jump on a plane and fly on her own. Her mother would easily do something as daring as that. Grethe too. But

Cecilie, who so often relied on her imagination to take her on adventures, was crippled by not knowing how to have them in real life.

> Arctic Fox: So where are you and your girlfriend off to tonight?

Hector didn't sense the disappointment in Cecilie's fifty-two characters. He didn't notice Pilar swear at her nailbrush because a little hair had dragged some oxblood polish onto her finger, and now it was on her beige bandage dress.

> I Feel You: Chupar. In a bar. Or not. She's just told me she doesn't want to go now.

He added an emoji of a face crying with laughter.

> I Feel You: Looks like we're staying in.

Cecilie didn't know what to say, so she carried on dreaming, imagining I Feel You's apartment or house: was it a shack or a hacienda? She'd looked at a few of both on Streetmap in the past day. She wondered what his girlfriend looked like. Beautiful, of course.

> I Feel You: Correction. She doesn't want me to go now. Looks like I'm staying in! Jajajajaja.

Two crying with laughter faces popped up.

Cecilie still didn't know how to respond. So she didn't say anything. She waited for the waving ellipsis to see what else I Feel You was typing.

> I Feel You: And she's gone!
>
> I Feel You: I pissed her off by going online. Never mind, we'll be OK.

Cecilie had a strange feeling of triumph, to have I Feel You to herself, so they could chat.

* * *

The next morning, I Feel You told Arctic Fox he was an illustrator and a cartoonist for the local newspaper, and he wasn't going out tonight because he had an early start tomorrow covering the student march to the Palacio de Gobierno. Oh, and his head felt as if the Cocos and the North American plates were groaning through his brain, such was his hangover of tectonic proportions. He had gone out after all. He'd had to find Pilar – his girlfriend had a name – to make up with her. When I Feel You told Cecilie that his girlfriend was called Pilar, Cecilie thought she'd better know his name, and asked again.

> I Feel You: Oh, didn't I tell you? Sorry, I was borracho the other night. Hector. Hector Herrera. Encantado. I like Arctic Fox for your name, maybe it's best I don't ask you in case I don't like your real name.

Hector Herrera.

Cecilie found Hector's blunt exchange endearing. She was so used to tiptoeing around people in the library. Polite talks with Fredrik about a new recipe one of them had discovered (Fredrik was a vegan, which always made Morten marvel: how could such a beefy man live on a plant-based diet?); whispering in the library; apologising to customers in the cafe for no particular reason.

In the silence of Tromsø library that morning, Hector Herrera made Cecilie feel bolder, without her saying a word.

Arctic Fox: Well I might not like your name!

I Feel You: You don't?

Arctic Fox: Actually I do. Hector Herrera. I like an alliteration.

I Feel You: Alliteration? Lemme look it up...

Hector Herrera's knowledge of British slang was better than Cecilie's, but her English was stronger.

I Feel You: Ahhh I see. Like Daffy Duck.

Arctic Fox: Greta Garbo.

I Feel You: Fred Flintstone.

Arctic Fox: Marilyn Manson.

I Feel You: Mickey Mouse.

Arctic Fox: I can tell you're a cartoonist!

Hector laughed. As his shoulders shook, he remembered how chaotic the night before had become, and he scratched the brown waves that licked his sore temples.

Arctic Fox: Well, I'm Cecilie. Cecilie Wiig. Pleased to meet you Hector Herrera. Hyggelig å møte deg.

I Feel You: Cecilie Wiig. Me gusta mucho. Encantado.

On day four, a Friday, Hector wasn't there. Cecilie frowned at the screen and she played 'Condemnation' through the PA system of the library. Dave Gahan's rough plea rattled through the building, making it feel like a church quivering in an earthquake. Nymph-like despite Dr Martens boots, Cecilie fluttered up and down the stairs, channelling her disappointment and yearning into very efficient tidying.

Fredrik was almost alarmed when he wheeled his repaired bike through the staff entrance to hear a choir on the ground floor.

* * *

On day five, Cecilie offered to work an extra shift, even though it was Saturday and she didn't usually work on Saturdays, but the internet was down at home. Two extra staff worked at the library on a Saturday, Pernille and Leif, and neither wanted the day off. But Cecilie went to the library on the pretext of doing an inventory of the 120 journals and magazines the library regularly ordered.

Usually on a Saturday, Cecilie would catch up on her chores; play the harp, clean the house and keep it nice for Karin if her mother was away; or if Karin were in town, they would see a movie or a play. Sometimes Cecilie would go to see her friend Grethe in the ice cream parlour, or meet Morten on his lunch break at the salon. Espen was far too busy at the i-Scand hotel to ever take lunch, but Cecilie liked her lunches with Morten, and sometimes they would go to the hotel restaurant so they could catch Espen while they ate club sandwiches overlooking the harbour and the Hurtigruten waiting to set sail.

As Cecilie looked at her watch and wiped newsprint on her brow, she couldn't think of anything other than Hector Herrera. It was 11 a.m. With a quick count back on the thumb and four fingers on her left hand and the thumb and index finger on her right hand, she worked out it must be 4 a.m. in Mexico, so the chances of chatting were slim. Still, she went back to the computer she had turned on when she first arrived that morning and checked the window of their conversation.

I Feel You: I mished you!

He was online. Cecilie felt a pang of relief, although she wondered how hard Hector Herrera must have been partying if he was still up at 4 a.m. Plus his English wasn't so good at this time of night/day. His words seemed to slur, even on screen, but she was relieved to read them, however chaotic. One day without a chat had passed by very slowly and Cecilie had a feeling that Hector Herrera made everyone's day a little bit more interesting; she felt a pang of envy that he wasn't her friend in real life.

Their conversation went around in circles, frustratingly. Cecilie preferred it when Hector made more sense. She liked his bluntness, his honesty, his humour. So she made her excuses.

Arctic Fox: I'd better get back to work. You go to sleep!

I Feel You: Yeah I can't really talk. Pilar just ask what I'm doing. I better get back to the missus.

Missus?

Cecilie didn't like it and regretted coming in and committing to doing the inventory of journals, all for this.

Arctic Fox: Yeah I'd better get back to work anyway...

Even though I'm not needed and this is my day off.
Suddenly, Cecilie felt quite unwanted and decided to cool off a bit.

Why am I wasting so much time thinking about this guy? Cecilie logged off and went back to counting magazines, annoyed that she couldn't get the word 'missus' out of her head.

* * *

On the Sunday, Hector and Cecilie saw each other for the first time.

Pilar had gone to Mexico City to get an inking on her thigh and was angry that Hector hadn't gone with her for this big life event. Espen was working a late shift at the i-Scand, and their mother was in the capital. Cecilie decided to use Espen's laptop to try her luck, to see if the internet was back up on this side of the fjord. She really couldn't get him out of her head.

Fuck it.

An impish smile fluttered across her cheeks. She'd been on her feet all day in the cafe, having worked a seven-day week, and was exhausted and curious. Her heart started to race. She opened the lid of the MacBook, negotiated Espen's predictable password (their date of birth) and discovered the broadband was back up. She counted back. It was 4 p.m. in Mexico, 11 p.m. in Norway. It was light outside in both countries.

Arctic Fox: Wanna FaceTime?

Cecilie worried that Hector's girlfriend might be there, but if she was, that could be a good thing – maybe they could become friends too. It's not like she was ever going to meet Hector Herrera, or be a threat to Pilar.

I Feel You: Síííííí!

Arctic Fox: OK, be right back.

They exchanged numbers and ended the chat, never to meet in the fan forum again. Cecilie turned on the camera of Espen's laptop and ensured her face fitted perfectly into the rectangle on the screen. She checked herself over before pressing the green button. She looked OK. Tired but OK. Anyway, this wasn't a dating site like the one Espen had tried to get her a profile on, when he'd tried to convince her to cut off her dreadlocked hair before he'd set her up with a nice account and picture. 'It'll give you wider appeal,' he'd said. Morten had told Espen off for that. No, this was just a friendly chat.

A shrill tone rang out and an ellipsis as wide as the ocean that separated them fanned in front of her. And then Hector Herrera filled the screen. They looked at each other for the first time, and both laughed nervously.

Hector spoke first, words Cecilie didn't understand.

'*A su madre, no mames...*'

Hector stood up and walked away from the camera, circling the room behind the chair with his hands over his mouth, as if he had just received shock news. Cecilie saw a glimpse of Hector's home. A bright, lime-green wall and a wooden chair with a holy cross cut out in the back of it. There was a filled ashtray on a counter to the right, and beyond that an open kitchen. A colourful rug hung on the wall in stripes of fuchsia, red and orange. It looked very different to her sedate and spacious home in the Arctic Circle. Muted tones of grey, brown and white. Wooden interior walls as solid and reliable as the oak of the coffee table the MacBook was resting on. Modern clean lines. The thick rug under foot. The motionless Calder.

Hector paced in a circle in the small apartment, what must have been three or four times, with his hands clasped to his mouth. Through the small rectangular window into Hector's home, Cecilie could see his strong arms curving, a tattoo, of a hand perhaps, peering out below the khaki sleeve of his T-shirt. He wore brown utility shorts; his legs were lean but muscular. The screen pixelated and Cecilie lost perspective, lost her sight, as Hector came back to the chair and put his face close to the camera, searching his befuddled brain for words.

The screen smoothed out and Cecilie saw Hector up close again, sitting back down, and she was struck by how he looked exactly like the man she'd imagined. Although now she could see the clarity of his features. His far-apart eyes, bronze and glimmering, more earnest than flirtatious. He kept rubbing his small nose and covering his mouth in disbelief.

Hector gathered himself. He smiled, and his face made Cecilie feel happy. As she smiled back, her cheeks rose into a love heart shape and her eyes shone, a dart of green flashing into the camera. Hector sat back in his chair, his arms dropping down by his sides in defeat, and sighed. All English escaped him and he paused for a few seconds while he remembered his vocab.

'You are not from this planet,' Hector said, marvelling at his cracked screen. Cecilie didn't know how to react. She tugged on her dreadlocks, pulling them over to one shoulder, and her pale eyes creased into laughter. 'Seriously,' he said. 'Yours is the most beautiful face I have ever seen in all my life.'

You look like home, Cecilie thought, and she smiled.

9

MARCH 2018, TROMSØ, NORWAY

Cecilie rubs the fuzz of her short white-blonde hair.

'I feel like an animal!' She laughs, looking up at Morten through his reflection in the mirror.

'You look like a forest sprite!'

'I feel as light as one,' she says with a shake of her head.

Morten sweeps up the heavy blonde locks, turned a dull shade of grey from eight years of matted life.

'You definitely dropped a few kilos,' Morten says as he sweeps methodically.

The door of the salon opens and Espen walks in, the front of his white-blond quiff swept up, forming a perfect arc that falls to one shorn temple.

'It's true! Hallelujah!' he exclaims, tucking his phone into his suit pocket. 'You look so pretty with all that grubby hair gone!'

'Doesn't she?' says Morten, leaning on his brush and gazing adoringly. Cecilie's exposed face is even more beautiful without the distraction of hair.

'You could come work at the hotel now!' Espen claps, before

giving it some thought. 'Maybe in a few weeks, give it a little growth time to look a bit less... severe.'

Cecilie thumps Espen on the arm as she stands to pull her coat off the stool. She is almost as tall as her twin.

'I don't want to work at the i-Scand. I don't want to wear a uniform. I'm happy at the Hjornekafé.'

Cecilie remembers a no-uniform pact she once made with Hector, and feels wretched and sad.

'What, with batty old Gjertrud bickering with Ole over cake every day?'

'Don't be mean, Espen. Gjertrud and Ole are lovely. Just because they're enjoying life at a slower pace. All birds cannot be hawks, brother. Some of us are cuckoos.' Cecilie gives a sarcastic smile and throws on her coat. She rubs her soft shorn hair again and realises she's going to have a cold head.

'Here, take this,' Morten says, throwing her his yellow and turquoise hat with a red bobble on top.

'Thanks.'

'But you could speak English all day at the i-Scand. And with me as your boss, I'd give you the best shifts.'

Cecilie's arched brows meet in the middle. 'I'm not bothered about my English any more.'

She thinks back to that first sighting of Hector, scrutinising her through his computer lens. It made Cecilie want to know everything about him; about his life, his body, his smell, his country; to make her English even better so there were no misunderstandings. Better still, she could learn *his* language.

Soon they were chatting through little green boxes on their phones, punctuating everything they did with a photo. At first, it was always in the safe parameter of pen pals learning about each other's culture. For months, they never mentioned Pilar unless it was a place Hector had been with her; Hector didn't ask if

Cecilie had a boyfriend, even though she secretly wished he would so she could tell him she didn't.

She so desperately wanted to touch the newspaper Hector was holding in his hand; inhale the corn and coriander of his lunch; stroke the raw skin of his latest tattoo; be able to converse fluently with him, some way or another. So Cecilie embraced any chance to improve her English: she read *Time* and *Newsweek* in the library; spoke to the British, American, Australian and Canadian customers who faithfully walked through the door of the Hjornekafé, flocking to Tromsø in winter in search of the lights, or in summer to marvel at the midnight sun. But she doesn't need to learn new ways to say bollocks any more now that Hector is married, and she doesn't need the heavy hair that's dragged her down for so long.

'I love your hair,' Hector had said once he'd recovered from the shock of her beauty.

Now the hair is gone, and with it, in a pile on the floor, the hope Cecilie felt as they'd grown to know each other, as they'd fallen for each other, as they'd admitted they loved each other.

'Why so sad?' asks Espen, looking at his watch to get back to the afternoon bustle of check-ins, chambermaids and restaurant bookings.

Cecilie's face crumples as she puts on Morten's bobble hat.

'You don't like it? Oh gosh, that's what I was worried about!' Morten drops his broom and rushes over to put an arm around Cecilie's shoulder while Espen looks on awkwardly. 'But I think you look divine. Only you could pull this look off, Cecilie. Perhaps when it grows a bit I'll shape it into an edgy sweep that...' Morten doesn't finish; he is winded by the emotion of Cecilie slumping her face into his chest and sobbing into his checked shirt.

Morten wraps both arms around Cecilie and gives Espen a

look of trepidation. Espen shrugs; he doesn't know what to say. He doesn't know what goes on inside his sister's head. She is the half of him he will never understand.

'It's not the hair...' Cecilie sniffs as tears tumble down her cheekbones and into the red and blue fabric of Morten's shirt. 'It's my heart.'

10

MAY 2018, SUFFOLK, ENGLAND

Kate stands on the driveway of number five The Finches, her arms folded, her back to the white door of the garage. She cranes her neck and shifts her weight from one foot to the other. She's too angry to appreciate the neatness of their front garden. The polite foliage. The recycling bins hidden tidily away in the bespoke timber cubby. She looks at her watch.

He said he'd be home by seven.

It is ten past, and Kate is panicking that the meeting at Claresham Church of England Primary School will start without her. She needs to be there because she has agreed to be chair of the PTA from September, so it won't look good if she is late for the summer fair planning meeting, which starts in five minutes. After the family fireworks night, the summer fair is the biggest fundraiser of the school calendar, where coconut shies and teddy-bear tombolas take over Claresham village green on the first (hopefully sunny) Saturday of every July. Tonight, Kate needs to watch outgoing chair Melissa Cox closely, to see how this meeting runs, because next summer's fair, and all of the events, will be on her watch.

'Argh,' Kate rages to herself, quietly and with restraint, as she watches lights go on in the cul-de-sac's prim houses.

Kate looks to the sky as she waits for George's little red car, his train station runaround, to turn into The Finches from the left, and notices it's lighter than it has been at this time lately, although the warm bounce of spring from earlier in the day has subsided and her arms feel chilly.

Kate wraps her cardigan around her spongey middle and lets out a sigh. She rushed the kids through teatime so she could leave George with as little of the bedtime responsibility as possible. And he's late anyway.

I shouldn't have bothered. He could have cleared up their tea.

A small red Aygo swerves into the road, heading towards their house.

Her harangued-looking husband gets out of the car, leaving the engine running, and raises his palms passively but doesn't apologise.

'You're late, I'm cold!' says Kate in anaemic anger.

'Why didn't you grab a jacket?' George snaps.

'I didn't want to go back in, I've had to shout at the girls too many times tonight. George, they were so vile, I just don't want to look at them right now.'

George rolls his eyes and then does a double take as he looks at Kate's face. 'Are you wearing lipstick?'

'Yes. I sometimes do,' Kate counters defensively.

Baby steps.

George's small grey-blue eyes contain both mistrust and mockery.

'Here,' he says, unwrapping a stripy scarf in three shades of blue from his neck and stuffing it in Kate's hands. A chivalrous gesture ruined by the execution.

'Thanks,' Kate says sarcastically, winding it around her neck, wondering when the last time he might have done that for her was.

Never mind.

She doesn't dwell on it for too long before getting in the car.

'Your dinner is in the oven, make sure Jack has finished his times tables.'

George nods. 'Don't sign me up for running "splat the..."' Kate doesn't hear the rest of the sentence amid the rise of the engine. She's late and she heads off down the road, wiping her Heather Shimmer lipstick off her mouth, onto the back of her left hand, before changing gear with a sharp grunt.

* * *

'Right, so we've got Mr Horsley's Punch and Judy show at the north end of the green, bouncy castle on the east flank, and retro games to the south. I'm thinking coconut shy, pin the tail on the donkey, that kind of thing. That means refreshments can go along... here.' PTA chair Melissa Cox marks an X on the A4 printout of a poorly reproduced map with a black Sharpie. 'I'm thinking retro refreshments like fondant fancies, coconut macaroons, ginger beer, elderflower cordial...'

'Ooh, the site manager's wife makes a wonderful elderflower cordial,' interjects headteacher Hilary Smith.

'Does it have to be Punch and Judy?' asks Venetia Appleyard, mum of Millie, the most precocious girl in Year 6.

Melissa Cox's bright pink cheeks flush in the warmth of the overheated staffroom. 'Sorry, Venetia, you've lost me.'

'Well, Punch and Judy will encourage the children to laugh at a man whose only interaction with his wife and child is based on violence. It's misogynistic.'

Kate, still smarting from Chloe and Izzy's attitudes, and

George's careless comment about her lipstick, starts paying attention. She even stops the click click clicking of her pen, which she would have felt terrible about had she known how much it was annoying the school business manager sitting to her right.

'Is Punch and Judy not a thing these days?' asks Melissa, turning even pinker. In fact, Melissa's yellow hair and pink cheeks make her look like the colour of a retro sweet herself.

Kate widens her kind eyes. It was news to her, but this meeting has just got a bit controversial.

'It's so politically incorrect.' Venetia sighs with vehemence. 'It doesn't really sit with the school's ethos... And it's saying domestic violence is OK.'

Melissa looks politely inconvenienced. 'Well, I'm not sure how to tell Mr Horsley that he needs to change the entire content of his much-loved puppet show.' She grimaces – he is the deputy head's husband, after all.

'I'm afraid Venetia does have a point,' says Hilary.

'I don't mind talking to him,' says Kate, signing herself up for something she will only regret. She can hear George's voice in her head, moaning about her moaning about the tricky conversation she's dreading. 'He and I worked on the egg-shell painting stall together at the Easter disco and we had a nice chat. I'm sure I can think of a way to say it without insulting his work.' Kate gives a hopeful smile. Always trying. Always people-pleasing. Always taking on the shitty jobs everyone else avoids.

'Brilliant,' says Venetia. 'Surely he must have some animal puppets or something, the little ones will like that.'

Hilary Smith knows Mr and Mrs Horsley best, and she knows it won't go down well, but is relieved that Kate volunteered to take on this one.

Kate clicks her pen and writes 'speak to Mr Horsley' on her

list of actions and draws some stars on the line next to it. 'So back to the refreshments table. Last year, do you remember, we had those little lucky dip bags of sweets...?'

Melissa continues and Kate's mind trails off again.

She wonders how she can build up to red lipstick when she doesn't dare to wear Heather Shimmer. She wonders how her daughters are so much more sassy and spirited than she was at their age – or still is really. Chloe already knows she wants to be a vet; she has gone off to Brownie camps and coped perfectly well with being away from home *thankyouverymuch*. Kate had never been further than France when she did the most daring thing she ever did the summer she graduated, going to a Third-World country to volunteer in an orphanage, and even then it felt as if she had scaled Everest.

I wouldn't have dreamed of talking to my mother like that when I was eleven.

Kate's neck gets hot and she loosens the shackles of George's stripy blue scarf from around her neck and slides it out from under her ponytail and onto her lap. She looks down. A long, blonde hair sparkles under the stark strip lighting of the staffroom, too long and too blonde to belong to either Chloe or Izzy. Kate pulls at the hair, unravelling it as it goads her. A misogynistic and belittling shrill, that no one else can hear, rings inside Kate's hot ears as she instinctively puts a hand to her own brown ponytail.

11

SEPTEMBER 2013, DAY 94

I Feel You: Who was your first lover?

Cecilie sat in the library after closing on a Thursday night. She'd worked the morning shift, singing lullabies and lending books; spent an afternoon at the Hjornekafé, with just Gjertrud and Ole for company, and had come back to the library to help Fredrik lock up. Cecilie increasingly offered to help Fredrik lock up so she could talk to Hector on his lunch break. Now Fredrik had gone home to mindfulness and vegan Malbec with his girlfriend, so Cecilie sat in silence, staring at her screen. She typed:

Arctic Fox: Why do you ask?

She was shocked by Hector's forthright question and looked around her to check no one could see over her shoulder in the empty library.

I Feel You: I want to know. It helps me draw you.

Arctic Fox: Draw me?

Yet again, Cecilie was disarmed by Hector's honesty, and surprised by how relaxed she felt about answering his question. It had been a forbidden subject in her past. Talking about current relationships seemed to be forbidden too. But a wave of liberation made sparks fly as her fingers danced across the computer keypad.

Cecilie thought back to the music room at school. The sensation of hands brushing against each other as she sat next to him at a keyboard. Accusative looks from boys in registration. Envious glares from girls at the bus stop. An obsessed ex-girlfriend with a determined face. His ashen expression when he walked out of the principal's office as Cecilie was summoned in. The shame her mother felt when the story went national.

Arctic Fox: His name was Mr Lind. Jonas. He was my music teacher at school.

Hector tried not to spit guacamole onto his sketching pad at his desk.

I Feel You: Your teacher? Wow.

Cecilie thought about her first time with her first lover. They'd been to see *Walk the Line* at the picture house and had walked back to his apartment with their hands in their pockets. He had so wanted to put his arm around her. She wanted to tear his jacket off. As soon as they'd closed the door behind them, Cecilie ran her fingers through Mr Lind's messy quiff and kissed his thin lips frantically.

He was a good teacher. Passionate about music. Passionate about his job. As first lovers go, he was pretty wonderful.

Hector felt a stab of jealousy like he'd never known.

I Feel You: Did you fall in love with him?

Arctic Fox: Of course I did. It was a big deal. It got us both into a lot of trouble, so I wouldn't have slept with him if I hadn't loved him. I was a good girl, always reading, always playing my harp. Mr Lind was my first lover.

And my last.

Hector imagined a man with grey hair putting his hands on Cecilie, and wished he hadn't asked. She continued typing.

Arctic Fox: He was 34, I was 17.

About the same age as me now. Puta madre...

Hector reimagined Mr Lind to look a little less grey, and let Cecilie carry on, glad for once that they weren't talking on FaceTime.

Arctic Fox: But you can't choose who you fall in love with, can you? We just had a connection. I felt it. In the music room, when he took me dancing. In his bed...

Cecilie wondered what Hector would make of this.

Hector pushed his lunch away and wiped his mouth on his arm.

I Feel You: What happened to him?

Arctic Fox: He lost his job. Had to leave. He was disgraced. The story made the newspapers because my mum is kinda famous...

She wondered what Hector would make of that too, but carried on.

Arctic Fox: So he went travelling. To Thailand. To Cambodia. To Indonesia. I got the odd postcard, but it broke my heart.

I Feel You: Wow, I'm sorry.

Arctic Fox: Don't be sorry, I'm glad it happened. And he's married with little ones now and teaching in Oslo, so it's all good.

Cecilie thought of the faded postcard in her harp case. A Buddhist temple with perforated stupas. A message saying she was worth losing his job for and he would love her forever.

Arctic Fox: What about you?

Hector couldn't shake the feeling of nausea. He so wished he hadn't asked. So he pretended he had a meeting to go to; he wasn't as honest as Cecilie thought.
Cecilie felt maybe it was best she didn't know anyway. It was hard enough trying to imagine the current girlfriend he barely talked about.
Hector didn't tell Cecilie about the English girl who volunteered at the orphanage. How he had given the impression of being so much more worldly, but actually it was she who took his virginity, just before he broke her heart. How he feels bad

when he remembers it. How he sometimes thinks about how the English girl's life turned out.

> I Feel You: Talk tomorrow, sorry, I have to go. Oscar's busting my balls.

> Arctic Fox: OK cool, you can tell me more about your drawings then...

> I Feel You: Drawings?

> Arctic Fox: Of me.

> I Feel You: Oh, they're beautiful. You're easy to draw. I didn't actually need to know about your first lover, I was just curious.

Hector couldn't shake the image of a young Cecilie entwined with an older man, so he logged off and went to the water cooler to fill his plastic cup.

Cecilie typed 'Goodbye', with a familiar urge to do something forbidden.

12

MAY 2018, SUFFOLK, ENGLAND

'Sorry I'm late, I had to go back for my notebook, just in case I miss anything.' Kate feels a drop of sweat run down her back as Melissa Cox, pink and yellow and calm because she's already been there for ten minutes, stirs her coffee.

'Oh, don't worry, I was just looking over my handover notes.'

Kate pulls up a chair in Jack & Jill's deli cafe and unravels her wrap scarf.

'I ordered a raspberry Bakewell slice. Do you want one?'

Kate feels the stretch around her thighs. 'I shouldn't.'

Melissa doesn't dwell on whether Kate is or isn't having cake and opens her notebook to get down to business. She talks Kate through the highs and lows of being chair of the PTA and gives her all the banking books, event notes and contacts for the annual list of fundraisers on the school social calendar. Kate scribbles diligently in her book, trying not to ask too many questions, trying not to witter, trying not to get in a flap.

'You know you've got this, don't you?' Melissa asks.

Kate looks up, as if she's missed something. 'Got what?'

'This chair malarkey. You'll be fine. You're good with

numbers. You're good at fighting fires. You're super organised. Everyone likes you...'

Everyone likes me?

'Just make sure no one takes the piss. Venetia has a knack of talking loudly so people *think* she's taking loads on, but she isn't as hands-on as she makes out. And Hilary does need nudging now and then, but she's OK with that, so don't feel you have to apologise to her all the time.'

Kate's very good at apologising all the time. She apologises to her daughters when she tells them off; she apologises to George if the veg is ever-so-slightly overdone. She even apologised to Jack's friend Samuel's mum when Samuel bit Jack in the back and left his dental imprint there for a week.

'OK, I'll try not to.'

Melissa's phone rings and she quickly rejects the call. 'Dave,' she says with a sigh.

Kate knows Dave Cox left Melissa last year, but she doesn't know why or how it happened. Genevieve Walton at Beavers said he'd run off with someone at work, but Kate doesn't know Melissa well enough to ask what occurred; how long she had her suspicions; whether she saw it coming.

A young waiter comes to clear the table. 'Can I just take your empty cups?' he asks.

'Sorry,' says Kate as she leans back.

13

JUNE 2018, XALAPA, MEXICO

'Baby, wake up, you've got school.' Hector is on his knees on the bed, rubbing the bony sierra of Pilar's spine, the contours of her flat chest anchored into the core of the mattress. He shakes the sharp blade of her shoulder gently. 'Pilar!'

A fist lashes out, restrained by a once-white sheet.

Hector ducks out of the way with a frown. 'Eh! Don't take it out on me! You gotta get up. You got kids waiting for you.'

An arching nose appears from under black matted hair. Pilar's Moorish skin looks pasty, and Hector can't tell if the black shadows under her eyes are caused by last night's mayhem or last night's mascara.

'What happened, baby?' he asks, eyes widened with concern.

Pilar flops back into the bed.

'Benny Trujillo happened,' she murmurs, her face seeking comfort against the pillow.

Hector slips off the bed as hatred and fear rise in his neck. *Cálmate.* Calm yourself.

He slinks out of the bedroom and into the open living room and kitchen space of their apartment, scratching his topless torso and looking for a distraction to calm his rage. Hector has surprised himself by how calm, how *tranquilo*, he's been lately, and he knows what his new demeanour is down to.

The morning after their wedding, Hector woke up feeling furry-tongued and foolish, and decided to stop drinking there and then. He didn't touch a drop during their honeymoon on the Gulf Coast – only water or watery fruit punch for the groom, while the bride drank daiquiris with her *desayuno* of eggs and pancakes.

When Señor and Señora Herrera got back from their honeymoon, Hector stopped smoking weed and, ten days later, cigarettes. It wasn't as difficult as he had thought; it was the habits that were the hardest to break, not the addictions. Despite seeming like someone who laughs happily through life's shitstorms, when Hector is determined to do something, he faces the struggle head on and does it.

He was determined to study art at university, even though Benny said art was for fags and university was for pussies; he was determined to get a job at *La Voz* as an illustrator, even though Benny said working for a newspaper would make him a weasel; and he was determined to get away from Benny and end their deepest of ties, even though he feared for his own life in doing so. And waking up a married man, Hector just knew that he had to quit drinking, and his determination alone would get him through it.

Hector was smart enough to know he had to change his habits, his patterns, before he could change anything else. So he stopped rolling from his newspaper office to the cantinas after work. He stopped taking Pilar for tacos and micheladas in a diner. He stopped looking for her, dancing in a club at 2 a.m. He told Ricky and Elias that he had work to do, commissions to draw. He started staying home and spent his evenings on the sofa sketching; sketching women, sketching animals, sketching mythical beasts, some grotesque, some beautiful. He joined *La Voz*'s five-a-side football team and saw improvements in his shape and agility every week that the editorial squad squared up to the advertising boys.

Yet now, three months later, out of pure muscle memory, in a moment of anger and exasperation, Hector feels the pockets of his cargo shorts in the hope that a packet of Delicados lies within.

Of course it doesn't.

The habit, and Pilar, were the hardest things about giving up. Ricky and Elias soon stopped asking Hector out and relied on Efrain and Heriberto to bring the whisky and the laughter to the party. But Pilar was less forgiving about him not wanting to go out any more.

Hector stood firm. He didn't miss the fog. He didn't miss the drama. He didn't miss the hangovers. He didn't miss the rows and the rages, although Pilar still rages on, as she did last night before she walked out.

Hector pads barefoot to the fridge to open a carton of orange juice and swigs from it to replenish himself.

Tranquilo, he thinks, aware that his left hand is scrunched into a fist. He opens his palms to release the tension and walks across the room to the panel of windows that overlook the noise of horns and smells of sizzling *huevos rancheros* below. It is 8 a.m. and already the town is bustling, children on their way to school.

Hector swigs again and lowers the carton of orange juice. On the box is an animated orange with arms and legs, dancing a conga at the front of a line of fruity characters. A lime with a cheeky smile. A muscleman mango flexing his arms. A sexy strawberry fluttering long eyelashes. The picture reminds Hector of Jugo's California, Benny's juice bar, and his first foray into business all those years ago. Hector chokes a little and puts his free fist to his bare chest to help ease out an uncomfortable cough.

He recovers and looks around the room. Torn sketches he tried to piece together with magic tape lie in a pile on the coffee table. He looks at the fragments; an iridescent eye on a shard of paper looks back at him, challenging him to speak up and fight for himself, even though he is tired of fighting.

Hector walks back into the bedroom and places the juice firmly on the rickety wooden bedside table.

'This will help,' he says.

Pilar emerges from under the sheet, turns gingerly onto her back, and raises a spindly arm to her brow. Hector fluffs up his vacant pillow next to her, taking his anger out on the synthetic stuffing, nursing his rage as well as her hangover. He props the pillow up against the rough spikes of the whitewashed plaster wall and Pilar rises to lean on it.

Hector passes her the orange juice and she sips clumsily. A trail of orange trickles from the corner of Pilar's claggy mouth and onto the sheet that clings to the blue heart above her breast.

Hector lowers his voice so he can speak calmly and sincerely.

'You know you shouldn't hang out with Benny Trujillo and his friends, hey? They're not good people.'

Pilar shoots Hector a petulant look but doesn't raise her voice. She is always quieter when her hangovers are really bad.

'You wouldn't come out with me, *viejo*. Who else was I going to party with?'

'You didn't *want* me going out with you!' Hector protests. 'You walked out. You were mad at me. Remember?'

A wave of confusion washes over Pilar's sallow silhouette. Even the sun streaming in through the wall of glass to the bedroom balcony doesn't lift her morning-after pallor. Hector perches on the bedside table, which strains a little under his thighs, and he watches Pilar as she tries to recall. All the anger she felt last night, that Hector spent the evening cleaning up after, and she doesn't even remember it.

'My drawings?' he prompts, not wanting to revisit the anguish, but shocked that Pilar could forget so easily. Or, if she does remember, how she can brush over it without apologising.

Of course she won't apologise.

'Oh, those...' Pilar shrugs.

Last night, just after Pilar had finished putting the finishing flick of thick black eyeliner to her hooded lids, she pleaded with her husband to join her for once, because he was turning into a boring old man.

'No, baby, I'm gonna stay in,' he said apologetically, trying to avoid a row. Hector told Pilar he was going to work on some drawings he wanted to send to a children's book publisher in Mexico City, and that she should meet her friend Xochitl as she had planned.

Pilar didn't tell Hector that Xochitl had just cancelled, which was the real reason she was particularly irked that Hector didn't want to go out last night – she hadn't seemed to mind earlier. But she *needed* a drink after what had happened at work. So Pilar had stalked the apartment like a panther, her black hive of hair swishing into a predator's tail behind her, sweeping and searching for an argument. She found it in one of Hector's A4 sketchbooks, carelessly left lying on the small round dining table in the corner of the living room.

Looking for something to take her rage out on, Pilar flipped open a book at random and found it. The book was filled, page after page, with sketches of Pilar. She was used to seeing herself in pencil, charcoal and ink. It was how Hector wooed Pilar in the first place, by turning her into a cartoon character and sending one of the kids from the orphanage to school with a sketch of SupaPila, folded up in his pocket, under strict instruction to hand it to Miss Cabrera. SupaPila was a kick-ass beauty, half superhero, half queen, lavished with bunches of flowers by a court jester with a Mexican eagle on his shoulder. After a few weeks, Hector pleaded with SupaPila to go out for a drink with him, and she sent a note back to the orphanage with her phone number on it.

Over six years, Hector's cartoons of Pilar became more sophisticated: from naked pencil sketches to a portrait in gouache that wouldn't seem out of place in the Prado in Madrid, her aquiline nose and high hair able to hold their own next to Goya's Black Duchess. Over time, Pilar had become indifferent to her portraits, but last night she scavenged her way through the book, picking out anything she could find to be angry about.

'My nose isn't that big!'

'My ass doesn't look like that!'

'Why did you put a *peinata* in my hair? I'm Mexican now.'

And as she flipped towards the back of the book, one of many that Hector filled years ago, her haughty, hawkish features dropped. Suddenly, her portraits looked different. The eyes were pale. The breasts were rounded. The legs were strong. The hair was piled in twists.

'This isn't me,' Pilar said in horror. 'Who is this?'

Hector rose from the sofa calmly to see what Pilar was looking at, hoping to rescue his notebooks, but he already knew.

'Who's this... this... *güera?*' Pilar almost spat the word. One part enraged, one part satisfied to have found something to take her rage out on. 'Is this the "pen pal" you talk to on your computer? Is this bitch the person you're messaging on your phone day and night?'

Pilar hadn't even noticed that Hector *hadn't* been messaging his pen pal for months.

Hector glanced up at his artwork in Pilar's shaky hands and saw *her* face again. His heart shrank.

I miss her.

His solemn eyes and his refusal to answer enraged Pilar even more.

'Did *she* pose naked for you? You having grubby little phone sex with some *güera* whore?'

Pilar's features became more jagged as she shouted, her face contorting like Picasso's *Weeping Woman*.

'No, baby, this is just my imagination, someone I made up. Someone from another planet.'

'Then it doesn't matter if I do this then, eh, Hector?'

Pilar ripped clumps of pages out of the sketchbook and tore them into fragments, like a child having a temper tantrum. When she'd finished ripping the pictures of Cecilie, she started on the pictures she didn't like of herself, before flipping through other sketchbooks, tearing, ripping, shouting.

Hector walked to his desk and unstuck his parents' wedding photo for safekeeping, then skulked into the bedroom, lay back on the bed and put his headphones on his ears. He scrolled his phone for his favourite song, *her* favourite song, and pressed play. Howling feedback, dirty blues riffs; 'I Feel You' ripped his heart out as Pilar tore the pages from his sketchbooks.

* * *

'You said you were meeting Xochitl. I wouldn't have been cool with you going out with Benny if I'd have known. It's too dangerous.'

The sun's curve floods through the window and into Pilar's face, finally lighting her brown eyes.

'Well, Xochitl is as boring as you. She wanted to stay in and catch up on her *telenovelas*.'

Hector, sitting back on the creaking bedside table, leans his elbows on his thighs and makes a triangle with his fingers as he pushes them together.

'I'm serious, Pilar. Benny and his friends are not the people a nice married lady from Spain should hang out with.'

Pilar lets out a husky laugh. 'You can say that again. Ayyyy, they party!'

'It's not funny. You don't know what he's capable of.'

'But Benny told me you two were like brothers when you were little. "Olmeca and Zapata", getting into little scrapes and adventures across the neighbourhood.'

Hector rubs his eyes.

'What happened with you two anyway? Why are you so uptight? He's always good to me.' Pilar turns to look up at Hector, and he sinks into her eyes.

Hector never elaborated on his history with Benny, only that it was history. He never told Pilar about the bad bits, because he thought those would become pretty obvious just by looking at Benny and his gang. But, Hector realises, like everything else with Pilar, her distorted way of thinking means she probably won't ever see this for herself. She doesn't even feel remorseful for ripping up sketches he spent years working on. That shrug told him she remembered perfectly well. But then Benny happened, and Benny Trujillo has a way of obliterating everything that went before him.

Hector ignores the question and concedes. 'Come on, I'll start the shower, you better get a move on,' he says, standing, as he goes to help Pilar up from under her armpits.

She flinches. 'Get off!'

'Pilar, you have to get up, get to school. You have thirty first-graders waiting for you.'

'No I don't.'

'What?'

'I lost my job.'

'You lost your job?' Hector runs a shaky hand through his hair. 'When? Why didn't you tell me?'

'I would have told you if you'd have come out last night,' Pilar says, lashing out.

Hector stands and looks out the window. He can see Orizaba's mighty peak, and he puts his hands to his mouth in despair.

Pilar looks up, ever more petulant, outraged by his shock. 'What's your problem? That fucking bitch Vicky said she had some complaints from the parents. I work my ass off for those kids and all their parents do is complain.'

'Shiiiiiiit.'

Hector scratches his fingers through the soft waves bouncing at his temples. His eyes dart from left to right, like the frantic Hector of old, trying to find a way to fix this; to fix Pilar. Since they got engaged, her parents stopped sending riches from the Old World and they've barely survived on two salaries. How will they pay the rent on his alone?

The pesos in the jar.

Every time Hector hadn't gone out *chupando* in the few months since he got clean, he put 200 pesos in a jar – his '*chupito* jar', he calls it.

There must be seven or eight thousand in there.

'My jar,' he says, walking out of the bedroom to get it from the cupboard under the television. 'That should buy us a few weeks for you to get another job,' he calls from the living room while Pilar stays static in bed. 'I was talking to Cintia and

Mariana in Lazaro's the other day and they were saying how rushed off their feet they were. Maybe you could ask there until you find another teaching job, or make an appeal to Vicky...'

Hector cuts off. The jar isn't there. He fumbles among the cables, a frantic hand searching in a dark and cluttered nook he can't see. Then he looks above the cupboard, behind the television, at the back of the DVDs. He knows it was near the television, because every time he sat on the sofa sketching, or watching TV, while he tried to ignore texts from his friends, from Pilar, urging him to join them in a bar or cantina – to be the real Hector again – he would look towards the cupboard, to his *chupito* jar stuffed with red and green notes, and imagine what he would spend that money on. A designer dress for Pilar from Mexico City? No, *he* had earned that money, not her. Converting the second bedroom into a studio? Pilar never showed any interest when Hector mentioned babies, so maybe turning the spare room into a place for Hector to paint would at least start that conversation. Or...

A flight to Europe?

'It's gone, baby,' Pilar calls out with a husky croak, sounding not the slightest bit remorseful. 'I needed it the other night.'

Hector leans his palms against the edge of the chipboard cupboard with the TV on top of it. His head hangs down and he looks at his bare feet on the cool tiled floor.

'You spent eight thousand pesos, of money I saved, on one night out?' he says quietly.

Calm yourself.

Pilar jumps out of bed and storms into the living room, wrapped tightly in the sullied sheet that trails behind her like a bridal train. She sees Hector's bare back arching, leaning away from her. His fake Calvin Kleins rising above the waist of his brown cargo shorts.

'Shut *up*, OK, Hector?' she snaps. 'My head is hurting and I don't need this shit right now. Stop being such a whining bitch.'

Hector turns and slumps down and sits on the terracotta tiles.

'Anyway, I told Benny last night. He said he'd look after us.'

The walls of the apartment start to sway a little. The TV cabinet Hector is leaning against bumps across the floor ever so gracefully, shunting Hector along a little, urging him to pull himself back up and get to work. The sofa facing him and the round dining table in the corner also move a few centimetres to the south; fragments of paper fall to the floor again and scraps of Pilar's sharp eyes and bitter smile taunt him. Tectonic plates shift, the earth quakes, and Hector Herrera's conflicted, angry heart rips into two as he wonders how the hell he's going to get them out of this mess.

14

When they were boys, Benny Trujillo was Hector's bunk buddy at the Villa Infantil De Nuestra Señora. They met when Hector was seven and Benny was nine. Benny had never known his mother, who fled town the night he was born, so Benny had spent his entire life being passed around, from aunt to grandparent to foster carer and back again, until they all had too much and he was left on the doorstep of the orphanage by an exhausted aunt.

'I'm sorry,' she said to Sister Miriam, the most senior of the three sisters who ran the orphanage in a town-centre villa, given to the diocese by a generous patron named Sánchez. 'We've washed our hands of him. Some people are just bad eggs. His father, whoever he is or was, must have been a bad egg,' said the woman with exasperated eyes.

Sister Miriam was horrified by how a child could be written off. But she took in the little boy with the square head, who wore a black bow tie over an orange shirt with ruffles on it, and showed him to his bunk.

'Hector has just got back from his grandfather's,' Sister

Miriam explained as she smoothed Benny's wiry black centre-parted hair. 'You boys will get on like a house on fire.' Alejandro Herrera became an old man the day his son and his wife died in a car crash, although Hector couldn't imagine his *abuelo* was ever a young man. He was already a widower and the only relative alive and able to take Victor and Lupe's four-year-old son on. Hector had been in the back of the car when it spun off the roadside and down a ravine at Las Vigas, after a Day of the Dead festival had turned rainy, as November days often did in the mountains. Hector's four-year-old bones must have been more pliable and able to take the shock than his parents'. At the bottom of the ravine, his mum and dad didn't speak, so Hector climbed onto the bench of the front seat to wake them.

'Mamá!' Hector had lumbered onto her lap, but it was hard to hug her with his brother in the way inside her tummy. 'Mamá!'

Hector looked at his dad but his face was distorted and red, his mouth locked wide open, and he looked a bit scary, so Hector snuggled around his mother's distended stomach, hugged it and cried, waiting for her to wake up while another life inside her was slipping away.

Alejandro took Hector on and learned to cook, and then rotate, three meals: *tamales*, *pozole* and *pollo a la Veracruzana*. He'd never cooked before; his wife Maria always had. Since Maria died three years earlier, Alejandro had got by on tacos and tostadas. But as he scooped Hector up in the hospital and took him back to his ramshackle little house on Calle Bremont, he knew he would have to learn to cook, to clean, to look after an only son again, as Victor had been.

Alejandro found looking after a preschooler back-breaking work at his age – his days in the gardens at the Museum of Anthropology were physical enough, but when Hector climbed onto his grandfather's back to ask Abuelo all the questions he was desperate to know the answers to, his spine would curve like a question mark until he thought it might just snap. The manager of the museum, a small and sympathetic man with a neat moustache named Felipe Hernández, was understanding, and welcomed the little boy at the museum. When Hector was six and started school, Alejandro found it even harder to work around the school day; dropping Hector off, picking him up and taking him back to the grounds of the *museo* to play hide-and-seek with the Olmec heads (Hector always won; those enormous stone statues were *rubbish* at hiding).

Soon after Hector had started school, Alejandro paid Sister Miriam a visit at the Villa Infantil, and she was kind and welcoming. She said she, Sister Juana and Sister Virginia would find space for Hector alongside the twenty other children, whenever Alejandro needed help.

Señor Hernández agreed for Alejandro to work at the museum, one week on, and then take the next week off so he could care for his grandson. He was accommodating; he'd felt terrible enough when Alejandro lost his wife to a heart attack, but to lose his son and daughter-in-law three years later...

'Of course, Alejandro,' Hernández said. 'You can work double shifts one week – in the grounds until the sun goes down – and then clean the interior of the museum after closing. Then you can have the next week off. Hector needs you,' he said with an avuncular nod. Hernández was sympathetic, but he wasn't *that* sympathetic.

On the weeks Alejandro worked at the *museo*, he pulled sixteen-hour shifts across seven days, working 6 a.m. until 10 p.m., until there wasn't a blade of grass too long, a plant unpruned, a gecko out of place or a display case smeared, and Hector would stay at the Villa Infantil De Nuestra Señora under the kind gaze of Sisters Miriam, Juana and Virginia. On the 'off' weeks, the weeks he had Hector staying back at his little house, Alejandro was a full-time grandparent; taking Hectorcito to school, cleaning, cooking, and darning the holes in his socks and on the knees of his trousers by day; then feeding him, bathing him, helping with his homework and reading him bedtime stories at night. Hector was exhausting but lively company.

'He keeps me young,' Alejandro said quietly to Sister Miriam one day.

There isn't much Hector remembers from his early years at the orphanage; he can't even remember the day he met Sister Miriam, when she gasped at how much Hector looked like Lupe Herrera, the friendliest of the girls who worked on the ground floor at Lazaro's, and pulled him to her bosom. The two most vivid memories Hector has from his childhood are of clinging to his mother's belly in the wreckage of the car, and the day Benny Trujillo, in his orange frilled shirt, black bow tie and thick square head, turned up at the Villa Infantil.

All the children at the Villa Infantil were orphans or had been abandoned, but Hector and Benny were the most alike and would have gravitated towards each other, regardless of whether Sister Miriam gave them a little nudge at the start.

The twenty-two children varied in age, from eighteen months to fifteen years, and many of them were siblings. Hector and Benny weren't the only seven and nine-year-old boys there, but they were the only ones without a brother or a sister, so they stuck together. They were also the most mischievous. Hector called Benny 'Olmeca' because his large head with its creased forehead, thick nose and wide lips reminded him of the colossal stone heads at the Museum of Anthropology. Benny called Hector 'Zapata' because his agreeable face and wide, bronze eyes looked like the man in the book Sister Virginia had shown them when she was teaching the children about the Mexican Revolution. Hector played up to this – he always did want to make Benny laugh – by painting a huge moustache on his face in ink that took five days to wash off.

When Hector was in favour, he was 'Zapata', and Benny would lift him on his shoulders like a war hero if he managed to meet one of Benny's challenges: to steal something from a visitor to the orphanage, or put a cockroach in one of the children's bunk beds, or turn pictures upside down to make Sister Miriam think she was going mad. Sometimes Hector would turn down one of Benny's challenges because he felt too guilty at the thought of the consequence; Nuria would miss her only toy, Sister Juana would be mortified if her *polvorones* made people sick, and Alejandro would be so devastatingly disappointed if Hector took twenty pesos from his wallet. When Hector refused a challenge, Benny's thick lips would curl and he would call Hector a dirty peasant and not speak to him for days. But their weakness was always each other. Olmeca and Zapata always came back to each other. They were best friends.

As teenagers, Benny's challenges got bolder, and Hector got a bit more carefree about meeting them, his hormones making him more cavalier. He didn't know why he wanted to make Benny Trujillo so happy. Hector could have plenty of other friends in the orphanage, or at the school they both went to; he got along well with everyone. But he mostly felt guilty because he knew Benny probably couldn't. People didn't warm to Benny Trujillo's craggy scowl or his clumsiness; girls didn't ever ask Benny to the movies, like they did Hector.

Hanging out one Friday evening in Parque Juárez next to the Palacio de Gobierno, Benny and Hector leaned against the back of a pop-up popcorn stand and Benny set Hector a challenge.

'See that guy there with the grey suit...?'

Hector looked at one of the officials, stepping out of the government building with an elegant woman on his arm, waiting for a car to arrive to take him and his wife for dinner.

'Yeah?'

'Get something from him. Anything. And I'll give you the top bunk tonight.'

Top bunk was the best prize because then you weren't on the bottom bunk, where you would never know if the person on the top bunk was about to swing down with a rolled-up comic book and thwack you round the head.

The man looked irked by the inconvenience of having to wait for a car, so he and his wife walked away into the after-work melee to flag down a taxi.

'Too easy.'

Egged on by teen bravado, Hector set about his challenge while Benny sunk back into the shadows of the popcorn cart to watch. Hector weaved between the ochre arches and grey pillars of the Palacio's façade, under the long balcony spruced up with green awnings above their heads on the grand first floor. He got closer to the dapper man with his slow walk: he must have been a minister – or even the governor himself... Hector didn't care who he was, he just had to meet Benny's challenge, so he tailed the couple for a few metres, his eyes darting left and right frantically, while he thought about his tactics.

He could get anything from the man: a button from his suit or his cigarette butt from the floor, but he knew he'd get extra kudos if it was something *useful,* something *valuable.* Benny liked Hector even more when he came back from a challenge with something they could spend or sell, because Benny always had a knack of turning something small into something bigger, such was his hatred for being poor.

As Hector weaved through the throng, he felt a metallic taste in his mouth and saw a gift before his very eyes: the elegant woman, wearing a woollen skirt suit with a chunky pearl necklace that matched the bracelet on her wrist, had her handbag *wide open*. Her bulging purse was bursting out of it.

Too easy.

In the rush-hour noise, as the bell chimed on the cathedral opposite, and drivers of the green and white Beetles tooted their horns with impatient passengers in the back, Hector removed his thin bomber jacket, slung it over his arm, and bent down to undo a lace on his red Converse boot.

'Ufff!' He stumbled over, falling and rolling at the lady's shiny beige stilettos to cause a distraction.

The man in the grey suit stopped suddenly but didn't say anything; he just looked irritated. The woman, with her soft caramel-blonde hair, bent down, knees together, with an anxious, maternal look in her eyes.

'Are you OK?' she asked, crouching and placing her hand on the knee of the skinny boy.

Hector feigned embarrassment and looked at his red boot and shrugged. He'd never taken it this far before. It was now or never.

'Yes, yes, sorry, I must have tripped on my laces.' Hector winced in pretend pain. 'All OK now though,' he said as he lifted the woman's bulky purse out from the bag under his bomber jacket. He dusted himself down with his free hand and the elegant woman took him by the arm. He had to stand up without using his concealed hand, but managed to, holding tightly to the purse under his jacket.

'Are you sure you're OK, young man?' asked the woman again. Hector could see his reprehensible reflection in a chunky pearl.

He nodded. He just wanted to get away. 'Thank you,' he said. 'I'm sorry.'

And with that, he walked back in the direction of the park while the woman gave her husband a look, pleading with him to show a little compassion.

'Silly fool,' he said gruffly. 'Kids can't even tie their own shoelaces nowadays.'

Hector skipped back to the park so the orphan brothers could split their haul. It was his biggest yet, and he was sure Benny would be proud of him.

Benny's eyes lit up as they counted the money.

'Wow, that's 1,879 pesos. Nine hundred each. I get the seventy-nine extra 'cause I set the challenge.'

Hector didn't argue. He was feeling pleased with himself, until Benny punched him on the arm.

'But you failed the challenge, you *hijo de puta* peasant.'

'Huh?'

'I said get something from the man. Not the lady. I keep top bunk tonight. And you're a fuckin' idiot.'

'Idiot? We have nearly a thousand pesos each!' Hector had never seen a thousand pesos in his entire life.

'Yeah, but when that lady notices her purse has gone, she's gonna know it was the orphan peasant who fell over and took it out of her bag, isn't she? And she's gonna see you again one day. Pretty soon, because you live here and you hang out here. Congratulations, Hector, you just did a big shit on your own feet.'

Hector felt angry. His left hand made a fist.

And as he lay on the bottom bunk that night, taking the intermittent hits when Benny swung down with a rolled-up copy of *Karmatrón Y Los Transformables*, he vowed never to honour another of Benny's challenges. At dinner, he hadn't been able to look at Sister Miriam and in bed, he couldn't get out of his head the face of the woman, a concerned and maternal gaze because she thought Hector might have hurt himself. She had children; he had seen the photo of them in her wallet – two teenage boys – and they would be feeling sad for their mother tonight.

Determination washed over Hector as he lay and took another hit from Benny.

Game over.

15

JUNE 2018, SUFFOLK, ENGLAND

Looking along the row under the darkened big top, Kate feels a swell of pride, even if Chloe is scrolling through her phone. *What's she looking at now? These tickets weren't cheap.*

But there they sit, three little eggs all in a row, increasing in size. Youngest first, Jack, leans into Kate's arm as he waits for the clown to come back, because Jack thinks the clown on the unicycle is the funniest. Izzy is next to her brother, trying not to show that she's impressed by the aerialist pulling her body up between two swathes of white fabric, but Kate can tell she is. Beyond Izzy, Chloe looks at her new phone, the one she got in anticipation of going to secondary school in September, like all her friends did for their eleventh birthdays. She's not impressed by the acrobatics in the air. She wants to see what Perrie from Little Mix is doing on Instagram.

Kate pulls Jack to her bosom. Her heart is proud but sad, the vacant seat to her left goading her. The one she decided to pile all the coats on, given George said he had to work today. Zippy Von Braun's Big Top always comes to Claresham during half-term, and the Wheelers have been coming since Chloe was four.

But last night, after they'd had a Chinese from the takeaway in the village, George said he had to go back into London tomorrow. On a Saturday. To tie up some sustainable or responsible investment deal or something, which didn't sound all that responsible, given Kate had been looking forward to this for months. The pile of coats looms in Kate's peripheral vision.

She gazes in awe at the aerialist. Her strong arms and muscular thighs, entwined in cloth as she climbs, rising through the air, while doing the splits upside down from a daring height. Kate looks at the acrobat's stomach, the naked space between her lilac satin crop top and matching big pants, as she uses every sinew of her core. Working hard, relying on her own strength to lift herself higher up towards the roof of the circus tent. Kate marvels at another woman's body. At her own inadequacies. At the acrobat's red lipstick in a shade she dare not try.

I wish I were her.

As twists of white cloth unravel, a flash of lilac and a whirl of red falls in a blur, violently towards the floor, stopping with an abrupt and expert tug of two muscular arms.

I will buy myself a new red lipstick and I will dare to wear it.

16

JUNE 2018, TROMSØ, NORWAY

'Grethe! I need your help, we've run out of ice cream!'

Espen tears through the double doors of the ice cream parlour like an actor in a hospital drama. Surrounded by the pastel colours of the walls and furniture, he seems to have wandered off set. Two teens spoon-feed each other sorbet and kisses behind a low table at the back; a party of three families from a faraway land go quiet while they tame the drips and drops of their cones; a father and his young daughters drink milkshakes in the window seat. Espen sees Cecilie sitting on a high stool at the counter, keeping her friend, Grethe, owner of 'Grethe's Iskrembar', company on a Saturday night in high summer.

'*Hei*, you OK?' Espen asks, giving his sister a loose hug. Cecilie smiles but doesn't reply as she stirs a long stainless-steel spoon into a blue sundae. Cecilie and Espen often don't answer each other because they can respond to chit-chat without the need for words.

Grethe, with shoulder-length blonde hair tied up into a headscarf and a colourful shawl fashioned into an apron around her heavily pregnant tummy, eases herself towards the glass freezer display and gestures to an array of pale peach, pink, brown and yellow ice cream colours, clinging to almost-empty tubs.

'We're practically out too, Espen, I can't keep up with demand today,' Grethe says with a shrug. 'Your selfless sister even volunteered to have Smurf flavour instead of cloudberry tonight so I didn't have to turn this party away.' She nods to the big group dominating the small parlour and wipes a tired brow with the back of her hand.

Since *Lonely Planet* put Grethe's Iskrembar in its latest edition and said the cherry ripple, Arctic cloudberry and peanut butter flavours were all 'to die for', the blue hue of the mysterious unidentifiable Smurf flavour does less of a roaring trade than it used to, and Cecilie doesn't mind having it tonight.

'Actually, it's OK.' Cecilie smiles with long, blue lips. This weekend is the weekend of Tromsø's annual marathon, which means the town is teeming with tourists from all over the world wanting to run under the midnight sun, in a town where it won't start setting again until late July. And then only for a few minutes. Carb loaders and support parties have filled the parlour all day ahead of the race tonight, and Grethe is about to close up.

Espen's neat quiff dips a little in panic.

'Shit, we're totally out at the hotel. I told Chef I'd do a dash here.'

Grethe looks at the baby-blue clock on the pink wall above a vintage poster of two animated ice cream cones and rubs her belly under its patchwork apron. She is thirty-three weeks pregnant and could do with shutting shop early this evening.

'Hang on, Espen,' she says, connecting to the kicks and flicks within her tummy. 'Let me look out the back and see what we have left in the freezer. I've barely had a chance...' Grethe presses her palms into her tailbone to propel her heaving bump forward to the churning room full of mixers and freezers at the end of the counter.

Oliver, the Saturday boy, is cleaning down the paddles since they ran out of milk hours ago and won't get any more from the dairy until Monday, so Grethe asks him to check the deep freeze as she can't squeeze into it easily in her current state.

Espen stands at the counter and leans on Cecilie's stool. 'So, what's new?' he asks.

'Nothing.'

'I thought I might see you and Morten for *kjøttboller* at lunchtime. Not that I would have had a chance to chat. These bloody marathon runners are so demanding...'

'*Nei*, I was playing harp and sorting out the house. Mamma's home tomorrow. I did a big clean.'

'Ah, yes. I need to talk to her about that delegation. It would be amazing to get that many diplomats into my hotel. I bet they're less high maintenance than runners. I had to send Camilla to the Spar three times to get more pasta – now the whole town is out.' Espen rolls his eyes.

'I'm sure that's not the first thing Mamma is going to want to talk about after an exhausting trip.'

'I know.' He nods as he smooths Cecilie's white-blonde, asymmetric fringe and tucks it behind the studded helix of her ear. 'I miss you, sister. Please come work at the hotel.'

'Is that how I get to see you? I have to work for you?' Cecilie gives a small laugh and sticks a blue tongue out at her brother.

Last month, Espen moved out of their mother's cosy home at the foothills of Mount Storsteinen and in with Morten, in the apartment above Nils' salon, just a stone's throw from the i-Scand.

Even when Cecilie and Espen started studying at the Arctic University on the outskirts of the town, they lived at home rather than on campus. It was easy. Karin always made her children feel welcome to remain there, even when they were no longer children. Actually, it was rather convenient for Karin, having her kids look after the house while she was in the capital or travelling Europe giving speeches and attending summits. When Espen said he was moving in with Morten, Karin worried that Cecilie wouldn't be able to look after the house on her own.

'It's not that you're not capable, my darling,' she said with a sweep of her hand, 'it's just your brother manages one hundred staff at the hotel. Running a house is like a smaller version of that. I know he can do it with his eyes closed.' For a progressive woman in a male-dominated sphere, Karin Wiig was surprisingly backwards when it came to their current domestic set-up, especially given it was she who had put out the dustbins, changed every light bulb and erected every piece of flat-pack furniture since her husband Kjetil had fled the family when the twins were four, becoming the seventh person to jump off the bridge that year. Unlucky number seven.

Perhaps that's why Karin wanted Cecilie to have an easier life, to have Espen look after her, although Cecilie hadn't shown any signs of ever wanting a man to look after her, not since the Mr Lind debacle. She was self-contained and content in her dreamy bubble.

'It'll be fine, Mamma,' Cecilie said. 'I'm always the one who does everything in the house anyway,' she added, making a face by crossing her eyes at Espen as she said it.

Morten couldn't help but agree. Espen put so much energy into empire building at the i-Scand that all he could do was sit back on the couch in his cashmere onesie when he was at home.

'Cecilie will be fine,' Morten had reassured Karin. 'Although

I'll insist on taking her to lunch more often if I'm not at the house so much,' he added with a wink.

Cecilie is managing the family home perfectly well, thank you very much. The fridge is always filled with fresh food, alongside Mette's leftover cakes from the Hjornekafé, the recycling is always ready for collection and the cosy cushions on the low grey sofa always look plumped up and pristine. Cecilie does leave her harp right in the middle of the living room when her mother is away, but that doesn't matter. And she does miss the chatter of Espen and Morten, curled up on the sofa late on a Sunday night as the three of them used to, watching a movie. Cecilie even came close to messaging The Mexican the other day, the house felt so quiet and private. She thought no one would even know, except for Hector of course. And maybe his wife. Which made Cecilie feel sad and silly, so she thought better of it. Picturing Hector Herrera in his new happy role as husband made it easier for Cecilie to step away from her phone.

I miss him.

'Come on,' Espen says with a click of his finger. 'It's Saturday night and you could be working a shift at the bar, earning money, meeting hot businessmen, making loads of tips... I need a good-looking mixologist like you.'

He looks at his sister and smiles. She looks so different to the girl with the dreadlocks, and he loves it. If only the sadness and inertia of that little cloud still floating above her head would fizz away.

'I don't need money,' says Cecilie, shrugging.

'Everyone needs money.'

'Well, I don't need any more money than I already have. I don't spend money. The library and the cafe pay me enough.' Espen looks down at his sister's dishevelled Dr Martens and rips on the knees of her light blue jeans and raises an artfully groomed eyebrow.

'Come on, look at you. Have some ambition. You could be anything you want to be; do anything you want to do. The world is your oyster, Cecilie, and you're eating blue ice cream on your own on a Saturday night?'

Cecilie's eyes fill up and she scratches the soft hair at the nape of her neck. Hector's face flashes in her mind, adding fire to the ice on her tongue.

I miss him so much.

'Be anything I want? What, like a "mixologist" mannequin in the dizzy heights of the i-Scand hotel? Letting diplomats or smug biotech boys touch me up, just for tips? Or listen to the banal shit of lonely businessmen while I pour them a whisky? You call that ambition, brother?'

The three families sitting together in the middle of the parlour stop planning their marathon vantage points and crane their necks to try to understand what Cecilie's terse tone is all about. Espen looks at them, quick as a flash, and they look away.

'It's a four-star international hotel,' he counters with a hush. 'Interesting people walk through the doors of the i-Scand every single day. What's wrong with wanting to welcome them to our town? To make them feel comfortable? To have pride in what you do?'

Cecilie looks at her brother in despair. His pale green eyes are the exact same shade as hers, but they have a determination within them that Cecilie has never known. She decides to diffuse the discussion with her usual whimsy.

'Look, thanks for the offer, but really, Espen, I'm fine. I like my life. What's wrong with being happy in your skin and just... *being*? I don't want to be in Strasbourg or Brussels with Mamma, or earning "megabucks" in your hotel on the harbour. When did being happy and grateful for what you have become a crime?'

Espen shrugs. 'It didn't. But you're hardly the poster girl for happiness, are you?'

'Fuck you, Espen.'

Grethe comes back to the counter. The teens in the corner clean the last of their sorbet from sticky lips; the tourists start putting their coats and scarves back on; the dad in the window lays a sleeping daughter down on the banquette while her sister slurps up the leftovers.

'Right, Oliver managed to find one tub of peanut butter, half a tub of triple chocolate and two and a half tubs of vanilla, but that's all I have,' Grethe says. 'You can take them if you want to. I'll close up soon anyway.'

Grethe looks up and notices tension between the twins. 'Everything OK?' she asks.

Espen glosses over it with businesslike panache.

'Grethe, you're a star. Can you put it on the account and I'll settle up Monday?'

'No problem,' she says, wincing at another kick from inside her. 'Oliver, can you help Espen carry it back to the hotel?'

'For sure,' says a languid teenage boy, tucking a blonde curl behind his ear.

'And don't let him steal you from me,' she says, giving Espen a playful look. Last year, Grethe lost her favourite sundae girl, Solveig, to Espen and his blasted hotel. Solveig had been wooed by the tips.

Espen nods his appreciation and turns to Cecilie. 'I'll call round tomorrow, yes? Catch you and Mamma.'

Cecilie doesn't answer. She spoons the last drips of Smurf-flavoured ice cream into her mouth and keeps her focus forward at Grethe as the bell above the door signals Espen and Oliver's departure.

Grethe wipes down the counter. 'Everything OK?'

'Just Espen being Espen.'

Grethe lets out a little laugh, but it soon turns to a wince as she takes another pounding from within.

'Here, what can I do? Let me help you close. You should call it a day. Sit down.'

Grethe gives a grateful sigh. 'Thanks, sweetie, you're the best. Can you turn the sign around to closed please?'

'Sure,' Cecilie says, slipping off the stool and walking to the door. The party of three families leaves as she does, and she sends them on their way with a smile. Only the father and his daughters, and the sorbet-sticky couple, remain. 'Hey, do you want to come back to mine and watch a movie?' Cecilie asks as she clears away napkins and detritus from the tables pushed together in the middle of the room. '*Dirty Dancing*, for old times' sake?'

Dirty Dancing was released on Cecilie and Espen's first birthday, and it was Karin and Kjetil's first night out after a gruelling year of twin feeding, weaning and teething. Karin begged Kjetil to take her to the cinema one night soon after the twins had turned one, and she fell in love with the footwork and the freedom that those one hundred minutes gave her.

When Cecilie was eleven, she discovered the old VHS on her mother's shelf, and she and Grethe must have watched it four thousand times as teens. Confused that the soundtrack to their infancy was like something from the 1960s, but loving how Baby was swept off her feet in a fantasy land far away.

In the spacious cosy living room of the Wiig family home, Cecilie and Grethe had eaten freshly popped popcorn, worked out the dance routines, and quoted the film, line for line, as they watched, tummy down on the rug, gazing with their heads resting in their palms. Sometimes they ordered Espen to try to lift them up and over his head during a particularly tricky manoeuvre, which he never could.

Almost twenty years later, Grethe's moved on.

'Sorry, I need to rest my swollen ankles at home. Abdi might even be back from the boat.'

'Hey, no problem, home is best for that bubba of yours. I'll tidy up out here for you.'

'Thanks sweetie, I'll just cash up.'

As Cecilie wipes down the vacant tables, she resigns herself to spending another Saturday night alone.

17

Walking back across the cantilever bridge towards the mainland, her homeland, Cecilie doesn't look at the peaks of the mountains, anchored reassuringly beyond the water and the houses ahead. She doesn't try to spot the moving cable car of the Fjellheisen, which will whisper up the mountainside into the small hours, so tourists can see what daytime looks like at midnight, as they try to spot miniature marathon runners from above. She doesn't look to the stained-glass façade of a white concertina building just beyond the bridge, the most northerly cathedral in the world and an Arctic accordion that plays its tune to lure Cecilie back over the windy strait. She buries her face into her snood, inside the collar of her long grey feather-down coat, and stares at the yellow threading on her black dishevelled boots as each foot propels her forwards. Cecilie thinks about how, in just a few months' time, she and Espen will turn thirty. He is already organising an elaborate party for the two of them in the largest function room at the i-Scand that Cecilie isn't particularly excited about but will turn up to and smile.

Thirty.

She thinks of Grethe, her friend since nursery. They went through every first together: first steps, first palm-print paintings, first books, first crushes, first heartbreaks... Cecilie didn't share these triumphs and tragedies with her mother the way Grethe told Mette everything. Cecilie would turn to her harp, or get lost in books: Ibsen, Hamsun, Austen and Woolf... She didn't have as many friends as Espen or Grethe had, because she was mostly happy in her own world; she had Peer Gynt, Emma Woodhouse and Mrs Dalloway for company. But there was no one like Grethe when Cecilie wanted someone to belt out 'She's Like the Wind' with.

Both girls went to the Arctic University; Grethe studied tourism and hospitality alongside Espen; Cecilie studied literature. Soon after graduating, Grethe's father, Tore, died of a heart attack as he was cleaning up the Hjornekafé one night after closing. His first career, pulling twelve-hour shifts on an oil rig, had taken its toll on his body, so he opted for a quiet life running a quiet cafe, until he died young at forty-nine. His devastated daughter put her inheritance money to good use and set up a business, deciding that an ice cream parlour could work in the Arctic. She had learned everything she needed to know about running a small business, not from her degree, but from her parents and their moderate success with the Hjornekafé. All Grethe needed to do was learn to make ice cream. Optimistic and practical as she was, she packed a bag and hopped on a flight to Florence, where she spent a month immersing herself in the art of gelato.

Grethe's Iskrembar was a huge success, despite the temperature rarely reaching fourteen degrees, even in high summer. But Grethe was the toast of Tromsø. Tore's girl had grown a business from scratch, she had brought something new to the town, and she had learned every stage of the process herself: from engineering the equipment to learning how to make the perfect ice cream base, then churning it and crafting it into delicious new flavours (with a little help along the way from an immigrant taste tester).

'Why don't you start a business, Cecilie? If you come up with a good business plan, I'll fund you,' Karin encouraged her when they were strolling over the bridge arm in arm en route to Grethe's grand opening. The conversation resonated with Cecilie. Not because of the pressure she felt to be something more than just a librarian or just a waitress, but because Mamma rarely walked anywhere. There was always a driver ringing on the doorbell to take her mother to the airport, or a car whisking her from one appointment to the next. Karin didn't drive, yet it was so unusual for her to walk. That evening, Cecilie pulled her mother's arm into her ribs for comfort, and her whimsical way meant she wasn't upset by the suggestion that she too should start a business. She was just happy to be walking arm in arm with her mother; happy for Grethe's success.

At twenty-six, Grethe met Abdi, a Somali immigrant fisherman, whose family had escaped war and ended up in the Arctic. Abdi had found work on the Hurtigruten, the expedition ship that sails up and down the Fjordland, netting the night's catch of the day for the tourists on board and stopping for a sundae whenever he was in town. Grethe was instantly taken with Abdi the day he walked into the Iskrembar in search of something to remind him of home. His favourite ice cream in the world came from a parlour in Mogadishu, where Italian rule had seen Neapolitan gelato reach the horn of Africa.

When Abdi stumbled across ice cream in the Arctic Circle, he was smitten with the woman behind the counter. Her eyes were bright blue and sparkling, and wisps of blonde hair poked out from beneath a colourful headscarf tied in a bow at the front, reminiscent of a fabric he would see back home. He had asked to try one tiny scoop of each flavour, on a plate, not a cone, so he could really find out which was his favourite – while also prolonging their encounter. He said he'd pay for it, of course, but Grethe was too speechless to charge him, so she leaned on the counter and watched him eat. She had never seen anyone with such beautiful creamy skin before. She wanted to lick her finger and touch his face with it, the way she would dip a digit into the ice cream mix to check its consistency. Abdi's skin was just right. When he finished, he looked up at Grethe, still watching him, her chin resting on her palm, and said he liked the yellowy orange one best because he had never tasted anything like it in the world.

'Is it a fruit?' he asked.

'Cloudberry. Have you never tasted it?'

Abdi smiled.

Before he left, he recommended to Grethe that she put cardamom in her vanilla ice cream and cloves in her chocolate, and Grethe nodded and smiled, knowing he would be back.

Soon, Abdi was no longer a stranger, and his spice advice turned out to be brilliant; his cardamom and clove-infused classics created big sellers.

Creating something out of heartache. Taking a chance on a business. Taking a chance on love. Both girls were fatherless, but Grethe's loss prompted another of her gutsy moves. Cecilie had never done anything with her inheritance fund; she'd never taken a risk in her life, nor dared to travel.

As the cathedral stands in full view before her, Cecilie knows that having walked the entire length of the bridge, she has walked past the point where her father was last seen, and she wishes she knew where it was.

At the end of the bridge, she turns right, walking past

nervous runners warming up their legs as they make their way to the start line in the hub on the island over the bridge. The pavements are clear of snow, and will be for the next few months before winter's white ink starts to hug the harbour. Although looking up at the green mountain to the tiny cafe terrace at the top, Cecilie can see small pools of snow dotted down the mountainside like spilt milk.

No use crying, Cecilie thinks as she edges left up a quiet side road to her house. She steps up onto the veranda with its waist-height white picket fence and elaborate lattice-front fascia and puts her key in the front door.

Home.

Home is quiet. Home is clean.

Home is precisely how Cecilie left it this afternoon when she decided to wander into town to see how Grethe was bumping along.

Cecilie puts her keys in a white oval bowl, takes off her Dr Martens and throws her coat onto a row of pegs in the airy hallway. She walks through a set of French doors to the living room.

Her harp is in the way, but that doesn't matter because Karin won't be back until tomorrow lunchtime, so she walks around it to turn the television on. Cecilie flicks through the channels, unmoved by the World Cup or wannabes auditioning for *Stjernekamp*. She goes back to the football match and mutes it.

When are Mexico playing? Where will he watch it?

Cecilie perches on the solid stripped-back wood of the coffee table her mother bought in Warsaw, sweeps her fringe behind one ear, and plants her bare feet into the thick sheepskin rug. She tilts her harp back onto her shoulder and plucks. *So, ro, lillemann...* pops into her head for the first time since that day – his wedding day. She'd banished it from baby rhyme-time sessions since then, and she banishes it again by going on a journey across the strings, dancing her gnarly fingertips along the timeline of her past.

It was a strange choice of instrument for a nineties kid with a penchant for eighties electronica, but their mother was gifted a harp from her Russian counterpart on a visit from Moscow, and for months it sat in a huge case in the unused dining room at the front of the house.

'Bloody thing!' Karin would say if she stubbed a recently polished toe on the hard external case. Espen didn't ever give the case a second glance; he was always too busy, even when he was a child. But one day, when Cecilie was thirteen and her imagination was running riot, she opened the box, plucked a string, and the noise that tickled back at her made her realise it could be the perfect soundtrack to the adventures in her head.

Cecilie and Espen's music teacher, handsome Mr Lind, told Cecilie, long before she knew him as Jonas, that the harp was a gift in more ways than their family could imagine, and he arranged for a teacher to come into school so Cecilie could have lessons. Soon she was playing everything from Delibes's 'Flower Duet' to Kylie's 'Can't Get You Out of My Head', and she loved how the music set her free when she played.

But this sombre Saturday night, alone in her mother's sprawling house, despite her argument with Espen, Cecilie doesn't feel sad striding her harp. She strikes up the plinky-plonky chords of Hans Zimmer, composed for a marimba, and dances around the room without even moving her bottom from the coffee table's edge. Her heart swells, her breath intensifies, her feet push down on the pedals, and she feels nothing but goodwill, nothing but a desire to speak to the man she loves.

You're so cool.

She looks up at the large clock on the wall and counts back seven, which is harder to do when all your fingers are in use.

Striding the strings, she continues, her head moving, then cuts the music short as she stands abruptly and pads across the room, through the French doors, to her coat hanging by the front door, and takes her phone out of her pocket.

Cecilie hovers her chapped thumb over the home button and scrolls through people she recently messaged. She doesn't message many people: Grethe, Morten, Espen, maybe Fredrik at the library or Henrik in the cafe if either of them is running late and needs to let the other know. A short scroll down and Hector Herrera's beautiful face sits in a tiny circle on the left. In the photo, he is laughing and looking to a person just beyond the camera, not directly into the lens. His eyes shine. His skin is warm and his cheeks are flushed with pink patches of elation and inebriation. His bow lips are sealed as if they are primed to kiss. Cecilie strokes the circle and opens up their last exchange, three months ago.

She doesn't read the conversation back. It's already etched into her eyelids when she tries to sleep at night.

Her harp-worn thumb, with a delicate silver ring at the base of it, hovers over the keypad.

Cecilie is no longer Arctic Fox, and Hector isn't I Feel You. They dropped those monikers years ago with familiarity and tech upgrades, and replaced playful names with playful pictures, faces in circles, and Hector Herrera is now just Hector in her phone. Cecilie's picture is impish and playful; her eyes are crossed and she's sticking her tongue out. Her heart-shaped face fills the photo. Her dreadlocks aren't visible in the picture; Hector wouldn't know she's cut them off anyway.

I can't not have him in my life.

> Hei stranger, how are you?

Send.

Two blue ticks indicate Hector Herrera received and read her message instantly. It is lunchtime in Mexico.

An ellipsis dances a Mexican wave as frantically as their hearts beat and Cecilie knows he is replying right now.

> Hola, guapa! How are you? I miss you!

I miss you.

> OK thanks. Working hard. You at the cafe ahorita?

> Nei. At home. A rare night off...

Cecilie pauses and decides to make herself sound more interesting.

He'll never know anyway.

> I've taken a third job, the one at my brother's hotel. Busy busy.

> Wow, what about our no-uniform pact, comadre?

Hector adds an emoji of a fist in solidarity.

> Things change! Espen talked me round. I work in the bar there now, I'm a mixologist.

> Mixolo… qué?

> I make drinks!

> Like Tom Cruise?

> Huh?

> Cóctel.

> Ah, yes just like that. I shake my little silver thing like a demon!

Cecilie adds an emoji of a Martini, followed by one of a cocktail she imagines she might conjure in her imaginary job.

> Jajajaja. I get to sleep with the clientele like Tom Cruise too.

Cecilie adds a winking face.

There is a pause. Cecilie wonders why the hell she's lying. What is she trying to achieve?

He married her. Is she there right now?

Hector sends a sad face and Cecilie slumps back into the low rectangular sofa with a sigh. She puts her feet on the wooden table and her eyes glaze over while she stares at the silent TV in front of her. The footballers become a blur.

Cecilie rises until she is in a corner between the ceiling and the wall of a high-rise apartment in a low-rise town, looking down at Hector on his phone as he watches the very same football match. She can only see the top of his head and so desperately wants to capture the flash of his eyes, but he's looking down at his phone. She looks around the room, and as she hovers from up high, willing Hector to look up, she can't tell if his wife is sitting on the armchair next to the sofa. It's all such a blur. Yes, that's right. Perhaps she's in the bathroom. Is there a figure of a woman in the kitchen making a *torta*?

The world's highest paid footballer curves the ball beautifully and the commentator's Spanish roar snaps Cecilie back into the muted silence of her living room. She looks up at the screen and sees a man elated, charging towards a crowd in triumph.

> So, how's married life?

He loves her.

> Good thanks, same as before.

Hector wonders why the hell he's lying. And changes the subject.

> Hey, I've been asked to illustrate a children's book!

> Wow, that's amazing!

> Yeah, I met this author in Mexico City and she wants me to illustrate her books, and the publisher is really cool... I'm working really hard on it.

> Wow. I'm so happy for you! That's wonderful, well done. What's the book?

> It's about a little panda cub called Pablito, he's really cute. He gets into lots of adventures and scrapes while he looks for a mate. I'm doing loads of drawings now, not going out chupando any more...

His wife must be an inspiration.

> Married life suits you.

Why did I lie about the job? He has always been honest with me.

> Something like that.

> Well I'm really happy for you, Hector, congratulations.

This hurts too much.

> Gracias. It made me happy. Hey you wanna FaceTime? It would be great to see you. That would make me really happy. And I could show you Pablito.

> Oh no, it's OK. I was just checking in really.

> You said you weren't going to...

Cecilie doesn't respond.

> But I'm glad you did... It was good to see your crazy face pop up on my phone.

Cecilie sends a crazy face emoji.

> Look, Hector, I have to go, I'm working a late shift. Loads of tourists in town. Better get over to the hotel.

> You said you had a night off.

Shit.

> I did. Well. Afternoon off anyway. I said I'd do a late. Those cocktails don't shake themselves you know!

> What's your uniform like? Traidora! Bleurgh. Tell me, I want to know.

Cecilie pauses.

Shit, what do Solveig and Camilla wear?
She remembers.

> White blouse. Black miniskirt. Black tights. Not very me.

> Sounds cool. As long as there's no tie though, right? Remember our no-tie clause?

> No tie.

Hector sends a wink face.
Cecilie sends a sad face as her own face gets hot.
This was a bad idea.

> I have to go now. Get across the bridge.

> Ceci nooo! We'll talk later yeah?

> Maybe.

It hurts too much.

> Don't say farvel. I hated farvel.

Cecilie tries to swallow but her mouth is dry.

> I hated it too.

> Hasta luego then x.

And with his kiss, Cecilie kills the conversation and sends her phone to sleep.

She didn't tell Hector that she is sitting alone in a sprawling family home on a Saturday night.

Hector didn't tell Cecilie that Pilar, who got fired from her job, went out with her friend Xochitl at 11.30 p.m. last night and hasn't been seen since.

18

JUNE 2018, SUFFOLK, ENGLAND

Under the shroud of her large, brown plastic sunglasses awkwardly perching on the bridge of her nose, Kate looks up and down the quiet platform like a really incompetent spy. With a niggling pain that makes her regret not going to the loo before she left the house, she hops up through the open doors and onto the train before they slam together behind her.

Kate looks left and right, to both sides of the half-full carriage, and turns left to sit where there seems to be fewer people.

Face forwards, Kate thinks as she slumps into a double seat, her hips chafing against the flipped-down table as she goes. She flips it back up as she lands in a plump puff of dust.

If anyone I know walks up the train they'll only see the back of my head.

She looks at her mobile. It is 9.51 a.m., the train is leaving exactly on time, and Kate, desperate that no one should see her doing something perfectly normal for a woman who might be shopping the summer sales, or meeting a friend for lunch, or going to a gallery while her kids are at school, feels her heart race as they pull out of the station. She leans against the window on a train she used to travel on daily but which now feels like an alien craft.

None of my family know where I am.

Kate removes her navy summer jacket and puts it over her small floral handbag on the seat next to her in the hope that no one else will want to sit there. So she can be on her own. So she can compose herself. So she can work out her strategy. This is only the second off-peak service of the day, winding through her rural idyll before bursting into the noise and chaos of London, and the carriage is only half-peppered with People In Less Of A Hurry. A retired couple, wearing gilets and cords, look relaxed as they head to the Wallace Collection. A smart, heavily made-up woman, who Kate assumes must be going to an interview, checks her reflection in a small compact mirror. Three women, not much younger than Kate, talk about how guilty they felt dropping their toddlers at nursery while they toted cool bags full of Prosecco, strawberries and cream. A man in a suit listens to a podcast. Perhaps he had a dentist appointment and is going in late.

The train before must have been much busier, Kate thinks, blowing a sigh of relief.

She removes her sunglasses and places them carelessly on the jacket next to her as she smooths down her fringe. She smiles wryly, and Kate feels a little bit bad knowing she would tell Chloe off for being so careless with her own sunglasses. Although Chloe's probably cost more than these make-do shades Kate got in the Next sale three summers ago.

She repositions herself in the seat and tugs on the seam of her black bootcut trousers. They feel uncomfortable between her thighs. She feels uncomfortable. Kate hasn't felt like such a fish out of water in a long time, but she has been waiting patiently for this opportunity, ever since she found a long blonde hair entwined in the fibres of George's stripy scarf.

That hair. It's consumed her. At first, Kate went back to scour George's diary, to look at the repeating patterns. 'Lunch B' came up several times since she first noticed it in March. Then Kate started to use the Find My iPhone app on her mobile – usually reserved for timing dinner, seeing where George is on the train line, so she knows when to put the chicken pie in the oven, so she doesn't overcook the veg. But since Kate found *that hair*, she's used her phone to track George more and more: to see whether he really was going to badminton (he was, although he did sometimes go to the Red Hart with the gang afterwards), or whether he took a detour when he popped to Waitrose (he didn't). But mainly to see where he was heading on the days it said 'Lunch B'. Sometimes it was Spitalfields Market, sometimes it was Galvin La Chapelle. Last Wednesday it was to The Shard, but Kate couldn't work out if he was back eating octopus at Hutong with 'B' – and clients, or whoever – or whether he was in a suite at the Shangri-La. Either way, he was there for over two hours and the infuriating little green dot couldn't specify which floor he was on.

Last Friday evening, when Kate was trying to work out when to put the pasta on and looked on her phone to see where his train was between Liverpool Street and Claresham, she noticed he was offline. Even after he came through the door, had watched *Newsnight* and gone to bed, his phone, sitting defiantly awake on the bedside table next to him, showed that he was offline. Had he disabled Find My iPhone so Kate couldn't find him? There wasn't a little green dot pulsating by their bed, and it agonised Kate as George lay with his back facing her. Even the brown moles on his pale skin started to look like green dots taunting her.

On Sunday morning, while Jack was playing cricket and George was standing on the rough chatting to Nigel Pickover, Kate sat on the soft grass at the edge of Claresham village green, sunglasses on, and slipped George's phone out from the inside pocket of his light blue linen jacket. She put the jacket over her knees and pretended to shiver on the fresh midsummer morning. Beneath it, she secretly tapped George's passcode into his phone so she could reinstall the app. 240576. His date of birth. It didn't work. His passcode had always been his date of birth ever since he got that phone. Kate tried hers. That didn't work either.

Of course it wouldn't be mine.

She tried each of their children's birth dates, then panicked that the phone might be disabled if she made one more attempt. It was at that moment, as Kate slipped the phone back into the inside pocket of George's jacket, as Jack shouted at his mum to bring over his gloves, that she realised she had no choice. Next time 'Lunch B' came up in the diary, she would go into London. She would sit in the sandwich shop – *if it's still there* – opposite the London HQ of Digby Global Investors, on a stool at a wooden bench attached to the glass window, and wait for George to come out. She would follow him. She would find out who B was, because she doesn't think it's Baz Brocklebank from the Sydney office any more – Kate looks at his dull Twitter feed every now and then, full of musings on margin deadlines and trade deals and pensions, but he's mostly 'Down Under' when these lunches crop up.

She didn't expect 'Lunch B' to appear again so soon, given there was one only last Wednesday. But on Monday morning, George's PA Bethany put one in the diary for 1 p.m. on Thursday, and given that today, Thursday 28 June, is a rare day without a PTA coffee morning or a WI planning meeting or a school sports day or a class assembly, Kate knows that today is her one shot.

She can finally find out what the hell is going on with her husband. George was never terribly communicative or loving, not like *him*, but he'd definitely been even colder and more awkward of late.

In the hazy carriage, Kate ponders her strategy: if George meets a city guy in a suit, she will head straight back to Claresham in time for the school run. If he doesn't... well, the school run will be the least of Kate's problems, and she's sure Melissa or Venetia would help her out in an emergency...

As the train rolls across the country and starts to gather speed, Kate feels increasingly nervous. She presses her head back into the headrest and feels the tie of her ponytail bobbling into the back of her skull uncomfortably, taunting her on her way. She shifts her head, turning towards the window as she hears the impending doom of familiar voices from the village, advancing through the carriage towards the front of the train.

'Keep going, sweetpea...' says a clipped voice knowingly. Kate slinks a little in her seat. She can hear it's Antonia Barrie from the WI, not just from Antonia's smug intonation but from the sound of her polished heels walking the dirty carriage floor disdainfully, in unison with another pair. Kate scrabbles to put her sunglasses back on before the heels arrive at the point where she's slinking deeper into her seat. In her peripheral vision, Kate sees a younger woman pass first. It's Antonia's daughter, Amber, equally sickeningly glamorous and as well put together as her mother.

Amber Barrie is the most poised twenty-two-year-old girl Kate has ever seen, and whenever Kate stumbles into her at WI fundraisers wearing pretty floral shift dresses, or at the supermarket checkout in skintight leggings and a bodywarmer, her basket filled with kale and quinoa, or walking her German Spitz Klein on the green with her hair effortlessly piled high in a bun on her head, Kate can't help but feel intimidated. Amber Barrie is everything Kate wasn't at twenty-two, and everything Kate isn't at forty-two.

As she glides past, fragrantly, ahead of her mother, Kate can't help but look up. Amber wears a blush pink skirt suit, and her long tanned legs stride through the carriage in elegant nude stilettos that won't be sullied by the capital's streets today. Amber's meticulous mane is the same golden blonde shade as her mother's, although Antonia's hair isn't quite as long and lustrous as her daughter's, but both always look as if they've *just* had a blow-dry. No one can always have *just* had a blow-dry.

Gosh, how does she walk in those?

Kate snaps the heels together of her black round-toe ankle boots that are looking a little like Cornish pasties they're so loved, but which were the most comfortable option for all the walking she might do today, and drags her feet under her seat. She looks back out of the window. She's seen enough, and doesn't want to be seen.

With a swish of her hair, Amber presses the button on the internal door and eases through to the next carriage, her mother following close behind. Kate holds her breath, willing Antonia not to stop and see her.

Phew. Although I'm sure she saw me out of the corner of her eye.

Once Antonia has passed, Kate quickly looks up at the back of her. She is dressed almost identically to her daughter, although her two-piece is cream and the elegant hemline of her pencil skirt is longer, to the knee, and more befitting a fifty-something. She wafts through the doors, confidently, dismissively.

Kate clutches her doughy stomach, easing her hand over her full bladder. She is nervous about what she's about to do, and irked that Antonia Barrie pretended not to see her, even though she pretended not to see Antonia Barrie.

She turns her gaze once more out of the window, at the sprawling green flats of East Anglia. The feeling of the unfamiliar envelopes her, and she rummages in her bag for a bottle of water.

This is ridiculous. I did this five days a week when I was pregnant with Chloe.

The tracks used to be familiar. Kate worked in London ever since she started her graduate trainee job at Digby's, but routines of motherhood and mundanity mean she hasn't been into London since…

Oooh, was it Wicked? *That was my fortieth, and George drove because we'd just got the S-Max. He wanted to give it a run-out.*

Kate unscrews the lid of the warm bottle of water and lingers over her fortieth birthday weekend. Dinner with Christine and Colin Leach on the Friday. The kids made her breakfast in bed on Saturday morning, then George surprised her with a trip to the theatre and a night in a London hotel. He'd got her parents over to babysit, and as Kate looked in the mirror and congratulated herself on her half-stone loss at Weight Watchers in the run-up to her birthday, she had a pang of guilt that she didn't really want to be in a dusty hotel room in Bloomsbury; she would have been happy with a takeaway at home with the kids.

That half-stone went straight back on in a birthday blowout. The show was amazing. The kids were fine for the night. Kate and George even had sex. It was the last time they had had sex, in fact.

Golly, over two years ago.

Kate looks at the clock on her phone and ponders whether it's worth doing something else before she goes and camps out in the coffee shop. Perhaps she should head to the big John Lewis to get the kids some summer swimwear? Maybe the National Gallery?

Then she remembers Him. The artist. The Mexican.

I've been cheated on before.

Kate's cheeks feel hot and she takes another slug of water. The butterfly motifs on her T-shirt retract through the fabric into her stomach and she feels them flying around her, uncomfortably trying to escape. Ahead, she can see a skyline of new shapes she doesn't recognise, and Kate wants to shrink with every metre she edges towards George's city, his street, his building, his corner office. She feels deceitful as she agonises over what she's about to do, yet proof of deception would be the only reassuringly familiar thing for Kate right now.

She remembers how small she felt that sticky night, when the boy she had been dependent on all summer, the life and soul of her trip, of the town, cheated on her, right in front of her very eyes. Kate had turned to say something to Hector, who was sitting next to her, but only saw the back of his head. His soft brown curls, his terracotta-toned neck, his torn faded band T-shirt, his trapezius she so wanted to touch. His arms, despite being just a boy of eighteen, were strong from arching and reaching to paint his mural he had been working on all summer. Kate had looked at the back of his warm body sitting on the stool next to her. She could smell musk and sunshine emanating from his skin, even in the smoke-filled darkness of the bar. She wondered who he was chatting to so intently, who he was sitting so close to. Kate cocked her head and felt a blow to the stomach. She withdrew her hand from his denim-clad thigh and gasped in a blaze of dry ice as the band played 'Sweet Child O' Mine', unaware that one girl's world had just stopped turning. Kate felt crushed and foolish to see her teenage lover, his tongue dancing with that of the beautiful girl next to him. He was cheating on her right in front of her.

At least I knew.

Kate had stood up and run to the toilets, shocked and embarrassed to see her summer romance in such a reckless and passionate embrace with Dani, the girl sitting on the stool on the other side of him, his paint-stained hands holding the girl's face in a brazen clinch. They didn't notice Kate noticing. They didn't see her get up and run off. The band carried on while Kate took deep breaths in a toilet cubicle as she clutched a palm to a heart that Hector Herrera had just broken.

There were no secrets.

Kate packed up and left the Villa Infantil De Nuestra Señora the next day, one week earlier than planned. She told Sister Miriam that she was going to make an impromptu trip to see friends in Guanajuato before flying home. She didn't have any friends in Guanajuato, but she was too humiliated to stay, to see Hector. She never did see Hector again. But Sister Miriam, Sister Juana and Sister Virginia, who had once had her heart broken, all hugged Kate tenderly and thanked her for her work helping to renovate and paint the villa over the summer.

'The kids won't believe their eyes when they get back from Coatepec!' Sister Miriam gleamed over her spectacles as she clasped Kate's hands. 'Thanks to you. And Hector, wherever he is... You were a good team.'

Sister Virginia gave Kate a sisterly hug. She knew what young Hector was capable of, and how vulnerable a twenty-two-year-old heart is. Sister Juana gave Kate a parcel of *polvorones* for her fourteen-hour bus trip to Guanajuato, which Kate unwrapped in the living room of her parents' home in Norfolk less than forty-eight hours later.

They were happy to have their daughter home and didn't ask why she had returned a week early. Kate's family didn't really ask each other questions.

19

In the window of the coffee shop, Kate reads the copy of *Woman & Home* that she bought conspicuously from the newsagent at Claresham train station. She flicks from the best wedding-guest cover-ups to a recipe for Normandy pork, without being able to focus on any of it. She looks up at the head office of Digby Global Investors, standing shiny and proud across the street. Six storeys of glass reflect white clouds bouncing against a blue sky. She wonders what George is doing inside and wishes she had gone to John Lewis first, because the past hour has been killing her. She looks at her watch – 12.45 p.m. – and turns to a headline that says, 'Ten things you should remove from your bathroom', before wondering if she should pop to the loo again.

No, he could be out any minute. Don't take your eyes off the door.

Fortunately for Kate, the entrance to the world headquarters of Digby Global Investors is a huge glass façade, through which employees can be seen heading down an escalator into an airy lobby as they leave through glass doors and down four concrete steps onto the City's streets for lunch. It's a step-up from the redbrick offices around the corner, where Kate and George met as nervous trainees on the graduate programme almost twenty years ago. Kate had wowed the selection panel the winter before when she said she was going to volunteer in an orphanage overseas the summer after her finals; George was an Oxford graduate with a photographic memory, and they both had their places secured by Christmas of their final year. They just had to get first-class honours, which they both did: George in mathematics at Magdalen; Kate in business management at York. They met in the subsidised canteen on their first day when Kate handed George a tray in the queue for lunch. Kate was sun-kissed but meek, fresh from heartache in Central America; George's small blue eyes jumped out against his Tenerife tan.

'Hello there,' he mumbled stiltedly.

Kate mustered up a smile and her kind, cried-out eyes crinkled.

Now her eyes scan the offices of Digby Global Investors. No sign of George. One o'clock and he still hasn't come out for lunch. Or had Kate missed him?

She looks back at her magazine.

Six royal baby facts you probably didn't know.

1.06 p.m.

Damn that app.

1.10 p.m.

I've come all the way here.

She looks up to the top floor, where George's office sits on the corner, and wonders if 'Lunch B' is happening right there, right now, in his office. Clouds dance across the reflection of the building, and a wind picks up on the thoroughfare.

Can't wait for lunch X

Kate stands, folds her magazine into a bag that's too small for it, and puts her navy summer jacket on over her V-neck T-shirt. Time for plan B.

* * *

In the light and spacious ground-floor atrium, worker bees descend the escalators fresh from cutting deals, ready for lunch. They look different to how they looked eleven years ago, when Kate left to have Chloe. The staff seem younger. More confident. Better dressed. Finely polished.

Two young women sit at a long low reception desk and Kate hits a glitch. She hadn't honed her plan B, seeing as she was sure she would be following George out of the building. He usually went out when he had lunch with B. And now, now that she's going to 'surprise' her husband with an impromptu visit, she can't announce herself or this will give him time to work out a cover story, if indeed he needs one.

She walks across the shiny dark grey tiles flecked with silver shards and thinks on her feet. The blonde hair, the B initial. Bethany must be her first port of call.

'Kathleen Timberlake to see Bethany Henderson,' Kate announces in a slightly different voice than usual, as if she's pretending to be a newsreader or an airline pilot.

Neither receptionist looks up.

'Just one second,' says the one with a sleek brown bob.

Kate looks at the escalators, to keep her eye on the downward traffic. If he sees her, if *he* catches *her* out, she will say, 'Surprise!' and pretend she just wanted to take George out for lunch.

'Hmmm, I'm not getting anything...'

'I'll wait,' Kate says firmly.

The receptionist looks put upon. She wanted to get back to telling the receptionist with the Pre-Raphaelite mane about whatever it was she was talking about in hushed tones, and again, Kate has the crushing sensation of being an inconvenience. A burden. She thinks of Hector holding the beautiful girl's face in the bar.

The receptionist dials again.

'Hi, Bethany? Oh, hi, Freya, is Beth about?'

Clearly all the receptionists and all the PAs know each other at Digby Global Investors.

'I've got someone down in the lobby to see Beth.' *Don't tell her who you are; she's one of them.* 'Sorry, what was the name?'

'Kathleen Timberlake,' Kate says with unusual authority. She sees the receptionist trying to repress a smirk. 'Kathleen Timberlake... Yeah. Is it not in the diary?' Kate can't hear the voice on the other end.

The receptionist covers her mouthpiece. 'Where did you say you were from?'

Kate has to think quickly. 'Office supplies.'

Kate's apple cheeks flush russet red, mostly in surprise at how quick she is to lie.

'It's the Staples rep.'

Rep? Rep? I'm his wife.

'You want to come down or shall I send her up?'

Please don't send her down, please don't send her down.

The receptionist hangs up.

'OK, just sign in on the iPad and you can go up. Take this escalator and you'll see lifts at the top. It's the sixth floor. When the lift opens, turn right and Freya will meet you through the double doors, Bethany's in a meeting with her boss. Freya said she'll see you.'

The receptionist looks Kate up and down as she types her name on the iPad to sign in.

Kathleen. Timberlake.

20

As the empty lift rises, the metallic taste in Kate's mouth grows. She looks out at the overpowering skyline. The Gherkin sits just beyond the end of the road. It was new and exciting when Kate left Digby's, but already it is dominated by newer, more exciting, more polished architecture. The Walkie-Talkie. The Cheesegrater. The Scalpel. Kate feels as though she is drowning under all of them.

The doors ding like the bell at the side of a boxing ring.

The moment arrives.

'Kathleen? I'm Freya.' A glossy Essex goddess with long, brown, poker-straight hair and plump gleaming lips stands in the doorway. 'Bethany's in with her boss at the moment, but I can deal with whatever you're here for,' Freya says, walking away so Kate has to follow her. 'As long as it's quick, I'm having my nails done at one forty-five.'

Kate's eyes dart to the closed door of the corner office. The blinds are drawn over the glass walls so she can't see inside. She has a fight-or-flight moment. She looks back at Freya's pert and purposeful bottom, striding away in front of her to a desk further away.

'I really need to see Bethany Henderson. Is she in there?' Kate stops, nodding to George's office. Freya stops and twists on the stiletto of her pointed heel.

'Yes. But you can't go in, she's in a meeting.'

She's covering for them.

'This is important.'

Freya's incredulous mouth hangs open, her plump pout gleaming five different shades of nude.

'So's her meeting. You can't just go in there... EXCUSE ME!' An English affectation turns to a full Barking drawl. 'They're in a meetin'!'

Kate pulls the brushed-steel handle on the door down and opens it wide, deliberately, vengefully. George is sitting on the edge of his desk, and a cascade of long blonde hair extensions lean in towards his crotch. Bethany is in the chair facing her boss and turns around clutching a tissue.

'Kate?'

'Hello, George,' Kate whispers through gritted teeth.

Angry, wobbly, vindicated.

'I'm in the middle of something!' George doesn't look flustered or flushed, just confused and irritated.

'Sorry, George, she just burst in, said she was from Staples to see Bethany...'

Bethany looks up, tears in her eyes.

George's confusion turns to panic. 'Are the kids OK?'

'The kids are fine...' Kate is overcome and starts to look around, lost for words, her body flooding with self-doubt. She feels a twitch in her left eye and puts her hand to her brow to try to quash it. The meek-looking girl in the chair doesn't look fresh from sex, or as if she's about to skip out of here hand in hand with George for a romantic lunch. 'I just...'

'You're George's wife?' interrupts Freya with a scowl and shoots Bethany a conspiratorial look. 'Why did you say you was Kathleen from Staples?' Freya lets out a confused laugh, then double-takes as she notices that her friend is crying. 'You OK?' she mouths. Bethany gives a small shake of her head as if to say no.

'Kate, I'm just dealing with something very important, give me two minutes.' George looks baffled and angry. Kate has never seen George look like this. And guilty, he looks guilty, but Kate can't understand why now. Gobsmacked and humiliated, she retreats and closes the door.

'Tell George I'll be in the lobby...' Kate says with a pull of her ponytail.

Freya tuts and strides back to her desk, her bottom even more pert and purposeful than before.

The shame. Kate knows everyone in the open-plan office will now be talking about George's embarrassing wife, bursting in to his office as Freya shouted at her not to, so she marches shame-faced through the doors to the lifts but takes the stairwell, down five flights of stairs, and an escalator, past the women on the front desk and out into the street, her horror blowing on the wind down Bishopsgate.

Deep. Breaths.

Three minutes later, George finds Kate leaning against a wall.

'What the FUCK just happened there?'

George's tiny eyes have turned from blue to steel.

'I'm sorry, I thought I needed to talk to you. Urgently.' A rash spreads from Kate's russet cheeks down to the V-neck of her butterfly top.

'Are you OK?'

'No!' she says with a wobble. 'I thought you were having an affair.'

'You thought I was having an affair?' George rubs his cropped grey hair. 'With Bethany? Jesus, Kate, I'm old enough to be her dad.'

'Well... I did think it was a bit of a cliché.'

'Actually, I was letting Bethany go. She's not up to the job. As you can imagine, she was upset. Nice one, Kate. You made a very tricky thing I wasn't much looking forward to doing even more difficult.' George walks away down the road towards the Gherkin, hands stuffed in his pockets. Kate is surprised by his temper. He's never usually this impassioned. If she wasn't feeling so mortified, she'd think it was sexy.

'George!'

She scurries behind him to catch up, battered boots scuffing along the pavement.

'Why didn't you tell me you were firing her?'

Kate catches up with George and tugs the arm of his blue shirt. They stop and lean into the exterior wall of Digby Global Investors.

'Why didn't you tell me you thought I was having an affair? Anyway, why *did* you think I was having an affair?' There are a million reasons Kate thought George was having an affair. The distance, the disinterest, that text, that hair, working on a Saturday, the vague blocked-out lunches, disabling Find My iPhone, the new passcode... And she knows all of them will sound ridiculous in the lunchtime hum of beeping buses and taxis.

Kate's eyes fill up. 'Oh, George, what have I done?'

'I don't know, but you've got to pull yourself together. This is ludicrous, not to mention embarrassing, for you as well as me.'

Freya walks out of the building, gazing at her nails as she sashays down the thin wide steps onto the pavement. She walks past George and Kate as she flits to her appointment in a hurry, shooting them a look of condemnation as she passes, shaking her head to herself. George manages to avoid her eyes.

21

DECEMBER 2013, DAY 183

> How are you spending Christmas?

Cecilie typed as she looked at the red and white votives stacked on the red and white runner on the dining-room table. She had spent the morning getting the decorations out of the summer house, which was covered in snow at the end of the vast garden and surrounded by white paper lanterns in the shape of stars. A triangular arch of seven stick candles was already in situ on the windowsill.

> We kinda got a tradition

> What is it?

> On Noche Buena my grandfather and I go to the Villa, the orphanage, where the sisters looked after me some of the time. They have us over for dinner. Sister Juana makes the best buñuelos

> Sounds dreamy

Cecilie made a note to google *buñuelos*.

> What about the kids at the orphanage? Where do they go?

> They don't go anywhere! They don't have anywhere to go. It's cool, it's one big feast. My grandfather makes pozole. I help with the turkey. All good. The kids love it. I guess they're like my little brothers and sisters.

As Hector scratched his temples and pressed send, he realised that, at thirty-three, he would probably be older than the kids' parents, were they alive or in their lives. He felt a yearning tug at his core and looked away from his cracked laptop screen, at the messy apartment he sat in.

> How old are they?

> Some are babies. Most are between four and twelve. Fewer teens.

> What happens to the teens?

> They become useful to the extended family. They can earn a buck. Or some rebel and leave.

Hector thought of Benny's thick square head and wondered where he was living right now. He hadn't seen much of him since that fateful night in the juice bar. The sinister appearances out of the blue on street corners, or in the dark of Hector's apartment late at night, had stopped.

> But you never left.

> No! The Sisters, the kids… they're my family. I'll always go back.

> How enchanting. I can't imagine what it must be like to live in an orphanage, but actually you make it sound lovely. More fun than here.

> It's all I know.

Cecilie put her feet up on a sable plastic chair and looked out of the window at the snowy expanse of her neighbourhood. She took a sip of milky coffee and hovered her fingers over the keyboard of Espen's MacBook, mustering up the courage to ask her next question.

> What about your girlfriend?

> She's going to Spain. She's Spanish. Last year was her first Christmas in Mexico so she stayed, but she missed the Reyes Magos too much. She missed her family.

> They must miss her.

Hector thought of the disappointment in Mari-Carmen's voice every time he, a Third-World peasant, answered the phone, and he laughed to himself at the prospect of her face when she saw the wall of ivy climbing up her daughter's thigh.

He changed the subject.

> What about you? What's Christmas in the Arctic like?

> Oh, you know, Santa is my neighbour... damn reindeer always shit on our lawn.

> Yeah? Can you tell him to send me some new pencils? I've totally run out of kit and my maldito jefe won't give me any expenses.

> Pencils? Are pencils all you want for Christmas?

Yip.

> You're so sweet, Hector!

He didn't say anything, so, self-conscious, Cecilie changed the subject, typing furiously at the long table.

> So, at Christmas my mum is always home. We host. My grandparents visit from the care home they live in. It's a few hours away.

Which grandparents?

> Mamma's. I don't know my dad's parents...

Cecilie wondered when a good time would be to tell Hector about her dad, that he didn't just die when she was young. That her father's parents were so heartbroken when he took his own life that they couldn't bear to see the grandchildren their son had abandoned, so they moved away, never to contact them again.

> And my Uncle Hakon and his wife Tove sometimes come. They live in Svalbard, which is even more remote than us, practically the North Pole!

Wow, cool.

> They have no one to celebrate Christmas with 'cause their kids live overseas.

Nice. Where?

> USA.

> Not so nice.

> Hahahahaha. You had a bad experience there or something?

Hector thought back to the disastrous trip he made to see Elizabeth, or *La Gringa*, as Benny scathingly called her. Hector had planned and saved up every centavo from working in Benny's juice bar so he could go to the US to see Elizabeth and meet her family. He hadn't planned to spend so much of the trip with Elizabeth's friend Megan, nor had he planned to ruin that particular friendship, but he knew he probably wasn't welcome back in the US any time soon. Probably not even now, some ten years later. But it was a story for another time.

> What do you eat at Christmas? Not reindeer? Please don't tell me you eat reindeer.

> Nei! We have belly of pork with crackling, and serve it with sauerkraut and potatoes and little Christmas sausages. I make a tasty hawthorn gløgg.

> ¡Guau! Wish I could come.

I wish you could come.

> What about your brother?

Cecilie felt bad for not thinking to mention him. But Espen was always there at Christmas; his presence was a given. He hadn't wanted to leave the Arctic north much either, although he had been on a few city breaks.

> Yeah he'll be here for lunch. He's a waiter in a big hotel on the harbour, but he's doing the breakfast and the evening shifts at Christmas – he works crazy hours, but he'll take a break to come home for lunch. He might bring his boyfriend, Morten. It'll be his first Christmas with us.

Cecilie wondered how Hector might react.

> I can't imagine what it must be like to be a twin.

> It's OK. People think you have this real closeness and connection. They expect us to do amazing mind-reading tricks, but we're very different. I can't get inside his head much. He can't get inside mine. But we coexist quite happily.

> Does he look like you?

> Yes, but without the long hair.

> Your hair is cooooool.

> His is much more functional! But it's nice to have a twin, it's nice to have a brother. But, like you say, if it's all you ever know then it's just how it is.

Hector paused and thought about his brother. He hadn't told Cecilie that when his mum and dad died, so did his chance to have a sibling, to coexist happily. He broke his train of thought with a smiley face.

Cecilie sent one back.

> ANYWAY, the most exciting thing I'm reading about in your country...

> What? Santa doesn't really live next door to me, does he?

> No! Depeche Mode play the Telenor Arena tomorrow, remember? You got tickets, right?

> No. Sad face. It's a two-hour flight.

> Mexico City is five hours on a bus! I saw them there.

Cecilie paused. She could feel the hard curve of the grey plastic chair digging into her tailbone, so she repositioned her feet, off the chair in front of her and onto the wooden floor.

> Actually, I have no one to go with.

She looked back out at the snow and wished Hector would ask her if she had a boyfriend. She wouldn't mind telling him 'No'.

Hector looked at the clock on the bottom left-hand corner of his dented Dell laptop and realised he had to get going for work. Pilar must have left for school over an hour ago, and his art director at the paper, Oscar, had been on his case again. All these late starts since the summer; since Hector had been online for a quick chat before he started work, between Cecilie's shifts at the library and the Hjornekafé, had made Hector late, and Oscar had given him another dressing-down the week before. He typed faster in the quiet of his apartment, high above the noise of the street below.

> Man! I wish I could go with you. Teleport myself.

He looked out of the window, to Orizaba's snowy peak in the distance.

Looking out of the large window, past the warm yellow blur of the advent candles, at the virgin snow beyond, Cecilie floated away. She floated out of the garden, up to the top of Mount Storsteinen, where she put her hand to her brow to see if she could see him, all the way from there. She wished that he could stand on a peak and reach out so their fingertips could touch. Touch the curve of his arm. See the tattoo of a hand on his bicep, its pointed finger igniting a flame. Feel the warmth of those arms wrapped around her, if he really stretched.

> Are you there?
>
> Estás allí? Ceci…?
>
> Ah no mames.
>
> Ceci…?

Cecilie loved that Hector sometimes called her Ceci, and seeing it appear on the laptop screen in her peripheral vision snapped her back into the conversation. She didn't know how to say it, but she took her cue from Hector's boldness.

> You asked me about my first lover. Why have you never asked me if I have a boyfriend now?
>
> Because I don't want to know if you do.

* * *

The next night, while their favourite band played her capital city, Hector sent Cecilie a link to a YouTube video of 'Enjoy the Silence' from his desk at *La Voz*. Espen was working a late shift waiting tables at the i-Scand and their mother was at a symposium in Gothenburg, so Cecilie synched the laptop to the slick speaker system and pumped music around the downstairs of the house while she played Hector's link.

She untied the thick band holding her long heavy hair and it cascaded from side to side as she shook her head to the beat. Standing barefoot on the thick rug, surrounded by white paper lantern stars, Cecilie felt softness envelope her toes. As she moved, she imagined roots rising from the rug, curling up her jeans, anchoring her into place, vines strengthening with every beat of electronica.

Meanwhile, eight thousand nine hundred and nine kilometres away, Hector sat at his desk in the disorderly office of *La Voz*. He couldn't focus on the Sagittarius illustration for the horoscopes page he was meant to be drawing, so he looked over his shoulder to check whether Oscar was still out at lunch. With a charcoal pencil in his right hand, and the fingers of his left hand tapping out a rhythm on his jeans, he started sketching out the contours of a love heart-shaped face.

22

JULY 2018, SUFFOLK, ENGLAND

'Ooh, nice lippy,' mouths Venetia Appleyard, exiting a cubicle as she pulls her underwear out from between her bum cheeks and straightens her wraparound dress. Venetia catches Kate's eye in the mirror above the sink.

Kate isn't sure. She's been feeling self-conscious all evening, but she's attempting to reapply her Estée Lauder in a shade called Envious without getting any on her teeth. She widens her eyes to say thanks while her mouth is incapacitated.

'Some people say red is submissive, that you're trying to make your mouth look like a vagina, but I think it's a good "up yours" to the patriarchy,' Venetia continues while she washes her hands in the long rectangular sink that runs along the small wall. 'Anyway, Pete hates me in Suffragette Red, which always gives me a giggle when I wear it.'

Kate finishes blotting and edges a little paint out from the corners of her mouth. Her cheeks are almost as crimson as her lips.

'I haven't worn red for ages,' Kate says apologetically. 'I had to dig it out of the bottom of my make-up drawer. Think I've lost my touch!' She twists the almost-perfect bullet back into its navy and gold casing before Venetia notices it's brand new. 'Is Pete here tonight?'

'No, he's at home with Mills. I'm taking this one for the team,' Venetia says, inserting her hands into the noisy air dryer. 'Although it's a good turnout,' she backtracks. Venetia enthusiastically encouraged Kate to be PTA chair from September and knows turnout will be Kate's headache for the foreseeable.

'It's great, I'm so pleased. Lots of people want to send Melissa off in style I think,' says Kate sweetly with a nod.

'Shall we?' says Venetia, opening the door and walking through it before Kate.

They snake back into dark and cavernous Corky's, Claresham's only wine bar that's been hired out for the PTA summer social tonight.

'Did George make it along? I haven't seen him,' Venetia asks, long pendant earrings swinging below her plum-coloured cropped hair.

'Yes, although I haven't seen him for the past hour. Can't for the life of me see where he is. Thought I might find him on my way to the loo!'

'He's probably having a cigar with Mr Horsley,' Venetia says, rolling her eyes towards the low ceiling.

'Well, I'm sure he went to the loo and...'

Venetia is already disinterested; she's spotted headteacher Hilary Smith at the end of the bar and has something she wants to chew her ear about. She turns back to Kate, who is shuffling behind her.

'Catch up later, just need to talk to Hilary,' she says with a dismissive squeeze of the arm.

Kate weaves through the crowd alone. She searches for her drink, for her husband, and finally sees the back of George's Superdry jacket, slung over his shoulder and hooked onto a nimble finger, as he leans in towards Amber Barrie by the fireplace. Amber is almost as tall as George, and their eyes are locked, deep in conversation.

What's she doing here?

Kate surveys Amber from the ground up. She wears knee-length black leather boots over black skinny jeans and her long golden hair weaves down her chest over a perfectly pressed cream silk shirt. Her face looks fraudulently make-up-free in subtle shades of nude and peach, and suddenly Kate feels like an overdone summer pudding, waddling over all plump and bursting with redness. She wants to quickly swipe her lipstick off onto the back of her hand, but knows it'll make an awful mess, even if she uses one of the antibacterial wipes in the handy packet in her bag.

'There you are!' Kate says, sidling up to George, breaking up their conversation about whatever it was. 'Amber, how are you? What brings you to the PTA?'

Amber flashes Kate a charming smile, illuminating the hearth with a row of straight white teeth.

'Hi, er, Kate, isn't it?'

You know it is. We chatted for at least half an hour by the simnel cake stand at the WI Easter Extravaganza.

Kate nods genially.

'Amber here is going to be teaching the Year 3 class come September,' says George proudly. 'I was just telling her to look out for Jack. "Here comes trouble!"' he bumbles.

'Jack's no trouble,' Kate says defensively, before turning to Amber. 'Gosh, how wonderful. I didn't realise you were a qualified teacher?'

'Seems there are many strings to Amber's bow,' George gushes. 'She was telling me she can speak Mandarin. Not much use at Claresham C of E, but we could use more Mandarin speakers at Digby's the way the markets are going!' Kate's eyes glaze over as she feels an invisibility cloak shroud her. 'Tell me, Amber, did you ever use your Mandarin at the High Court? Amber here worked in her dad's chambers...'

Claresham's largest house, on the village's most expansive piece of land that edges onto vast Suffolk meadows, belongs to Amber's father, Archibald Barrie, rumoured to be the next Master of the Rolls, and certainly master of his Rolls, in which his driver Ken ferries him to his pied-à-terre in Chancery Lane three times a week.

Amber's peachy cheeks flush as her doe eyes look into her Prosecco flute before she realises Kate doesn't have a drink in her hand. There is something both awkward and consummate in Amber's faraway eyes.

'Kate, you don't have a drink. Shall I get one for you?' she says, looking for her exit strategy.

Kate gives George a scornful look. It was embarrassing enough having to listen to him fawning over Amber, but now Amber has pointed out his negligence.

The chink of a fork on glass draws all three of them out of the fireplace with a sigh of relief.

Melissa Cox stands in the middle of the bar with her back to a wall and taps the fork on her glass of Beaujolais five times swiftly.

'Before I hand over the reins to the highly competent and completely unflappable Kate Wheeler, I'd like to say a few words of thanks...'

Kate looks around the room to see everyone look for her fleetingly but unable to find her in this clammy corner of

Corky's, and they all look straight back to Melissa as she says her thank yous and her farewells. Kate's face feels hot and her throat parched.

I need a drink.

23

JUNE 2014, DAY 357

Click, click, click went the bank of plugs as Cecilie started up the machines. She sat down at her favourite terminal, the second one in on the first row, and realised she had a few minutes to spare before the sands of the egg timer would stop flipping and get her to middle-of-the-night Mexico.

She jumped up out of her white plastic chair and skipped down the stairs, two at a time, as elegant as a fairy in clumpy boots could be. The long ropey twists of her hair tangled themselves into the neck of her cream jumper and she freed them as she walked to the ground floor to get herself a drink from the coffee machine behind the reservations desk.

She had a giddy feeling in her tummy. One of excitement. Today was a packed day of events at the library, all of which Cecilie had coordinated. Baby rhyme-time at 10 a.m.; a visit from a class from her favourite infant school at 11 a.m.; an author talk, which she would come back for in the evening. Today was also the first time that Cecilie had known Hector Herrera on his birthday. When they met in a fan forum almost a year ago, she didn't know he had just turned thirty-three.

Yesterday, during a particularly quiet shift at the Hjornekafé, Cecilie had messaged Hector on her phone to ask him what his birthday plans were, and he said he would be out *chupando* that night, to get the party started early, with some friends, his girlfriend and all the other people Cecilie imagined Hector knew in town.

As she stirred a third splash of milk into her coffee and swizzled her spoon into a cyclone, she looked at the time lighting up the drinks machine. It was 8.15 a.m.; 1.15 a.m. in Mexico. She had fifteen minutes before Fredrik the man mountain would carefully wheel his bike through the back door.

Cecilie thought that although today was a new day for her, and it was Hector's birthday, it would still be yesterday to him. He would still be out *chupando,* or he might be partying at home. Wherever he was, Cecilie knew to expect one of their more stilted, unclear chats: the ones they had when Hector forgot his English and talked about being *muy bien pedo* – which Cecilie had googled, and the translation hadn't made much sense either. But her excitement about her day ahead, as she climbed back up the open staircase to get ready to log in, meant she was prepared for one of their more awkward chats, and she could take that in her dreamy stride.

As she sat down at the terminal and inhaled a slug of milky coffee, she tried to picture where Hector was – would he answer on his phone or his laptop? – would he be waiting for her or would she catch him by surprise? She tried not to think that he might be otherwise engaged, making love to Pilar... and she typed in her password with both a furrowed brow and a glow of excitement.

Let's see...

Cecilie didn't want to see Hector's beautiful bronze face all drunken and slurring, so she decided not to FaceTime. They rarely spoke with the cameras on, unless it was an unusually quiet afternoon on the art desk at *La Voz* and Cecilie was home alone for the evening. In fact, they had only talked face to face a handful of times in the past year since they'd met. They would mostly stick to chatting in green or blue boxes, and send silly pictures of themselves, or snippets of their favourite music videos or funny clips from movies they both loved – it was safer like that.

> Are you there?

Siiiiiii.

> Are you 'very well fart'?

Cecilie loved the literal translation Google threw her for Hector's drunken state.

Siiiiiiii.

> HAPPY BIRTHDAY/FELIZ CUMPLEAÑOS/GRATULERER MED DAGEN!

Cecilie added some balloons, party poppers and gift emojis in the box.

Thanks! It's started well.

> Glad to hear it. Where did you go?

Octava – a bar in town. Hang on, I'll send you a foto...

> You there now?

Hector didn't answer. Instead, a picture pinged onto the screen. Cecilie looked straight into the far-apart flirtatious eyes of the drunken man in the middle, strong arms up in the air. He made a peace sign with one hand and the other arm was tucked around the neck of a friend, and they were surrounded by more friends. Hector was wearing a khaki T-shirt with a white skull-and-crossbones illustration on it and Cecilie looked at it, knowing it was probably still clinging to his back right now, with a heady scent of turbulence and tequila embedded into the fabric. She wished she could inhale it.

> Looks fun! Who are they all?

Cecilie wondered which of the girls Pilar was.

> OK, gimme a second... Ready?

> Ja.

> OK from left... that's Anael, Xochitl, Ricky, Elias, Edgar, Nayeli, meeee, Heriberto, Luis, Efrain, Armando, Pilar...

So that's Pilar.

She was half cropped out but Cecilie could see she had very black, very big hair, almost bigger than Pilar herself, that seemed to drown her tiny face and frame. She was wearing a tight black dress with a sweetheart neckline. She looked like she was from another era. A pin-up from the fifties – not a girl from the same continent as Cecilie – only Pilar looked frail and spindly, not buxom like Ava, Bette or Jane. Her cheeks were sallow and sunken, her hooded eyes large and dilated, or was she just startled by the flash? She was not the sexy school-teacher Cecilie expected, and it made her sad to see that Hector loved a woman who looked so different to her. She knew at that moment that she would come back to that photo, to linger on it, to torture herself, but she snapped herself out of sadness with the excitement she felt, wanting to tell Hector about his birthday surprise.

> They look like a funky bunch.

> They are. Most of them are back here now hassling me to get off the computer.

> You home then?

> Síííííí.

But not making love to Pilar.

> OK, so I got you a present.

> Un regalo? For me?

> A little present.

> Un regalito then!

> Hahahaha.

In their last conversation, Hector had explained to Cecilie the Mexican obsession with the diminutive. *Hectorcito. Ahorita. Mañana por la mañanita.*

> Cool, how do I get it?

> Tomorrow in the little morning go to the post office. The correos. You know where that is?

Hector laughed.

> Mañana por la mañanita. Of course I know where it is. It opens at 8 a.m. I won't be there at 8 a.m., but thank you, I will go on my way to work!

> Ask for 'Post Restante', there's something with your name on it. Take ID.

> It's OK, I know everyone who works in the correos.

> Don't take ID then. But your regalito will be there. It should be there, I sent it three weeks ago.

> Wow, I'm honoured.

> It's just a small thing. And I didn't know your address.

Hector felt relieved Cecilie hadn't sent anything to the apartment on Benito Juárez, even though he had nothing to hide, of course...

Hector was sitting in the bedroom of the apartment, at the laptop on his bed, while Pilar and Elias each rolled a joint on the sofa in the living room and Nayeli was raiding their fridge for snacks.

'Pilar, no wonder I can see your bones, there's no food in here!' Nayeli hollered.

'There are *totopos* in the cupboard, *gordita*!' shouted Pilar from the sofa as she put the spliff to the corner of her lips and closed her eyes.

Ricky and Edgar walked into Hector's bedroom to see where the birthday boy had disappeared to.

'You jerking off in here, *güey*?' asked Ricky, a tall man in a sleeveless white hoodie that showed off his sepia skin.

'Are you fucking Ricky's *mamá* online again, *cabrón*?' said stocky Edgar, laughing, as he tried to look at Hector's screen and anticipated the punch on the arm from Ricky.

Hector hadn't told anyone about his online chats with Cecilie yet. Not even Pilar. He always gave Pilar the impression he talked to several different people in art, music and political chatrooms, rarely going back to the same discourse.

'Fuck off outta here, guys!' Hector slurred, relieved that neither Ricky nor Edgar knew English as well as he did, so they wouldn't be able to read the words on the screen.

Besides, the boys were sidetracked by Nayeli, shouting that one of them should go down to the convenience store on the street below for snacks.

'*A su madre...*' cursed Ricky, knowing he had little choice if he wanted to keep his girl happy.

> Look I gotta go! All crazy here. Thanks for the regalito – I'll pick it up tomorrow!

> Hey no problem, gratulerer med dagen! Have a fun night.

> Gracias.

Hector closed his laptop and gave a sigh, taking a moment to appreciate the peace a conversation with Cecilie brought him before heading back to the party.

In the quiet of the bright library, Cecilie's eyes filled up. Of course Hector was having fun with his friends. With his girl. He'd told her as much. Why was it bothering her anyway? She was nothing more than a friend to him, and if she was a good friend she would be happy for him.

Cecilie felt a wave of dejection and despair wash over her, then she remembered the gift waiting for him, and she felt a swell lift her and thought that even though she would never meet Hector Herrera, she wanted to make him happy. And *that* made her happy.

Cecilie gazed across to the rows of bookshelves beyond the computers, and in one corner of the silent library she could hear a muffled, muted noise. Figures were stumbling over each other with mirth and laughter to get imaginary drinks from the reading tables. She watched dreamily, the hum of smoke rising into the high recess of the curved ceiling. She saw Hector, sinking back into one of the colourful cushions people sink into and read on, while she watched faceless friends ruffle his hair and a diminutive girl lean her head on his chest...

Suddenly, Cecilie heard the back door to the ground floor entrance slam shut and the calm reassurance of spokes revolving. The figures in the library faded up into the atmosphere, distorting and shapeshifting like the smoke rings Hector exhaled.

* * *

In the morning, Hector woke alone to the sun streaming down on him through the curtain-less window overlooking his and Pilar's bed. His head was fuzzy and his tongue furry. Pilar had already left for school without waking Hector to say happy birthday, so he got up, threw on a clean T-shirt, a yellow one with an illustration of a red and orange sunset on it, over brown shorts with pockets on the side. He walked past Edgar lying on the sofa and saw Elias through the open door of the spare bedroom, lying on a mat on the floor. He grabbed a tall carton of orange juice out of the fridge, put on his military cap, slung his hessian satchel over his broad shoulders, and slammed the apartment door shut as he left, to deliberately wake and irritate his friends.

On his way to the offices of *La Voz*, Hector planned to call in on his grandfather at the ramshackle house on Calle Bremont for a birthday breakfast of *huevos rancheros*, but before that, he walked into the post office.

'*Hola*, Silvia,' he said to the woman behind the next available counter.

'Hectorcito, good to see you. I have a parcel for you!' she said with glee in her eyes. She went out the back to fetch it, knowing exactly where it had been sitting for a week, and came back hastily. 'It's from *Noruega*! Look at the stamp!' she said, pointing to a picture of a Viking ship on it, as if the letter had come over the seas on such a vessel. '*Maravillosa*,' she muttered under her breath while she pointed at a line for Hector to sign on.

Hector scribbled an illustrator's signature, then smiled and doffed his cap to Silvia. 'I'll pass on your best wishes to Abuelo,' he said with a twinkle in his eye. Silvia blushed. Hector stepped outside and sat on the steps of the *correos*, pushing his hessian satchel to one side so he could open the parcel. He looked at Cecilie's writing. He had never seen it before and it certainly looked like a stranger's handwriting. The alphabet was the same, but the letters took a different curve. Hector stroked the picture of the Viking ship softly with his thumb, then tore open the hard-backed cardboard envelope. Inside was a book. Hector pulled it out carefully. It was a graphic novel called *The Left Bank Gang* by a man called Jason. He had neither heard of the book nor the author, so he flipped it over and read about Jason, or John Arne Saeteroy, an illustrator from Norway. Hector flicked through, devouring the artwork, mesmerised by the brilliance and the politics of it, by the thought put into sending this, this work of art, across seas and an ocean.

This was the first birthday present of his thirty-fourth birthday, and as Hector carefully slid his new book into his satchel and made his way to meet Abuelo for breakfast, walking with a spring in his step, he knew that no present would touch this today. If ever. Apart from the photograph Alejandro gave Hector on his eighteenth birthday. One he'd held back for a special occasion, as it was the only family photo with all three of them in it. Of Victor and Lupe Herrera holding Hector on the beach at Veracruz as a young toddler. Apart from that, he had never been given anything he treasured as much.

24

JULY 2018, TROMSØ, NORWAY

'Thank you, Cecilie, that was wonderful as ever. Liv's whole being lights up when we come here, I'm so, so grateful to you.' Cecilie looks at the woman with the tired face and pointy chin. Her greying hair is scraped back and her delicate toddler is balanced on one hip as the mum leans down to pick up a soft giraffe from the floor of the library basement.

Cecilie takes Liv's hand in hers, to steady her as an anchor as her mother bends with difficulty. She looks into the little girl's far-apart eyes and slides a finger down from the flat bridge of her nose to the delicate tip, where she gives an affectionate double tap.

'You sang beautifully, Livvy Loo,' Cecilie says to the little girl. Enchanted eyes gaze back. Her mother stands and hands the soft toy back to her daughter. 'Come back and see me next week, yes?' Cecilie smiles.

The girl nods with an open mouth. An indebted mother smiles and slips away to gather bags, cardigans and coats and put them all on the buggy.

Cecilie collects the books scattered around the floor and stops at the feet of a pair of familiar tan-coloured brogues.

'Did you collect your order at the desk?' she asks, looking up.

'Yep, got it from Fredrik,' says Morten as he raises a puckish eyebrow above gnome-like eyes. He looks around conspiratorially to make sure the mothers, babies – and Fredrik up the short flight of stairs to the ground floor – can't hear him. 'He is so darned hot, Cecilie. Is the man not for turning?'

Cecilie gives a flustered smile. Twenty babies and toddlers in the basement of the library left her a little hot.

'For you or for me?'

'For you, my darling,' Morten says, tucking his book into his messenger bag. 'Although I wouldn't say no. Has he dumped that dreary yoga teacher yet?'

'India's OK, they're very happy together.'

'But you would make *such* a beautiful couple. And have you seen his thighs?'

Cecilie smiles and deftly changes the subject to the book in Morten's bag. 'What was it he called in for you anyway? Anything I need to know about?'

Morten thinks Cecilie must have read most of the books in the library, so she will know about this one, although Fredrik did have to call it in from Deichmanske Bibliotek in Oslo, and they only had an English-language copy.

And then it occurs to him that this book might be a bit sensitive for Cecilie right now.

'Oh, I'm sure you've read it already,' he says, pushing his frameless glasses up his snub nose and reluctantly opening his bag again to take the book out. Cecilie takes it out of Morten's soft hands and looks at the unfamiliar cover.

Instead of a Letter.

'No, I don't know this...' ponders Cecilie as she reads the blurb on the back out loud.

Morten talks awkwardly over her, as if that will distract her from what she's about to find out. 'Oh, she's an English writer. She wrote about how she was engaged to an air force pilot but he stopped writing to her, then she got a letter out of the blue saying he wanted to marry someone else...' Morten feels terrible.

'Oh.'

'*Ja*, she's amazing. Saucy old woman. I read one memoir she wrote about ageing – it made me want to fit a lot more in during my life – but I wanted to get my hands on this. Apparently, it's quite uplifting,' he says with a hopeful smile. 'I can pass it on to you?'

Cecilie busies herself tidying away the iPod dock with all the nursery rhymes stored on it and *So, ro, lillemann* pops into her head. 'Yeah, sure, no hurry,' she says, looking more sheepish than heartbroken.

Morten's eyes narrow. He can tell Cecilie is keeping something from him. She's a terrible liar and won't let him see her face as she bends down to pick up the last of the soft books.

'What is it? Cecilie...?'

She stands and looks at him, cheeks flushed. 'Oh, we're back in touch. The Mexican and me.'

Morten already knew who she meant. 'Is that wise?'

'Probably not.'

'So why do you torture yourself, sweetie?'

'Because talking to him and being sad is better than not talking to him and being sad.'

Cecilie's hot flustered face drops and her eyes well up.

'Here,' Morten says, bringing her to his chest.

'Don't tell Espen, hey?'

A man mountain lingers at the top of the stairs.

'Oh, Cecilie...' says Fredrik quietly.

She breaks away, looks up and smiles. Fredrik runs his fingers through his tied-back hair and rests his hand at the back of his vast neck. His forearm swells under his ribbed jersey top.

'I'm just going to the first floor to reset a machine for Mr Mosvold. Can you cover the desk please?'

'Sure.'

Fredrik walks off and Morten looks at Cecilie and mouths three words.

'So. Fucking. Hot.'

25

AUGUST 2018, XALAPA, MEXICO

'Sorry to interrupt, Cintia, but will you take a photo of me please?'

The woman from the ground-floor *perfumeria* sits at a small square table with a colourful stripy cloth over it, slurping the soup of the day from the *comida corrida* while she catches up on celebrity gossip. She puts down her spoon and dabs her deep burgundy lips.

'Sorry, Hector, how rude of me. I was in another world.' Cintia closes her magazine, feeling terrible that she hadn't been her usual chatty self.

Since Lupe's boy started working at the top-floor restaurant of Lazaro's, Cintia has liked their chats. He's made manic weekend shifts much more enjoyable. In fact, most of the women who work in Lazaro's now eschew a torta and a can of Boing in Parque Juárez on their lunch break for the *comida corrida* in the department store's restaurant. But the room was so busy when Cintia came on her lunch break she took the last available table and, not wanting to disturb Hector, picked up a copy of *Vanidades* another diner had left behind.

'Of course I can take a photo.'

'No, don't apologise, *guapa*, you're OK,' says Hector in a reassuring tone. 'I've been super busy, it's crazy today. That's the last chicken you've got there,' he says, sliding the *pollo a la Veracruzana* across the colourful cloth, lining it up for when Cintia is ready for her next course. Hector places his phone on the table next to her soup spoon.

'You're not a fan of the selfie, Hector? My girls are always taking selfies, my grandkids too.'

Hector laughs. 'A selfie is no good today. I need my entire body in it please, *guapa*, shoes and all.'

Cintia looks Hector up and down appreciatively.

'I'll do my best!' She gives a cheeky smile and narrows her eyes to focus on his phone screen. 'Is this to show Pilar? You certainly do look the part.'

Hector stands taller and straightens his buttons. His white short-sleeved shirt is perfectly pressed and doesn't have a single splash of red tomato and onion *Veracruzana* sauce on it, despite the bustling service. The creases of his Lazaro's grey strides point proudly towards the camera, hems resting on the polished brown shoes he wore on his wedding day. He smooths a white cloth on the bend of his left arm and raises a black circular tray out to the side with his right hand.

'Something like that.' Hector smiles, feeling bad that he asked Cintia to take a photo of him so he can send it on for a joke. Cintia is a proud woman.

She rises from her chair and bends at an awkward angle. Her grey pencil skirt strains under her hips. Her hair is heavy and immoveable thanks to hairspray.

'OK, smile.'

I am on the inside.

'Three, two, one...' Cintia stops abruptly. 'Hector, you look so serious!'

'Sorry,' says the austere waiter, trying not to look so formal.

Hector's eyes connect with the lens on his camera phone, flirtatious and playful.

'That's better. Three, two, one... *ay qué guapo*.' Cintia hands Hector the phone.

'Thank you.'

'No problem,' she says with a quick flick of her hair as she sits back down and straightens the magazine. Crispy curls don't move.

The lunchtime rush has ended. Hector puts the last rice pudding aside in the fridge for Cintia, and Lazaro's restaurant, with its colourful *papel picado* strung across the ceiling above their heads, is about to close for the day. No one eats dinner in Xalapa; it's all about lunch and the *comida corrida*: small plates comprising a four-course set menu, served with red salsa, crispy triangular *totopos* and a large glass of Jamaica – hibiscus water from a lime-infused jug. When the lunch has all been served and the chairs have been stacked in the restaurant's entrance to indicate it's closed, Hector will throw a grey jacket over his white shirt and walk across to the homes department, selling towels and toilet brushes to men and women who look about as bored as he feels.

This is Hector's third weekend working at Lazaro's to try to boost his income; to cover the shortfall of Pilar's lost teacher's salary. He hasn't had a pay cheque yet, but when he does he knows that weekends in Lazaro's won't be enough. He will need to do something else as well. But he doesn't want to get an evening job in a bar; he can't go back there. He can't serve his wife *micheladas* and *mezcal* while she's drinking away their rent money. It would be enough to turn him back to booze. And there aren't any days left in the week for Hector to take a third job.

Hector had encouraged Pilar to go for the job at Lazaro's, but José Luis, the third generation of Lazaros to manage the family-run store, wasn't so keen. José Luis had seen Pilar on nights out. He wouldn't mind if he saw Hector propping up a bar, or slurring and shouting obscenities at cantina staff, but he doesn't think women should behave like that, and Pilar isn't the kind of woman he wants associated with the Lazaro's name, whatever her heritage. José Luis knew Hector; he was happy to take him on. When he told his father that Hector was the new Saturday assistant, he waited for the story of Lupe Herrera again, to hear about what a terrible day it was when they realised why she hadn't come in to work.

Cintia closes her magazine and makes a start on the tepid chicken. 'How's that strange brother of yours getting on?' she asks as Hector walks back in from the kitchen. She heaps a spoonful of tomato and coriander salsa from the withering pot on the table and regrets not coming to lunch earlier.

'Brother?' Hector thinks back to the tumbling Beetle; how he clung on to the brother he never got to meet. 'I don't know about that.' Hector shrugs as he folds tomorrow's napkins and puts them under the counter that divides the kitchen from the dining area.

'I remember when you two were little. Running amok in the toy department! He wore that funny shirt with the frills on it. He did look a picture!' Cintia chuckles. 'He had this angry little face...' Cintia tries to compose herself and not show her mouthful of chicken as she laughs.

'I don't really see him, he's a busy man.'

'He must be doing well for himself. I saw him in a huge Dodge the other day.'

'I don't know,' Hector says. 'I don't even know where he lives now. I heard he moved out to a ranch.'

'A ranch? Sister Virginia was in the *perfumeria* last week, she said he was hanging around the Villa Infantil.'

Hector's cheeks flush pink and he gives Cintia a confused smile. 'The villa? I don't think so. I was there this week fixing the boiler. There were lots of little kids, definitely not a big ugly one like Benny.'

'Well, I didn't think it could be right. No one drives a car like that without having a palace to match. And I doubt Benny's much of a handyman to have around the place.'

Hector shakes his head and remembers the axe.

'No, no, I don't think he is.' Hector feels an uncomfortable taste rise in his mouth. 'I'll go get your rice pudding.'

As he walks to the kitchen with a feeling of foreboding, he remembers the dapper photo of him in his uniform on his phone and how much it will make Cecilie smile – *that* smile – to see he too has sold out and broken their pact.

26

AUGUST 2018, TROMSØ, NORWAY

'Mr Hansen, please meet i-Scand Arctic's most recent acquisition and newest member of the team... our bartender Cecilie. Erm, who also happens to be my twin sister.'

Cecilie dries a large red wine glass with a pristine white cloth and places it on the shelving above the ambient-lit bar. Her asymmetric sweep of white-blonde hair complements the white crisp shirt of her uniform perfectly. Iridescent green eyes flutter as she smiles, but she doesn't extend a hand.

Espen pulls up two bar stools and invites his guest to sit down at one while he stands and gently leans against the other.

'Cecilie, Mr Hansen is a regular at the hotel, commuting between here and Copenhagen.' Mr Hansen, a dashing man with noble lips and mink-brown hair that's greying at the temples, sits on his bar stool and smiles, looking from one twin to the other in awe. People often do that when they realise Espen and Cecilie are twins as they piece together the jigsaw puzzle of their features. 'He's an esteemed scientist; in fact, Mr Hansen knows more about your brain than you do.'

'Espen, please, it's Andreas...' Andreas says, removing his

navy-blue suit jacket. 'And he flatters me, Cecilie. I'm no brain surgeon, I merely import fish oil, and up here you have the best.' Mr Hansen – Andreas – shrugs and drinks in the bare-faced beauty behind the bar.

'Nice to meet you,' says Cecilie, drying another large glass. Espen is always polite and effusive to guests at the i-Scand, but she can tell her brother is keen to impress this one in particular.

'Can we get you a drink?' Espen asks. 'Your usual?'

'Actually, I think I'll need something stronger, Espen.'

Andreas widens his weary eyes and then looks at his watch. 'As of, ooh, two hours ago, I became a single man again. I think I need to drown my sorrows.' He lets out a wry laugh.

'Or celebrate perhaps?' fawns Espen, seeing an opportunity.

Espen!

Cecilie turns around to look at the offering of spirits she's not yet familiar with, standing neatly on the glass back wall, and hides her cringing face.

'Perhaps,' Andreas says, flinging his suit jacket on the back of his stool like a cape.

Cecilie gives Espen a sideways glare.

'Usually, Mr Hansen – sorry, Andreas – likes a cold pilsner, but how about a whisky today? Have a Yamazaki on us.' Espen points his finger. 'That one there, Cecilie. It's twelve years old.'

Cecilie picks the bottle from the line-up, scoops ice into a square glass and pours a measure with her free hand. Espen tells Cecilie to stop pouring without uttering a word. She can hear his voice in her head telling her that this whisky is 1,500 krone a bottle.

'I'm sorry for your turmoil,' Cecilie says with a sympathetic smile. The ice cubes crack under liquid gold.

'Oh, I'm not really. I am sorry Iben fleeced me for the house, the summer house, the kids and the dog... But I'm not sorry her personal trainer boyfriend is about to find out just how high-maintenance she is. I give their relationship till Christmas.'

Andreas gives a wistful shrug and rubs the end of his nose.

'Here. Well, I'll have a drink with you, to celebrate or commiserate. A sparkling water please, Cecilie.' Espen never drinks on the job. In fact, he rarely drinks off the job. Many an evening Morten and Cecilie have sunk a bottle of red and Espen has barely got through a glass.

Cecilie blinks three times in an attempt to hide her fatigue as she searches the low fridge for a bottle of Voss. She's exhausted and can't wait to get home and put her feet up when she clocks off in three hours' time. Cecilie was up at the library at 7.30 a.m. to help Fredrik clear the basement area for a children's writing workshop; she left the heaving basement at midday to work the lunchtime and afternoon shift with Henrik at the Hjornekafé, and now she's at the i-Scand, looking for Espen's favourite brand of fizz and getting ready to pour whisky – not all Yamazaki – for the evening arrivals from the capital. She catches her reflection in the fridge door.

Uff.

'And can I have some ice in that, please?' Espen asks, even though Cecilie already knew that's what he was about to say.

Cecilie stands and shovels another cluster of cubes, this time into a longer glass, and pours Espen his drink. She looks at the downbeat man sipping his whisky and finds something comforting in his acquiescent face. Perhaps it's that he looks like he's in a daydream, because Cecilie likes to have those too.

Fizz, fizz, crack. The ice breaks the silence.

Espen raises his glass and snaps Andreas out of another world.

'*Skål*, Mr— Andreas,' Espen says, raising his effervescent glass. 'To pastures new.'

Andreas smiles and nods and looks at Cecilie.

'Cheers,' he replies, lifting his glass but not taking his eyes off her. 'Hey, you need a drink too. Espen, what about your sister?'

'Oh, I'm OK.' She smiles reassuringly.

Cecilie feels flushed and busies herself by fitting the lid of the ice bucket back on.

'So, Espen, I didn't realise you had a twin, how fantastic.'

'Yes, I've known her all my life.' Espen laughs, even though it's a joke he has told a thousand times. Cecilie rolls her eyes.

Andreas studies Cecilie's face. 'Wow,' he says, almost to himself.

One of the hotel receptionists approaches Espen cautiously. At twenty-nine, he is the youngest manager in any of the chain's fifteen hotels across Scandinavia, but staff are still respectful of him; he worked his way up from bell boy to waiter to restaurant manager to hotel manager. He cares so much about customer satisfaction; he's passionate about the i-Scand brand.

'Can I have a word?' asks Camilla, her dark blonde hair in a neat bun.

'Sure,' says Espen, putting a fist to his mouth and clearing his throat. 'Excuse me just a second,' he says, putting his hand on Andreas's shoulder before walking off to a discreet corner of the room with Camilla.

Cecilie feels under pressure to make chit-chat. She loves singing lullabies to babies, or watching children in awe of authors in the library; and the Hjornekafé is a home from home. Just stepping inside it and wiping her feet on the coarse mat feels like a warm hug. But the stark and dark décor of the businessman's current favourite Tromsø hotel is less comfortable. Cecilie isn't very good at chit-chat. It's one of the reasons why she always felt so contented chatting to Hector online. She likes a safety barrier of screens.

'How long are you staying for?' Cecilie asks stiltedly. But there is something about Andreas that puts her at ease. It makes her understand that whatever it is he does with brains or fish oil, or whatever business he's in, he's obviously very competent.

'Just a few days. I'm only ever here for a few days. But I like it up here. Your people are a bit mad.'

Cecilie laughs as she straightens mats on the black granite bar.

'I can't argue with that. It's all this daylight followed by darkness. It sends us a bit loopy,' she says as she crosses her eyes and sticks her tongue out to the side.

Andreas laughs, which takes him by surprise. His smile is warm and he's bemused by an absurdity he's never seen in Espen.

Cecilie stops abruptly and looks back down at the bar mats. She straightens the same ones again, in the same order as she did before.

The bar area is quiet apart from the two of them, and Camilla and Espen mulling over a clipboard in the corner. Thursday's late-afternoon arrivals won't start filling the bar for the next hour or so, and Eirik, who is working the early evening shift with Cecilie, isn't due in until six o'clock.

Andreas sees the flush of shyness in Cecilie and wants to put her at ease.

'You live in such a beautiful town, although I never get to see it as I'm always working.'

'Have you been up the Fjellheisen? The view from the ledge up there is pretty spectacular.'

'No, I must have been to Tromsø twenty times and I've never been. I bet it's beautiful to see the lights from up there.'

Cecilie nods dreamily.

'Not this time of year.' She takes a cloth and pretends to look busy by drying already-dry glasses. It's easier to make chit-chat if she's doing something with her hands. 'What's Copenhagen like?'

'Really cool, really colourful, my sons have a good life there – it's just a shame I'm not at home as much as I like, I guess...' Andreas drifts away for a second, then his eyes light up. 'The restaurants are amazing. You've never been?' he asks with surprise.

Cecilie feels embarrassed again. 'No, no, but I heard it's awesome.'

A beep goes off on Cecilie's phone under the bar and she tries to ignore it.

It wouldn't look professional.

Then another.

Is it him?

'Would you like a top-up of ice?' Cecilie asks under a pretext, fumbling for a scoop.

'Sure, thanks.'

She looks down. Her screen is lit. It's not Hector. The texts are from Grethe and they come in a stream of five or six.

> Hei Cecilie!
>
> Can you talk?
>
> Are you there?
>
> Are you at work?
>
> It's happening. I can't get hold of Abdi.

Cecilie gasps.

'Shit! Espen!' she calls across the bar. 'Oh, I'm sorry, Andreas,' she says, putting her hand to her mouth.

'Is everything OK?'

'My friend, I think she's gone into labour.' Cecilie teeters between protocol and primeval. Then she shouts across the bar again. 'Espen!'

He turns around, breaking away from his conversation with Camilla, and gives his sister a look.

'Just a second,' he says, raising an irked palm. Cecilie doesn't wait.

'It's Grethe, I think she went into labour.' Espen's face softens. 'Abdi's out on the boat and she can't get hold of him.'

'Excuse me a second, Camilla,' Espen says, straightening his suit jacket as he strides over. 'Have you spoken to her?'

'No, I just had a text.'

'Well, you must call her,' Espen says, in a strange concoction of fire-fighting mode and inconvenience. 'I'll get one of the dining staff to cover the bar for a minute. Actually, Camilla, can you just cover for a second please?'

The girl with the neat bun nods and follows Espen's trail. 'Excuse me, Mr Hansen – sorry, Andreas,' says Espen, bowing. 'It's practically a family emergency. Our friend is heavily pregnant.'

Andreas smiles.

'Would you like another Yamazaki?'

'No, no thanks,' Andreas replies as he watches Cecilie walk away to make a call. Andreas sees her for the first time from the ground up. Dr Martens boots. Black tights and a short black skirt. Crisp white shirt. Even in her uniform, she looks edgier than her twin brother.

Cecilie walks into the function room, a room with big mesh spheres for lightshades, and closes the sliding doors behind her as she presses Grethe's face to call her.

'*Hei*, you OK?'

'*Nei*, I'm at the hospital. Abdi is at sea. I can't get hold of him.

It hurts so much, Cecilie. My mum is at the Iskrembar. I told her Abdi was on his way so she wouldn't worry.'

'Want me to come? I'm sure Espen won't mind.'

'Will you, I want to die...' The line goes silent and then Cecilie hears howling, like a wolf at the moon, followed by a retching sound and the splat of liquid – vomit, she assumes – hitting the floor. Cecilie knows she must go to her.

'I'm coming!' she shouts, hoping Grethe would have heard her from a phone that's now on the floor of the delivery suite. 'Espen, I need to get to the hospital, she's on her own – can you cover my shift until Eirik gets here?'

'Don't worry about here, go go go – where's Mamma's car?'

'It's at home, I walked.'

Mamma's car is actually Cecilie's, given Karin doesn't drive, but she certainly pays for the family runaround.

'You might struggle getting a taxi.' Espen tries to remain cool and calm in hotel manager mode, but even he is starting to flip and the quiff of his blond hair is waning.

'My driver is out front,' says Andreas coolly. 'He knows these roads. Take my car.'

'Really?' asks Espen. He's clearly uncomfortable about crossing an imaginary line with a hotel guest.

'Yeah, sure – he is only sitting there bored, waiting to see if I want to eat out tonight, which I don't. I'm going to have a club sandwich in my room.'

Andreas always has a club sandwich in his room on the first night.

'If you're sure...'

Cecilie flutters to the door at the end of the bar, goes through it to grab her coat and bag and comes out looking flustered. She sweeps her fringe behind one ear. Andreas stands.

'Come on, I'll show you to my car, I'll explain everything to Svein.'

Andreas puts a reassuring hand a few centimetres away from the middle of Cecilie's back to help usher her out. She doesn't feel it touch her, but she knows it is there. Andreas and Cecilie guide each other out of the bar area: through the atrium-like dining room to the sleek and shiny tiled floor of the reception area and through the automatic doors onto the harbour. There is a large space where the Hurtigruten is usually docked, where Abdi will return tonight, perhaps as an unwitting father.

'Here we go,' Andreas says, opening the rear door of a sleek black Audi.

'Svein, take Miss Wiig wherever she needs to go please – although I assume it's the hospital, yes?' He nods at Cecilie as she slides into the back and gives a grateful smile.

'That's right, the hospital please.' She looks up at Andreas. 'Thank you,' Cecilie says as she closes the car door.

27

> I delivered a baby!

Cecilie types as she walks over the bridge in the chilly wind. The August sun barely set last night and Cecilie didn't go to sleep at all. She spent most of the night clutching Grethe's pale tense hand, navigating her through the pain and the terror of every wave, until baby Ahyana Cecilie Margot arrived into the Arctic Circle, her father still out at sea. Cecilie attaches a photo of a pink and brown newborn with swollen eyes and beautiful lips. She doesn't expect a reply, but one comes straight away.

> Beautiful! Congratulations! Is Mamá OK?

> She's fine. She was amazing. So strong. Abdi arrived at 5 a.m. I'm already on my way to work, I only had 45 minutes at home but I was so wired, I couldn't sleep!

> Well you're strong too. Mi héroe. Well done you. A new career perhaps? Not sure of the word for partera... Midwife, I think.

> Sí, midwife.

> You've found your calling, Midwife Ceci.

> Ahh, thanks. Not sure I could go through it again.

> Well done my love.

My love?

Cecilie is thrown.

I thought we left that behind.

It's late over there. But Hector doesn't get drunk and careless any more. In fact, since they started messaging each other again, Cecilie has loved chatting to level-headed Hector. Always sober. Always coherent. Whether he's stealing five minutes from the art desk at *La Voz* or sending pictures of himself in his uniform from Lazaro's, Cecilie loves talking to solid, sensible Hector even more than she did before.

Maybe it's a querida *thing.*

Yes, Hector probably calls everyone *querida* or *mi amor*. Cecilie's not sure why, but 'love' still cuts through her like a knife.

I'm tired.

A black Audi pulls up on the other side of the arching cantilever bridge, heading the other way. Cecilie recognises Svein, the driver, his silver hair curling softly at the nape of his collar. The rear window lowers and Andreas is revealed, looking pleased to see Cecilie. The driver of the car behind him beeps his horn, but Andreas is unperturbed.

'Everything OK with your friend?' Andreas shouts across the traffic.

'Yes.' Cecilie laughs gratefully. 'A girl. "Ahyana". Born at 4.21 a.m. I cut the cord!'

Andreas looks impressed. 'You want a lift?'

The horn beeps again, twice in quick succession. Or was it a second car joining in?

'No thanks, don't worry. You're going the other way.'

Andreas's car *was* heading away from the town, past Mount Storsteinen to the roads that lead to the Finnish border, but he imagines Cecilie won't fancy the biting wind of the bridge at 8 a.m., especially on so little sleep.

'Jump in! It's fine, it'll take Svein, what, ten extra minutes? It will save you a lot more time than that.'

Cecilie is tempted. Her bones ache. She didn't reply to Hector's confusing comment and she's too tired to try to make sense of it. Besides, he's probably about to go to bed, to spoon his bony wife, so she nods across the traffic at Andreas, who moves along the back seat to make way and winces while Cecilie dodges the cars heading into town, towards the library, the cafe, and the hotels on the harbour. She opens the car door and slides in as a succession of three SUVs behind them beep, making Cecilie feel flustered, although Andreas and his driver aren't. The car is warm and the plush leather seats are a comfort; the smell of clean upholstery reminds her of how this night she will never forget started.

'Thank you,' she says, looking across the back seat to Andreas.

'Svein, why don't you turn around in the car park of that cathedral there and head back across the bridge?'

The driver nods compliantly.

'The i-Scand, yes?' Andreas asks.

'No, the library actually. The big white building at the back of the town, with the undulating roof.'

Svein nods again; Andreas doesn't know Tromsø very well but he knows that impressive building.

'The library? Wow. Delivering babies at 4 a.m. and studying by 8 a.m.'

'No, I work there.'

'At the library? As well as the hotel?'

'Yes. The library in the morning, a cafe in the afternoon, and at the hotel recently, during their busier evenings.'

'You are as hard-working as your brother.'

'More so; I'm a midwife too now, you know.' Cecilie winks through her sweeping fringe. The strange concoction of happiness and fatigue make her feel unusually bold.

Andreas looks back at Cecilie, sitting in her regular clothes and not her uniform. She looks fresh, despite not having slept, and he likes how her blue jeans, frayed at the knee, and green Converse boots offset the stuffiness of the car, his driver, their suits.

'So how was the birth?'

'Not pretty. But I saw a miracle happen before my very eyes. Not many friends get to experience that.'

'Brutal, isn't it? I was at both my sons' births and they were pretty gruesome. It would have put me off having kids if I were a woman.'

Cecilie swallows the lump in her throat. Until now, it hadn't put her off, or made her feel sad, but a defensive fog rises from the pit of her stomach and the wind has been taken from her wings. In two months' time, Cecilie will turn thirty, and she's never even had a proper boyfriend. She has never been able to walk hand in hand with the man she loves.

As the car turns around in the jagged shadow of the white concertina of the Arctic Cathedral, Cecilie suddenly feels a little naïve, a little intimidated. Not by Andreas himself, but by his age, his experience, by what he's been through in his business, his life, his divorce. It's a feeling she had before. But her tired, dreamy mind digs deep into her resilience reserves.

Not many people can say they delivered their friend's baby.

'It didn't put me off, it was magical,' Cecilie says, looking up at the crisp blue sky as the car rolls back onto the bridge. Cecilie always has a knack of putting a magical spin on something, and flashes of what Grethe, Ahyana and she went through in the night tell all those uncomfortable feelings to be gone with a wriggle of her nose.

Andreas glances across in awe and they lock eyes.

Cecilie feels for her phone in her pocket, just to check it's still there, as it didn't vibrate again after Hector called her 'my love'.

He must have gone to sleep.

'So, the cable car. I've not been up there.'

'Yes, you said.'

'Will you show me around? I leave Saturday night – shit, that's tomorrow – but I have tomorrow morning free. Is the cafe any good at the top? I could buy you lunch...'

Cecilie's face flushes pink, making her green eyes look as bright as her shoes. She feels flattered, if a little scared. But tomorrow is Saturday, and on Saturdays, Fredrik, Pernille and Leif cover the library, and Henrik and Stine have everything in hand at the Hjornekafé. Cecilie searches her brain for an excuse.

'Well, I'm not working until the evening shift at the hotel, but Grethe's mother Mette might want some help at the Iskrembar...' Andreas's gracious smile wanes. 'But that's OK, I'm sure Mette will be fine with Oliver,' she adds, feeling guilty. Grethe had ordered Cecilie *not* to work at the Iskrembar while she was on maternity leave, not when she had three other jobs and barely any time off as it was. Plus, Cecilie hasn't been up the Fjellheisen herself in months. It would be nice to show off the view to a tourist.

'So...?' asks Andreas with an eyebrow raised playfully.

'Sure,' Cecilie says, to her surprise. 'That would be wonderful.'

As Svein navigates through the morning traffic to the library, Cecilie and Andreas sit in comfortable silence. A flash of a smile appears in the corners of their mouths as they look out of their respective windows.

'This is it,' she says, pulling her bag across her body as Svein pulls up. Cecilie pulls the sleek silver handle and edges out. 'Thanks for the lift. Again!' Her nose creases up nervously as she looks at Andreas. Cecilie breaks the tension by turning to Svein. 'Thanks so much.'

Svein nods.

'See you at the Fjellheisen. Say 10 a.m.?'

'Ten is good.'

'Shall we pick you up?'

'No, it's fine, I live right near it. I'll see you tomorrow morning, at the ticket office at the bottom.'

On no sleep, tomorrow morning seems so far away that it takes the edge off Cecilie's nerves, and she walks down the side of the library to the staff door, without looking back at the smitten businessman in the black Audi.

28

AUGUST 2018, SUFFOLK, ENGLAND

'So lovely of you to invite us into your stunning home, Antonia, it's just superb out here.' Kate drinks in a little too much from her flute, and perfectly chilled pink champagne runs into her doughy bosom, dampening the V of her swallow-print dress. She thought the white bird silhouettes on navy cotton was rather natty when she picked it up in M&Co when she was getting Jack a gilet last autumn. The dress had become a bit snug by spring, but since Kate decided to snap out of her rut, to stop being suspicious and needy, and to get back to Weight Watchers, she's actually felt better. And the dress fits her again, so she decided to wear it to Antonia and Archibald Barrie's annual cheese and wine party. In fact, Kate's honoured to be invited this year. Last August, she and George didn't cut the mustard, which was a bit of an outrage given all the hard work Kate had put into the WI summer jamboree, but they were on holiday in Lake Annecy so they couldn't have made it anyway, as Kate kept telling herself.

This summer, the Wheelers have arrived, and Kate is standing on the terrace under a pagoda trimmed with fairy lights, admiring the sweeping view of the Suffolk countryside alongside WI, PTA and NCT chums. Even George has come willingly – he's been much more compliant lately, which is great for Kate as she hates turning up to drink parties alone – although he is skulking around in the kitchen, talking hedge funds with Nigel Pickover, who runs the cricket club.

It's not quite dark, so Kate surveys the pink sunset that's peppered by the silhouette of a church steeple as she sips champagne with Antonia Barrie, lady of the manor, who is regaling Kate with her plans to have a set of stables and a paddock installed at the far end of the field. It was when Antonia told Kate that she'd fallen for a sixteen-hand grey Hanoverian that Kate choked on her drink. She had no idea what any of it meant.

Antonia gives Kate a smile to veil her pity – she saw the champagne trickle into that inelegant cleavage of hers but decided to carry on talking about her architect's plans for the stables and horses to fill them with.

'It'll be so wonderful for the children – all of them. Alistair and Bertie really ought to be riding by now,' she says, but she can't hide her disdain any longer. 'Chen!' she calls to a woman topping up glasses. 'Napkin please, we've had a little accident...'

We. How thoughtful.

Kate blushes and apologises, fumbling to take the crisp white linen from an obliging servant.

'Sorry, Antonia, I got a bit carried away! Big gulp. I'm just so pleased to be here, it's such a beautiful evening.' Kate presses the linen into her cleavage to absorb the moisture. 'So, how many horses will the stables house?' Kate asks, not interested in horses in the slightest, but doing her best to pretend she is.

Amber Barrie sidles up to rescue them both and Kate doesn't see the knowing look dash between mother and daughter.

'Sorry to interrupt.' Amber nods at Kate, not sounding in the least bit sorry. 'Marta has managed to get Alistair and Bertie down. Clarissa has just gone over to Meadow's house.'

'Meadow's house? At this time? What could possibly be more exciting at Meadow's house?' says Antonia in high-pitched outrage, laughing. 'Meadow ought to have come here.' She strokes her daughter's long golden mane. 'Thank you, sweetpea. Oh, have you met? Darling, this is, er, Kate, Kate *Wheeler*, from the WI. She's *very* talented with a spreadsheet.' Kate tries not to look offended, but this time she does notice a loaded look between Antonia and Amber, right about the point when Antonia said 'Wheeler'.

You thought my Battenberg was the best in the blind tasting.

'Kate, this goddess of a girl is my daughter Amber.'

'Yes, Mummy, we've met...' the goddess says, glowing.

Kate is both fascinated and intimidated. How does a woman as fragrant and floaty as Antonia Barrie have two grown-up daughters and two young boys – who would be in the same school as Jack and Izzy if they weren't at the private school in the next village? Antonia must have been well into her forties when she had Bertie, but she doesn't look like a woman who's harangued with homework and sticker charts and cricket practice. And now her daughter is standing next to her, like Antonia v.2. A younger, more charming, more attractive clone, with swishier hair and peach-perfect skin.

'Nice to see you again,' Kate bumbles, trying not to spill anything else from her flute. 'Looking forward to the new term next week?' she adds keenly.

'Can't wait.' Amber smiles.

'It's Amber's first teaching job – and in a state school! It'll be quite a different environment to what *you* experienced at school, darling.'

'Oh, it's OK,' Amber says, slightly flustered that her mother might not know that Kate's son will be in her class. She's preoccupied by a secret she's trying to conceal. 'I trained in East London, Mummy, I'm ready for anything!'

The quiet lioness in Kate feels slightly riled by the implicit criticism, and emboldened by champagne.

'Well, Jack is raring to get back to school. And Claresham might not have the facilities of Saint Felix's, but it's a really lovely school. My eldest daughter Chloe was sad to leave this summer. She's had a marvellous time there.'

'Oh, I'm sure it'll be wonderful.' Amber smiles without using her eyes.

There is a lingering pause in the conversation and Kate feels scrutinised by the two polished women, looking her up and down with pitying smiles. Suddenly, Kate's Weight Watchers success doesn't seem like such a triumph, and she shuffles from one foot to the other before deciding she ought to move along now, to make it easier for Antonia to mingle. She knows when she's not interesting enough.

'I wonder where George has got to,' Kate says, looking back over her shoulder to the guests behind her on the terrace.

'He's in the kitchen,' Amber replies in a flash.

'Oh. Thanks. Excuse me...' Kate smiles meekly as she walks away with uncomfortably damp nipples.

* * *

In the vast expanse of the beige and black kitchen, guests mingle around a huge granite island, while Chen, and Antonia's other minions, glide around with platters full of manchego tartlets and quince.

Nigel Pickover walks towards Kate, standing in the wide doorway as she surveys the room looking for George, and raises a hand as if he has something important to say to her. He looks sozzled and sweaty, with a plump red face. Kate pauses to see what Nigel wants to talk to her about.

'Where's the big white telephone?' he stumbles, putting an unwieldy hand on Kate's shoulder to steady himself, desperate to find one of the seven bathrooms.

'Oh, I don't know,' says Kate, shrugging. 'Where's my husband?'

Nigel walks past without answering, and Kate wonders if she really might be invisible after all. In the kitchen, she is horrified to see George hanging off one of the double doors to the fridge, leaning in and helping himself to a beer. He looks quite at home for someone who usually eschews such parties. 'George!' Kate scolds, embarrassed by his overfamiliarity but relieved that she can't see Archibald, Antonia or Amber anywhere in the vicinity. 'What are you doing?'

George rummages before he finds a brand he likes. One of the waiting staff rushes over with a bottle opener.

'You can't just help yourself to beer in someone else's home!' Kate says as she studies George's flushed face.

'Why not?' He shrugs.

'I think we'd better start making a move. I told Susannah we wouldn't be late.'

'She's all right,' George says with a cavalier gleam in his eyes.

'Well, I'm not, and you look like you've had enough already.'

'Party's only just getting started,' he slurs, looking out the kitchen window onto the terrace outside.

Kate can't put her finger on it, but after hankering for an invitation to Archibald and Antonia Barrie's annual cheese and wine party for years, she doesn't like being in Claresham Hall, or Barrie Manor as everyone in the village calls it. She just wants to get home.

29

NOVEMBER 2016, DAY 1,232

> Are you OK Hector?

Yeah I'm fine. You?

> Where are you?

DF.

> DF?

Mexico City. My friend Efrain had a birthday party here last night.

> Ah, happy birthday Efrain.

I'll tell him. Thirty-five yesterday. An old bastard like me. We're about to go get some breakfast. You OK?

It was a cold Sunday afternoon in November. The library was closed, Karin was in Geneva, and Espen and Morten were huddled on the sofa, legs stretched out and entwined in front of them, drinking a bottle of red and watching a movie on a rare day off. Cecilie sat at the long wooden table in a silent conversation with someone on the other side of the world, her own glass of red perched proudly next to her own new MacBook. She didn't have to use her brother's any more. Espen and Morten punctuated her quiet conversation with chuckles at the television.

Cecilie lingered on Hector's words.

I'll tell him.

That would mean that she was an acknowledged friend of Hector's. In his life.

As Cecilie looked out of the window onto the snowy expanse of their garden at the foot of Mount Storsteinen, she floated through the howling wind and grey clouds to a sunny November morning over Mexico City. She paused for breath atop mighty Aztec pyramids before continuing until she could see the green, white and red of the giant flag rippling in the Zócalo and smell the tamales and tacos from the street vendors around the vast plaza.

> Ceci?

She didn't reply.

> Ceci, you OK? Wanna FaceTime? Efrain's brother has wiffy here.

The sun burst through slats in the window and warmed Hector's face – the thought of seeing Cecilie's while he was hungover already felt like something of a tonic, so he lingered on the sofa in Efrain's brother's apartment.

A squeeze of fresh lime from a street food vendor burst into the sky and Cecilie snapped out of her dreamy state and back into the warm toasty living room within the safe confines of the Arctic Circle.

> Oh no, it's OK, you get going, sorry. I forgot it was the boys' night out. I just wanted to check you were OK, I was worried. But you're OK.

> Worried?

> About something I just read on the news. Nine severed heads, thirty-two bodies...

Hector leaned back into the sun-dappled sofa and looked up at Efrain, his brother Raymundo, and their friends, all heading out of the apartment door. Efrain gesticulated at him to *vamos*.

> Hang on, Ceci...

'Guys, I'll catch you up, I need to make a call.'

'Eh *cabrón*, you gotta eat!' said Efrain, looking disappointed.

'Checking your *mamá's* porn hub out again, Hector?' Efrain's brother, Raymundo, said, laughing. Efrain winced. Hector ignored them both and looked back at his phone.

'Order me *huevos al abañil* and a nopal juice. I'll be right there,' he lied.

Efrain felt bad for his brother's careless comment to a motherless son, so he smiled and nodded compliantly.

The door slammed. The air smelled stagnant under the vaulted ceiling of the Centro Historico apartment, but it was silent, he could talk. Hector lit a cigarette and messaged Cecilie back.

> OK I'm here. What's up? I can call you...?

Cecilie didn't want to say it out loud in front of Espen and Morten. She typed furiously.

> It's just, I'm scared for you.
>
> I keep reading horrific stories. Things happening in Mexico.

> OK so where did these things happen?

Hector put his feet up on the coffee table in front of him and inhaled as he looked at his phone. Perhaps it was best this conversation wasn't voice to voice or face to face; Hector didn't know how to be calming about something that fizzed away murkily in the back of his mind like a constant feeling of impending doom. Like the thwack, whack, whack of Benny's rolled-up comics on the back of his head in the bottom bunk.

> Somewhere called Zitlala?

> OK well Zitlala is nowhere near Xalapa. It's, like, seven hours away. That shit doesn't go down near me.

Again, Hector was lying. Two weeks ago, a taxi driver was decapitated and his severed head left on the dashboard of his abandoned car, right near the city centre. Hector thought of the nopal juice he had ordered, and his mouth went dry with thirst and fear. But Cecilie was reassured and took heart as she looked across the room at Espen and Morten, laughing on the sofa.

> Ah OK. I just seem to be reading more and more stories about violence and massacres and mass graves, I just wanted to check you were OK, that none of this world touches you.

Hector felt relieved that she hadn't read the story about the taxi driver, just 200 metres from his grandfather's home.

Hector thought of the axe.

> I hear about this shit all the time at the paper, but trust me, these guys keep among themselves. I don't mix with them, no amount of money is worth that.

Hector thought of the deliveries he used to make for Benny. Of the times Benny knocked at his door, or let himself into Hector's apartment, sitting, waiting in the dark, asking for a pair of helping hands.

'It's good money, Zapata. You'll get you a proper place to live, a ranch like me.' When he'd said this, Hector wondered where Benny had moved to, since where he lived had become a closely guarded secret. But Hector didn't actually want to know. He didn't want to sully his visits to Sister Miriam at the Villa Infantil with chit-chat about Benny, which grand hacienda he had bought, or what his latest business venture might be. And Benny's unannounced visits to Alejandro's house on Calle Bremont, or to his apartment in the tall building on Benito Juárez, had got less frequent as the years went on. He couldn't remember the last time Benny Trujillo let himself into the apartment and sat waiting in the dark. It hadn't happened since Pilar had moved in anyway. Hector knew that every time he said 'Thanks, man, but I'm OK...' and turned down Benny's offers of work, he was making himself more of a foe. But saying no to Benny put Hector in less danger than saying yes to Benny. And their relationship had always been about survival.

Hector leaned his head back against the sofa and looked up at the fan on the high ceiling of the Mexico City apartment.

> Don't worry princesa, I'm fine. Hungry and hungover, but fine.

Cecilie let a sigh of relief out at the screen of her laptop. Relieved that this was a world Hector didn't inhabit, relieved that he had been on a boys' night out and his girlfriend must be miles away back at home.

> Phew, well that's OK

Cecilie took a large sip from her glass. Calmness flooded her as Merlot travelled to her bloodstream.

> You go get breakfast, nourish yourself Hector!

> OK, me voy.

> Hector?

> Siiiiiiii...

> I love you.

> I love you too.

30

AUGUST 2018, TROMSØ, NORWAY

Andreas inhales the view as the cable car rises.

'Amazing, my boys would love this!' His face is that of an enchanted little boy himself, although his minky hair is greying at his temples.

Cecilie smiles. She finds other people's smiles infectious. 'You'll have to bring them!'

They marvel at the rising view of the green slopes, the blue fjord, and the bridge connecting the mainland to the town. Despite the dark secrets the bridge keeps, it surges majestically out of the water. Cecilie is glad she agreed to this date; the view is breathtaking, and living at the foot of the mountain means she takes it for granted and doesn't summit the peak nearly as often as she should.

'Look!' She points to the white roof of the library, a tiny wave across the water. 'It's easier to spot it in summer. Come December, everything looks white over there!' Andreas leans into Cecilie so he can look down the length of her arm, her finger. Their sides touch.

'Wow, you're so lucky to live in such a magical place.'

At the top of Mount Storsteinen they sit on metal chairs at a table at the cafe on the terrace, crisp thin air filling their lungs with feelings of newness, of excitement.

'Ready to order?' asks a stout woman wearing sunglasses and earmuffs.

'What would you like?' Andreas asks, looking down at his menu and stroking his nose.

Cecilie, still exhausted from not having slept the night before last, needs comfort food. 'Burger for me, please,' she says with a smile.

'Bacon and cheese?' asks the waitress, smoothing down her pinny.

'Yes please.'

'Potatoes and coleslaw?'

'Yes please.' Cecilie laughs and closes her menu.

'And I'll have the fish gratin please,' says Andreas, handing the menu back to the waitress and lifting his sunglasses onto his head. In the lunchtime light of day-and-night brightness, Cecilie can see white glasses tracks wrapped around Andreas's crow's feet, highlighted by a summer tan. His eyes are blue and kind.

'Anything to drink?' asks the waitress. 'How about a bottle of white? Cecilie?'

'Sounds great, thanks.'

Andreas turns to the woman wobbling at their table. 'Whatever your best bottle of white is please.'

Fresh air and fatigue make Cecilie feel happy to be looked after today. And there's something very comfortable about Andreas that doesn't make her want to ruin the moment with chit-chat. But he is intrigued by the beauty in front of him and wants to know more.

'So, your brother. Wow, he's quite a whirlwind. You seem very different; much more...' He makes a gesture with his hand to indicate a calm, steady line. Cecilie looks calm, but Andreas doesn't know how she can rage internally while she delicately plays the harp.

'We are – I am!' Cecilie laughs, her cheeks rising playfully. 'He's very driven, like our mother. She's a politician. She works harder than any woman – any man – I've ever met.'

'You work pretty hard! Three jobs?'

'Keeps me out of trouble.'

'So, what do you do when you're getting into trouble?'

'I come up here,' Cecilie lies. She hasn't been up in ages. 'I read. A lot. I play my harp.'

'I've never met anyone who plays the harp. How does one learn to play the harp?'

Cecilie remembers Mr Lind and smiles fondly.

'With patience. Which is another difference between me and Espen – he never sat still long enough to learn a musical instrument.' Cecilie always finds it easier to talk about Espen than herself; he is the easier half of her to talk about. 'My mother isn't very musical either, she is always so super busy, so... *away*.'

'So, do you take after your father?'

Cecilie looks down at the bridge taunting her and lowers her own sunglasses over her eyes. She feels a tug inside her chest for a man she doesn't know.

'I guess. Anyway, what about you?' Cecilie says, swerving the question. 'What exactly is this business that brings you to the Arctic from cool Copenhagen?'

'Well, I'm no brain surgeon as your brother seems to think, however many times I tell him. I import fish oil. And up here, in these waters, it's the purest in the world.'

'Fish oil?' Cecilie curls her delicate nose as she remembers being spoon-fed the stuff as a child by her mother. Espen made an even bigger fuss than she did and insisted on putting a clothes peg on his nose before Karin went near him. 'Is it really worth it? I stopped taking it as soon as I could.'

Andreas laughs. 'Totally worth it!'

'Why?'

'Heart health, brain function, kidney function, lower cholesterol, healthy skin, hair, eyes...' Even as he's saying it, Andreas's eyes sparkle, and Cecilie suspects that he is a man who practises what he preaches. 'The results are unbelievable. Recent research has shown fish oil can even help ease symptoms of certain genetic disorders. The benefits are just incredible.'

As Andreas extols the virtues of his virtuous business, Cecilie closes her eyes and listens. As she listens to his measured, comforting voice, she drifts, over the bridge towards a faraway land, to another fatherless child, an orphan, who she can't locate right now. She can't see through the haze and clouds; Popocatépetl's mighty peak obscures her view. She can't see Hector sleeping alone in his marital bed. She can't see his eyelids flicker as he dreams about her.

31

OCTOBER 2018, XALAPA, MEXICO

Hector mounts the pavement on his moped, turns off the coughing puht-puht of the engine and kicks out the stand. A short man with a round face and a big nose presses his knuckles into Hector's and the men loosely hug.

'Eh, Hectorcito, we don't see you round here no more. *Qué pasó?*'

Marriage happened. Sobriety. And another headless corpse. All of which made Hector more insular.

'Ah, you know, Tote, my body is a temple...' He shrugs.

Tote's tiny confused eyes shrink behind the thick bridge of his nose.

Hector tries again. 'I've been working hard, buddy,' he says as he pats the bouncer's stocky shoulders.

'Yeah, man, I heard you work in the restaurant at Lazaro's now. What's going on with your little drawings?'

'Oh, I'm still drawing. Still at *La Voz*. I did a kids' book too. *Pablito the Panda*? But...' Hector notices Tote's eyes glazing over and stops himself. 'Pilar in there?'

'Yeah, man, she's with Benny.' Tote gives Hector a sympathetic look as Hector swallows hard.

'See you later, *compadre*,' Hector says, pressing his knuckles against Tote's again as doors are pulled open and he's welcomed into the dark and crowded tavern.

Hector snakes through beyond the bar to his left, past a DJ cramped in the window to his right and little round tables full of empty vodka and tequila bottles, shot glasses and plastic cups. A reggaeton beat pumps. The air is heavy with dry ice, revelry and fear. Hector inhales, drinks it all in, and realises he doesn't miss it one bit. He rubs his temples to attempt to shield his face from all the people he doesn't want to engage with. In the back corner, around three little circular tables pushed together, sits Benny Trujillo and his crew. Hector can't see the conflicted face of the little boy who arrived at the Villa Infantil all those years ago, the day both their lives changed forever. Only the anger remains. Hector's wife is at Benny's side.

Pilar's tight white dress clings to her bones like a bandage.

She looks up.

'Hey, baby!' she says, half startled, half bemused, beckoning Hector to the tables where she and Benny hold court with six other men. Hector looks for signs of another woman in the group. He can't see Xochitl's handbag on the table and he didn't see her earthy-brown Nahua skin and deep red lipstick smouldering quietly at the bar as he walked in.

Hector scratches the back of his head and his T-shirt tightens around his arm.

'Xochitl went home?' he asks exasperatedly, while trying to keep his cool.

Pilar and Benny give each other a conspiratorial glance.

'With Draco!' Pilar lets out a husky cackle.

Hector looks uncomfortable. 'Was Xochitl OK with that?'

'*She* led *him* out! We couldn't believe it, baby, could we, Benny?'

Benny sits back. The lined wide front of his square head creases further as he looks teasingly, knowingly, challengingly at Hector as he puts his hand on Pilar's leg next to him.

* * *

If there's one thing Hector was ashamed to admire in Benny it was his audacity. Benny was the one who dared them to steal mementoes from the officials outside the Palacio de Gobierno; Benny was the one who made things go missing from inside the Villa Infantil; Benny dared Hector to take money from his own grandfather's wallet. And although he turned down that particular challenge, something in Hector admired Benny's bravado for suggesting it. Fortunately, Hector had his grandfather's 'off' weeks, time away from Benny, to dampen that admiration. Even though at times he was tempted to rise to Benny's challenge, he wouldn't take twenty pesos from Abuelo's wallet; he couldn't do it. And Alejandro would quietly and stoically drum into Hector the importance of an education over friendship and tomfoolery. 'Education is a light in complete darkness,' he would say as he stirred his *pozole*, knowing that Benny had already failed his exams, that he was trying to get Hector to skip school ahead of his. 'If you have a good education, then good friends will come to you.'

Alejandro would tell Hector about how Hector's father was the first person in a family of peasants to go to university. 'Abuela and I were so proud of him. I'm *still* proud of him – because education can never be taken away, even if the people you love are. And it was through your father's education that *you* came to be.'

Hector's father Victor Herrera had met Lupe Treviño in the faculty of medicine at the Universidad Veracruzana. Lupe had wandered in from the Fine Arts building next door and blushed when she walked into a lab and couldn't see a single easel or paint tube as she scanned the room with her huge smile and wild curls. She locked eyes with Victor, setting up his work station with a microscope, a new notepad and pencils, and the look lingered that bit longer than any exchange either of them had experienced in their eighteen years. A look that would ignite a love to last for the rest of their lives.

'But what's the point of university, Abuelo?' Hector asked one evening when he was struggling with his maths homework. 'It didn't serve Mami and Papi very well, did it?' Hector laughed and Alejandro slammed his fist on the table in outrage. It was the only time Hector heard Alejandro raise his voice in anger.

'Oh, yes it did. Your father was a doctor! He was respected; he was an honourable man. Your mother was an artist before she had you. That's what you come from. Education and honour! Imagine if you were that bastard Benny and you didn't know where you came from? You do, and you should honour that.' Hector was so taken aback he never forgot it.

Hector did go to university, to the same Fine Arts department his mother had studied in. He sketched, refined and exhibited in the same building Lupe Treviño had, next door to the science block where Victor Herrera had studied medicine. And although he knew that was where it had all begun, Hector would never fully understand just how bright the sparkle was in Lupe's eyes when they widened that day she first looked at Victor, quiet and serious, setting out his belongings in the lab.

Even though he had heeded his grandfather's advice, he still couldn't leave Benny behind. While Hector was studying animation and illustration, he took a job in Benny's juice bar on the high street. It was another reason to admire his bunk-mate. Benny had shunned education, but he had the audacity to open

Jugo's California, a juice bar under the arches next to the Palacio de Gobierno, opposite the cathedral. It was tiny, but it had three stools at a counter and two *licuadoras* that whizzed up fresh blends of papaya, mango and maracuyá for townspeople on the go. Benny was rarely there, but it was his business, and it was doing well, which was another reason for Hector to admire Benny's bravery to invest what little money he had into a business.

Sometimes, Sister Miriam and Sister Juana would come in for a juice while they were doing their errands, while Sister Virginia watched the children back at the Villa Infantil. Miriam liked a 50/50 blend of strawberries and watermelon juice; Juana liked a few leaves of chepil thrown in to her 100 per cent mango. A girl called Gabriela opened Jugo's California on the mornings Hector was in class. Gabriela managed the production line, deciding which fruit needed using first, and would tell Hector when she handed over to him for the afternoon shift which fruit and herbs needed reordering for the next day. Benny would pop in around sunset to cash up; his visits increasingly felt like they were something to fear and Hector couldn't work out why. But Sister Miriam and Sister Juana were always delighted to find Hector behind the counter so they could catch up, hear about university life, ask after Alejandro and the home on Calle Bremont, where Hector now lived permanently. Except he was so busy between university life, the juice bar, and going out dancing with girlfriends in the evening, Hector barely saw his grandfather.

When Hector graduated, he got a second job on the local newspaper, *La Voz de Xalapa*, illustrating stories and horoscopes, or helping out on the picture desk when they needed it. Hector noticed another shift in Benny around that time. He'd come back from trips meeting fruit suppliers and pace around the tiny *jugeria* like a hungry jackal.

'What's new in news then?' he'd ask Hector suspiciously.

'Nothing, I'm just on the art desk, Benny.'

It was around that time when the shift went from bunkmates and equals, from Olmeca and Zapata, to something more sinister.

'I want you to start delivering juices, Hector,' Benny said one day, pointing his finger while a thick gold watch jangled on his wrist and a faded pink moustache of watermelon hugged the curve of his wavy, thick top lip.

'Deliveries? We're slap bang in the town centre, everyone comes to us. How would we deliver?'

'Leave the logistics to me. I'll set you up with a moped. You won't even need to use your own, but I need a reliable driver.'

It was that look again – testing eyes. Benny was asking Hector to prove himself; to see if he would steal a memento while Benny watched on from Parque Juárez. Much to Hector's discomfort, he was rising to these challenges every time. He needed the money to help support Alejandro, and he always wanted extra money to give to the sisters at the Villa Infantil. And still he didn't want to disappoint Benny. Meanwhile, Benny's menace and hold grew like the verdant mint plant on the counter.

Sometimes police officers would come into Jugo's California. Without saying a word, they would tick the thin white sheet of paper indicating which fruit and herbs they would like in their *jugo* and hand it over to Hector while they studied his face. Sometimes, Hector found himself delivering vats of maracuyá and lime juice to their houses after hours; he didn't speak to them then, either. They'd just wipe their dinner from around their mouths as they accepted the deliveries and closed the doors. It didn't sit well with Hector; he was streetwise enough to know something wasn't right, but he knew it was best not to ask.

He didn't want to get involved. He wanted to make his *abuelo* as proud as Victor Herrera had.

After two years working for *La Voz*, Hector was entrusted with attending daily editorial meetings. He loved feeling more like part of the team, rather than just being instructed by his art director to draw something. But he didn't like the photos he saw of headless bodies as they arrived on the picture desk. He didn't like the fact his editor wouldn't discuss the photos in their meetings; that he didn't want to report on them in the newspaper. So Hector stuck to court profile pictures, political cartoons, caricatures of sports stars or illustrations for the horoscopes page. He divided his time between the offices of the newspaper, Jugo's California, or the student digs of the Australian, the American, or whichever *extranjera* he had met in a bar the night before. Hector was only twenty-four, but already he felt burned out, mostly from the pressure of being at Benny's beck and call, without feeling able to question why.

Hector's final test came the day he went out the back of the juice bar to find a fresh watermelon for Sister Miriam's blend and saw an axe next to the sink. Benny had popped in and out that morning, delivering some crates of limes and chepil, and had left just as Sister Miriam and Sister Juana had arrived, kissing them on their tiny foreheads, although he wasn't much taller himself. The axe had been placed next to the sink out the back, its head propped against the wall. It was visible to patrons at the counter if the green and fuchsia floral beaded curtain was parted. Benny had left it there, as a test. For Hector? For the women who had brought them up? He wasn't sure, but he looked at it with a quick flash as he searched for fruit. A shiny brown hue licked the blade. Hector went pale as he thought of Alejandro and how disappointed he would be in him; how Sister Miriam and Sister Juana shouldn't be anywhere near anything so murky.

'Are you OK, Hectorcito?' asked Sister Miriam, seeing the sickly shade on Hector's face as he turned and tried to ignore the axe. He couldn't pick it up to secrete it or they would see, so he stood in front of it as he turned on his feet, pretending he had forgotten what he was looking for. 'It doesn't have to be watermelon *cariño*, I can just have *fresa*.'

'It's all right, there are loads back here.' Hector floundered as he made himself as big as possible and closed the beaded curtain behind him while he went out the back. Hector was always trying to please, always trying to calm a situation. He did it in Jugo's California that day, and he was still doing it whenever he tried to keep up with Pilar, to put a happy face on a sad situation.

All that afternoon, Hector thought he was going to be sick, waiting for Benny to come back and cash up.

Enough.

As dusk hit, Benny walked in through the open façade of the front entrance.

'Eh, Zapata, good trade?' he asked, his creased forehead rising into crumples above questioning eyebrows.

'Benny, I quit.' Hector exhaled in soft exasperation. 'I have more and more work on at the paper. I can't be there, here and do deliveries at night too. I'm sorry.'

'Is this to spend more time with that... *gringa*?' Benny spat.

'No, man, we broke up, she went back to America.' For a flash, Hector wondered if he ought to have blamed it on a relationship. Women were a handy scapegoat for Benny; he didn't seem to like them much. 'It's time, man, I'm wiped out, I can't lose my job on the paper.'

Benny looked incensed. He needed someone loyal like Hector, and now his oldest friend was betraying him. He turned around to pull down the grille on the façade of Jugo's California and Hector could see veins bulging in his thick neck. The slow high-pitched screech of the steel door rolling down felt like fingernails on a blackboard, hurting Hector's temples. Benny anchored the grille into place with slow, purposeful precision and clicked the padlock as he pondered his next move. Hector looked at Benny's wiry black hair, slicked back to the nape of his short, wide neck.

Benny turned around with a forced smile. 'C'mon, Hectorcito, now why would you do that?' His new gold tooth sparkled under the strip lighting.

Hector looked at the little exit door in the rolled-down façade and wondered how the hell he could get out for good. He decided honesty was the best policy.

'Come on, brother, this is beyond me. I can't do this any more. That axe? It doesn't look like it was used to chop papaya.'

Olmeca eyed Zapata, his thick brow feeling that familiar horror of rejection for the first time in a long time. It stirred an anger in Benny that was so powerful, he wanted to pick that axe right up and chop off Hector's thumb and forefinger to see if he could draw now, anchor him to the business; teach the *hijo de puta* about loyalty.

Hector looked at Benny with the pleading, sparkling eyes of his mother, stains of strawberry, melon and nopal all down his apron front. And Benny softened. For all his anger and rising hate, Hector's had been the only real face of love Benny had known since he was nine – and he knew Hector wouldn't betray him. Plus, it was better to have a friend on the paper.

Benny stepped to one side and Hector opened the little door and walked out, feeling the weight of four thousand watermelons lifting from his strong shoulders. As he headed through town to his grandfather's ramshackle house, he heard glass smash as Benny took the axe to the interior of Jugo's California and pulverised it.

* * *

Hector looks at Benny's thick hand resting provocatively on Pilar's knee. In the crevice between his thumb and forefinger sit two inked holy crosses, poorly drawn and badly executed. His hand rests on the ivy that crawls up Pilar's thigh before it creeps out of sight under the tight white canvas of her dress. 'Baby, I think we'd better go look for Xochitl,' Hector says, his eyes as cold as the ice in Benny's *michelada*.

'She's fine, she took Draco off to Parque Juárez. What's the problem?'

'She's not that kind of girl.' Hector extends his hand. '*You're* not that kind of girl, Pilar. Come on, let's get out of here.'

Benny stands. His leather waistcoat sticks to his wide sweaty shoulders.

'You gotta problem, Hectorcito? Lookin' down your nose at me again?' Benny's friend Robi rises out of his chair next to him.

'I think my *wife* has had enough and needs to come home.'

'Calm down, baby,' Pilar says, rising, pressing her hand into Hector's groin to get him to sit down. She's seemingly enjoying the conflict, as her protest is hollow. Hector takes a step back. 'Come on, *viejo*, we're just having a bit of fun. Sit down and join us. You two would get on great – Benny said you *did* used to get on great. Don't be so boring, have a drink and tell me about the good old days. Olmeca and Zapata, no?'

Hector had tried to keep Benny from Pilar; to hold details of their past back; to protect her from the path of self-destruction he always feared she might take.

Hector stands firm. He doesn't look at Pilar. He doesn't break eye contact with Benny. Those same wounded, conflicted, angry eyes Benny had in those first weeks at the orphanage, and with a flicker and a flash, Benny's eyes show a glimmer of mischief. Or is it the audacity Hector once admired?

Benny sits back down and starts to slowly run his hand up the inside of Pilar's leg, following the trail of ivy. Pilar's heavy lids flounder and she smiles coquettishly, as if Hector can't see what's right in front of him.

Still, Hector doesn't break Benny's gaze. He doesn't acknowledge the creeping hand. The anger rises in Hector's throat and he can't breathe.

You win.

'I'm done,' Hector says, staring at Benny, then nodding to Pilar, and turns around to leave. He walks through the smoke, through the crowds, through the people all wanting to say, 'Hector, so good to see you! Let me get you a drink!' and they all blur into faces and noise and all he can think of is *her* face. Purity and brightness, the face of home half a world away, and anger dissipates into comfort with every step.

32

OCTOBER 2018, TROMSØ, NORWAY

That Same Night

'I'm so glad you could make it!' Cecilie hugs Grethe carefully, while her baby sleeps curled up and snug in a sling on her chest.

'Well, what difference does it make at this age? She still doesn't know night from day yet, and we wouldn't miss Auntie Cecilie and Uncle Espen's party for the world!' Grethe and Cecilie release their embrace and look down at the baby cocooned between them. They laugh. Ahyana's lips pucker rapidly as if she's dreaming of her mother's milk and, like tired Grethe, she doesn't look all that party ready.

Cecilie on the other hand is glowing. Peacock-green eyeshadow sparkles across her feline lids. Her sweep of platinum-blonde hair is pinned to one cheekbone with a diamanté clip; a sparkling black ear cuff whispers up the elegant curve of her other ear. Gone are the woolly jumper, jeans and clunky DM boots. She wears a long black dress cut deep at the V of her décolletage and, underneath swathes of black silk, Cecilie stands strong in petrol-green heels. Even her hands are elegant, her nails painted a sleek shade of oil slick. Grethe, make-up-free in her patchwork dress and stripy baby sling, looks at her friend in awe and pushes the loose strands of hair back into her crocheted hairband. 'You look stunning!'

Cecilie isn't used to being called stunning, so she smiles and blushes.

'No wonder Andreas looks like the cat who got the cream.' Grethe nods, aiming her gaze towards Andreas and Abdi, shaking hands stiltedly by the table of devilled eggs, marinated herring and glazed trout.

'Now I know Espen has been thirty for, like, nine years, but look at you! All grown up!' Grethe laughs in admiration as she strokes the shoulder of Cecilie's black dress.

'Shut up, you're next,' says Cecilie, laughing.

'But, seriously, isn't this lovely?' Grethe marvels, almost in surprise, as she looks up at the ceiling. Huge white globes that look like balls of lace light the i-Scand's party room and soften the dark circles under Grethe's eyes.

One wall of the room has floor-to-ceiling glass that overlooks the harbour, the bridge and the Arctic cathedral in the distance across the water. A ship sails past so close it gives the illusion of the room moving gently along the harbour the other way.

'You know Espen, never one to do things by half. But he went to such an effort, I had to get on board. Have you had a drink? Eirik has created a signature cocktail especially, the Double Wiig.'

'A Double Wiig? Your own cocktail?' Grethe laughs.

'You must try it! *Can* you try it?' Cecilie nods down to Ahyana.

'One won't hurt,' Grethe says with a wink. 'Might make her sleep better later.'

As if on cue, a waitress walks past with a tray full of Martini glasses, filled with a peachy syrupy drink.

'Ah, Solveig!' says Grethe, deftly taking a glass from the tray. 'Any chance I can steal you back? The hours are more sociable at the ice cream parlour.'

The waitress laughs and leans in to look at sleeping Ahyana.

'She's beautiful, Grethe. Congratulations,' she replies diplomatically.

Grethe smiles and Solveig weaves away into the crowd full of friends, family, regulars from the library, the Hjornekafé and the hotel, and Espen's former flames. Espen and Morten look dashing in his-and-his tuxedos with thick silk bow ties, and Cecilie, happy not to be the centre of attention at her own birthday party, likes the feeling of having wandered into their wedding.

'So, how's it going with Andreas?' Grethe asks excitedly as she raises a Double Wiig to her lips. 'He looks smitten, Cecilie. You can tell he's totally not listening to a word Abdi is saying; he keeps looking over here because he can't take his eyes off you.'

Cecilie plays with the olive in her glass. 'Oh, it's OK...'

'I have a good feeling about him, Cecilie. He has a nice face. He's super into you. And how amazing he came to your party, all the way up here, all the way from another country. When are you going to Copenhagen?'

Cecilie has had a fun few months – and she's finally had another lover since her first and last, Mr Lind – but she can't help wishing another man had crossed borders to be here with her now, at her birthday party. She feels an emptiness in the pit of her stomach. A feeling of doom she knows might sour the party atmosphere later.

'Oh, it was coincidence. Andreas was here this week for work anyway, he just stayed an extra night.'

'Yeah, but clearly he wouldn't have missed this for the world,' Grethe gushes, her tired face illuminating a little.

Cecilie sighs. 'He wants me to go to Copenhagen next weekend, to meet his kids.'

Grethe's blue eyes widen encouragingly. 'What do you think?'

Cecilie scrunches up her nose and goes to say something, but the women are distracted by Karin's chink chink of a glass as she stands at a microphone on a small stage, her back to the twinkling lights of the harbour.

33

Cecilie's sore soles teeter across the footpath of the bridge. A cold wind whips down the strait and dishevels the clean lines of her hair some more.

'You should have let me call a taxi, honey,' says Andreas as he places a suit jacket over Cecilie's shoulders. She's already wearing her long thick down coat and thinks to herself that his jacket won't make any difference.

'I wanted to walk,' she says irritably.

Cecilie is thirty years and six hours old, and although the dawn sky is still dark, she can almost hear the sun starting to wake up behind the mountain in front of her.

The party was everything Espen expected it to be and a million times better than Cecilie had thought. She wasn't up for a big song and dance, but boy, did she dance. She drank more Double Wiigs than she should have, but managed to hold it together by replenishing herself at the buffet and shake it off to Taylor Swift, Gwen Stefani and A-ha.

Karin made a polished yet touching speech before her driver whisked her off to catch a flight to Helsinki; Grethe and Ahyana managed to stay for a good few hours, and as Abdi set sail on the Hurtigruten at midnight, he made sure the captain tooted his horn right by the window of the i-Scand function room.

At 2 a.m., the Northern Lights put on a stunning celestial show, for which Espen bowed and took the credit. It was 6 a.m. when Espen and Morten stumbled home to their apartment above Nils' salon in town and waved Cecilie and Andreas off onto the bridge, towards the peaceful house at the foot of Mount Storsteinen.

Cecilie tried to get Espen and Morten to join her and Andreas for a *nachspiel*, to prolong the night so she could put off the inevitable. She even offered to serve bacon and eggs on her home-made rye bread, toasted into little triangles the way Espen likes best, but it was all to no avail.

Now her feet are sore and her limbs are tired. And she still doesn't know how to say it.

'Want me to give you a piggyback?' Andreas smiles blearily, his tie undone around his neck.

'No, Andreas, it's fine, I can walk.' Besides, Andreas isn't much taller than Cecilie, who is pretty solid on her feet.

'You're practically hobbling. Come on, I'll carry you. The quicker we get over this bridge, the quicker I get the birthday girl to bed.'

Andreas leans down to lift Cecilie from under her bottom and sling her over his shoulder.

Resistant and heavy, Cecilie protests. 'No, Andreas, put me down.'

Andreas continues, lifting Cecilie higher over his shoulder in a fireman's lift. 'Ah, come on!'

'I said NO!' Cecilie hammers her fists on Andreas's back like a Nutcracker drummer.

Andreas stumbles in surprise towards the edge of the bridge

as Cecilie balances perilously close to the top of the railings that were raised to prevent suicides; too late for her family. The wind makes Cecilie's long coat flap frantically like the flag at the cafe on the top of the Fjellheisen. A feeling of fear envelopes Cecilie, like she's choking under the ripping tug of synthetic fibres.

'*Put me down!*'

Teetering on Andreas's shoulder at the very edge of the bridge, Cecilie doesn't know that she is at the exact spot her father jumped.

Andreas is taken aback. He lowers Cecilie and gently places her on the ground, then straightens out her coat. He puts his hands on her shoulders and lowers his head a little so he can look her in the eye.

'I'm sorry, I was just trying to be funny. I was only trying to help.'

'Well, it wasn't funny and I don't want your help, OK?' The Arctic wind fills Cecilie's lungs with a chilly hit of boldness. 'I don't want to go to Copenhagen with you and I don't want to meet your kids.'

Andreas looks winded.

'I'm sorry.' Cecilie's lips wobble as she tries not to cry. Andreas removes his hands from Cecilie's shoulders and looks down at his feet in dejection. 'I really am.' The horn of a ship passing under the bridge accentuates his silence, which in turn agitates Cecilie. 'Why do you even want to be with me?' she snaps. 'I'm a barmaid. I'm a waitress. I'm a librarian. I still live in my mamma's house. I'm like a bored teenage girl. Who's in love with someone she's never met. Look at me! I'm ridiculous.'

The green eyeshadow and black mascara tearing down her cheeks do make Cecilie look somewhat ridiculous.

'You're beautiful, Cecilie. I don't care what you do. Fish oil doesn't make me *me*. I think you're amazing. You're the highlight of my working week. I can't wait to see you.'

Cecilie thinks of the highlight of her day. The messages.

The conversations. The photos. The stolen moments.

'Did you not hear me?' she pleads, wiping make-up from under her eyes. 'I'm sorry, but I'm in love with someone else.'

Andreas nods. 'Is it the person you're always texting?' Cecilie's silence confirms it.

'I thought he was just a pen pal. Someone you'll never meet.'

'I won't ever meet him.'

Her heart lurches in her chest.

'Then come to Copenhagen. I'm here. I'm real. I'm in love with you.'

Cecilie bites her lip. She had felt it coming and wanted to get out before he said it. Planning the party had been a convenient distraction.

'I'm sorry, Andreas, you deserve better. I'm not for you. I'm just the first girl you fell for since Iben. You need time to heal.'

'That's bullshit. I'm in love with you.'

'Oh, Andreas,' she groans. 'You deserve to be with someone who loves you back. Someone who would appreciate your exciting life, your children, your kindness. Don't waste any more time on me.'

The phone deep in the pocket of Cecilie's long down coat beeps and she instinctively pulls it out so she can read it. She counts back seven hours.

Can you talk?

Iridescent eyes sparkle. 'Is that him?'

Cecilie nods guiltily, then plants a kiss on Andreas's lips. She really did enjoy spending time with him; talking to him; making love to him in his hotel room, even if she was trying not to think of Hector. So she tenderly savours the taste of him.

He closes his eyes and inhales, wishing it weren't the last. 'Go back to the i-Scand, Andreas. Get some sleep. I'll make it over the bridge OK.'

Cecilie picks his suit jacket up from the floor and hands it back. 'I'm sorry...'

'I'll see you home.'

'Don't, it's fine. The sun's coming up. The mountain will look after me.'

Cecilie strokes Andreas on the cheek, belts up her coat, removes her heels and runs barefoot the rest of the way across the bridge. Through biting wind and freezing temperatures. Run, run, running, past the Arctic cathedral, along the road towards the Fjellheisen and left on the track to the grand slate and wood house lit by Mount Storsteinen's snowy peak. As Cecilie leans on the lattice-trimmed veranda to catch her breath, her feet numb, she types back furiously.

> FaceTime. Five minutes.

34

OCTOBER 2018, XALAPA, MEXICO

That Same Night

At the little desk in the cramped living room of his apartment, Hector wakens his laptop and checks the camera works. He studies his face in the monitor. Wide-apart eyes of darkest brown that crease into laughter lines like contours of the Sierra Madre. His hair looks dishevelled and his khaki T-shirt sits tightly around the tops of his arms.

Cálmate.

Hector clicks on a green square to start FaceTime with the only number he's ever called. It still says Arctic Fox on the caller list of one. He smooths the waves kissing his temples and is pleased to see peace in his face. Rage has passed. The shrill dial tone only soothes him.

A love heart-shaped face fills the rectangle. '*Gratulerer med dagen, guapa!*' Hector says sloppily.

Cecilie's smile fills the screen, and she's touched by his efforts, however clumsy the pronunciation. They messaged each other throughout the day, punctuating her thirtieth birthday with good wishes and photos. Hector bought a slice of *tres leches* cake on his way to work at Lazaro's and sent a photo of it to Cecilie before he ate it; Cecilie sent Hector a photo of the new harp her mother had bought her, a shining blue bow atop it; Hector sent Cecilie a message to say he wished more than anything that he could be at the party; Cecilie sent Hector options of her wearing two dresses reflected in her bedroom mirror and asked him which he preferred.

Now, Cecilie slumps into the sofa and Hector's favourite black dress has a dampness rising from the hem as she plunges her frozen feet in a hot bubbling foot spa next to the thick brown rug. They see each other's faces for the first time in weeks.

Hector leans in closer to focus on the slightly pixelated image.

He gasps.

'Wow, you look amazing!' he says, his palm scratching the back of his head. Even with twelve-hour make-up blurring Cecilie's bleary eyes, Hector is spellbound. He's never seen Cecilie's face in full make-up before. Even though green dust dances under black smudged eyes, it looks dramatic and stunning. And it suits her.

A real-life angel.

I look a mess.

Seeing her face in the corner of her laptop makes Cecilie rub under her eyes.

'Anyway, how was my pronunciation?'

'It's not my birthday any more, silly!'

Cecilie has a feeling of relief: that she turned thirty and the world didn't stop turning; that the party is over; that she said what she had to say to Andreas.

'It looks like you had a good party.'

'I did. We did. Espen did a great job.'

'Are you home now?' Hector asks nervously.

'Yip. Soaking my dancing feet. Heels do not suit me...'

Cecilie lifts the laptop to pan the camera around the living room. Hector sees his Black Swan disappear in a whirl as a pile of unopened presents come into view on the long wooden dining table; sunlight starts to enchant the vast garden beyond the window, and a large television sits flat against a wall; the Calder doesn't move above the fireplace; a stationary harp, gilded and golden; then back to Cecilie's face as she places the laptop back on the oak coffee table, above her soothed feet. Hector didn't see any sign of anyone else in the room with her.

'You?' Cecilie says as her face refills the screen.

'*Sí*. Solo,' Hector confirms as he ducks his head out of the way to show the fuchsia, red and orange stripes of the wall hanging.

She's not there.

Cecilie scans the screen frantically, drinking him in while she can, as Hector picks up his laptop and gives a twirl around the room. The wall hanging blurs into the kitchen, which blurs into the lime-green walls, which blur into the night sky that looks into the top floor apartment, then Hector places the laptop down and returns to the wooden chair with the holy cross cut out of the back of it.

'So, tell me about the party...'

'It was awesome. I had such fun!'

I wished you were there.

'Did you take pictures?'

'Of course! I took them for you. I'll send them in a second. The room looked amazing. The food was great, and I danced so much my feet hurt!'

'Great,' Hector says, feeling a pang of envy, his body pulled by longing. 'I wish I could have danced with you; I wish I was there to rub your feet.'

Sadness flits across Cecilie's face, but she doesn't say anything. Bubbles in the pedi spa provide a comforting, rhythmic hum.

'Was Mister Denmark at the party?' Hector tries to sound casual, tries to make it a joke. When Cecilie mentioned her Danish friend a few weeks back, Hector knew what it meant, and it's played on his mind ever since. He raises one quizzical eyebrow and gives Cecilie a playful, desperate look.

'Yes.'

'Is he still there?' he asks, trying to keep envy and urgency out of his voice. He knows he has no right to feel the jealousy he does.

'No. He's back at the hotel.' Cecilie smiles at the screen, which pixelates. She can't see the relief on Hector's face as he shuffles on his old church chair; he can't see how reassuring her smile is.

He settles down so the screen can sharpen.

'Did you pick up my parcel yet? Is that it on the table?'

'No, I was decorating the party, and it's Saturday. Well, Sunday now, but the post office shuts early on a Saturday. I'll get it Monday.'

'Well, it doesn't matter now because I got you something else. Something cooler.'

'What? Now?' Cecilie starts to laugh at the screen, then looks around her living room to see what surprise Hector might have planted.

'Listen closely.'

'What is it?' Cecilie puts the sparkling black cuff that runs up her left ear towards the camera on her laptop and closes her eyes.

Giddiness has overcome guilt for Andreas and fatigue in her feet, and she is filled with happiness. So much so that the image of That Person They Never Talk About doesn't even pop into her head.

Cecilie's ear cuff sparkles on Hector's screen.

He puts his lips to the camera. His voice lowers to a whisper and he mumbles something about soya.

He got me soya?

Cecilie can't seem to hear what he's saying without seeing him say it, so she fills the rectangle with her face again.

'What is it?' she repeats, searching Hector's beauty for reassurance.

He says it again. 'It's me. *Soy yo.*'

A whisper travels across a gulf, an ocean, a sea and a fjord, and arrives in Cecilie's living room, filling her eyes with meltwater.

I must have misheard.

She takes a deep breath and puts her hand to her lips. 'You? You're my present?'

'*Sí.*'

Condemnation turns to elation.

I can't believe it.

'How?'

'I've saved money. Everything I earned at the newspaper just about covered living, and I managed to save enough from the department store for a flight. Abuelo said he'd give me a little to help with hotels. I'm coming to Europe.'

'Oh my God! Where?'

'London? Paris? Oslo? Wherever is easiest. I could fly direct to London, Amsterdam or Paris. Madrid is probably too far for you. But I can connect to Oslo.'

'I could meet you wherever, and bring you here.'

Could. Cecilie doesn't believe this can be real, though she wants to.

'I *will* meet you wherever, and bring you here.'

Hector smiles.

'What about... What about... Pilar?' There, she said it.

'It's over. We're done.'

Hector ponders just how far up Pilar's leg Benny's hand has reached by now; if they're still in the bar, that is.

Cecilie doesn't want to ask how, not now anyway. 'When?'

'How's Christmas?'

Green lids flutter frantically. 'I want to see you tomorrow.'

Hector laughs. 'Christmas is my best chance of getting time off. The paper shuts down for one week, and I'm sure they'll give me another off. The women in Lazaro's will cover me, I know it.'

They never liked Pilar anyway.

Cecilie sinks back into the low grey sofa as warm bubbles fizz around her feet and her stomach.

'I can wait,' she says with certainty.

Minutes ago, Cecilie thought she'd never meet Hector Herrera, but at thirty years and seven hours old, she's just received the best birthday present of her life.

35

Hector closes the cracked lid on his laptop, leans back in his chair with fingers interlocked behind his head, and exhales at the ceiling.

Relief.

Europe isn't cheap, but that's six weeks to save everything he can. It'd be worth it for just one day with Cecilie Wiig. Paris sounds good. Meeting under the Eiffel Tower. He's sure he can fly to Paris from Mexico City.

Hector's phone rings, interrupting his racing brain. Unknown number. He assumes it's Cecilie calling him with a flirty postscript.

'Paris, *mi amor*,' Hector says as he answers. 'I'll find out about flights from DF to Paris.'

'Hector?'

It's not Cecilie's voice at the other end. His heart sinks.

'What do you want? I said I'm done.'

'Come get your whore wife.'

'What?'

'She shat in my bed when I was fucking her and now she's not breathing.'

'*What?*' Hector rises, kicking back the old wooden church chair, and stands, alert.

'She's not breathing. She shat and she puked and now she's lying here like the dirty whore she is.'

'Do something, Benny. Get her to the hospital. I'll go straight to *Urgencias*, I'll meet you there.'

Benny is silent at the other end of the phone. Weighing up his options.

'*Do it!*'

'No, man, come and get her, clear up her shit. I'm going out.'

Hector races down five flights of stairs from his apartment, through the arcade and out onto the street. Taxis, drinkers, revellers are crossing the town with plans and purpose, going from bar to bar on this busy Saturday night, and the traffic is thick. Hector has no idea which way to turn and looks up and down the street at the cars and mopeds beeping at him.

La Villa.

He starts running – it'll be quicker on foot; even mopeds are getting stuck in the melee – to the Villa Infantil three streets away at the quieter end of town. Past cars snaking nose to tail. Away from the main roads onto pretty cobbled streets. Running, running, racing to get to Pilar before she stops breathing forever, although he doesn't even know where she is or how the hell he can find her before it's too late.

Shit.

Bang bang bang. Hector's fist rattles on the door of the orphanage, knowing that Sister Miriam, Sister Juana and Sister Virginia will all be asleep at this time on a Saturday night.

No answer. Bang bang bang. 'Come *on!*'

Hector's fist is clammy and cold.

'It's me! Hector!' He rattles on the thick wooden front door, flailing like a child treading water, trying not to drown. A startled Sister Miriam opens the door. Her exposed hair is as grey as the habit it's usually hidden under. Her mole-like eyes widen with worry.

'Where does Benny live? I have to get to Benny's hacienda. *Now!*'

'Hector, *cálmate cariño*. Whatever is the matter?'

'It's a matter of life and death. I never asked and you never told me, but please tell me you know where Benny's hacienda is. I have to get there...'

Sister Miriam puts her small wire glasses on tiny confused eyes, magnifying them and waking them up.

'Hacienda? Benny doesn't live in a hacienda. Benny lives at the back here, *cariño*. In the former Patrón's quarters.'

Hector is gobsmacked – but relieved.

She's here.

'Here? Benny's lived here all along?'

'He lives here now, yes, but there's no access this way. And the children are all sleeping. You'll have to go round to Hidalgo and knock there. But what's the urgency...?'

Before Sister Miriam finishes speaking, Hector is already running to the end of the block. He turns left out of sight and Miriam closes the front door, confused and concerned. She knows all of Hector's faces, but she's never seen him in such distress.

Please don't stop breathing, please don't stop breathing.

Left again, onto the cobbles of Calle Hidalgo, past colourful houses of bright green, yellow and blue, and a thud thud thud on the door of the former Patrón's house.

No answer, but the door is unlocked, so Hector charges through. The Patrón, Eduardo Sánchez, gave most of his land to the church so they could open an orphanage, and he lived a humble life in the small home that backed onto it. But he had long since died, and Hector assumed the house had been bought by a private landlord. He had no idea the church owned it all, and Benny's squalid and murky existence was going on right under the nose of the women who brought him up.

Hector scans the dark room. Cockroaches whizz out from underneath pizza boxes. Empty bottles and dirty needles litter the floor. Ashtrays teem over. This isn't the grand and gaudy ranch Hector pictured Benny conducting his dealings from. It looks like a low-grade narco has been squatting there between deliveries. Hector bursts into the bedroom and cries out when he sees Pilar's naked soiled body on the bed.

'*No!*'

Through thin skin and bone, he can see that Pilar's chest is just about rising and falling, but she's struggling through vomit stuck in her windpipe.

'*Pilar!*' Hector shouts, climbing onto the bed. He straddles her and coughs as he inhales the acrid mess around her. Hector lifts Pilar's grey chin to tip her head back and help clear her airwaves. She splutters vomit in his face and her hollow chest convulses; the blue heart tattoo pulsates ever so slightly. Hector slaps Pilar's cheek, at first gently, repeatedly, growing stronger until she attempts to open her eyelids. 'That's it, deep breaths...'

Hector hears the familiar huskiness of Pilar's voice, rattling in the depths of her cough.

She's alive.

He finds the corner of a less sullied sheet on the floor and flicks it for cockroaches, then pulls the shit and vomit-smeared mess out from underneath Pilar, trying to wipe any off her as he does, and wraps her up like a parcel in the sheet from the floor. Hector lifts his corpse bride with ease onto his shoulders and stands.

'Come on,' he says to no one. 'Let's get out of here.'

36

NOVEMBER 2018, SUFFOLK, ENGLAND

'Oooooh!' says the crowd as a peony shell of purple sparks rains down over the school field.

'Ahhhhh!' says Kate into Jack's ear as she pulls him tight into her faux-fur trimmed parka. Chloe was too cool to come to the annual fireworks party at her old school, but Izzy is sipping a mug of tomato soup as she curls into her dad's fleece, and Jack seeks solace from the noise he's pretending he's not scared of in the comforting folds of his mother's waist.

Kate turns to George to savour the moment. Bright lights in the night sky illuminate his eyes and she feels *connected*. This is the first time in months Kate has felt any real unity with George and total harmony in their family. He keeps looking up, fixated on the fireworks, and doesn't notice Kate's contented glance.

It's the annual Claresham Church of England Primary School family firework night, the first Kate has organised since she became chair of the PTA. Three months of blood, sweat and tears and her gunpowder plot has paid off. Practically the entire village has turned out for a brilliant event, and Kate feels as triumphant as the supernova rocket they're watching head into orbit.

'Mum, your phone...' Jack's freckled face looks up towards his mother.

'What was that, poppet?'

Kate can't hear it under the whizz bang boom, but Jack feels a vibrating hum against his ribs as he hugs his mum's dimpled thigh.

'Your phone's ringing.'

Kate decides to ignore it. It's probably the same withheld number that has called six times this week, and the person at the other end hung up every time. On the other hand, it could be one of the suppliers at the school tonight, needing to reach Kate because the kitchen has run out of frankfurters or the DJ has locked his Minion costume in the van with his keys.

Please, no, it's all going so smoothly.

'Give Daddy and Iz a cuddle, they'll keep you warm. I need to see who this is...'

Kate walks inside the school building and pulls the bobble hat off her head. She takes her phone out of her jeans pocket as it stops ringing.

Withheld number.

She feels a mixture of annoyance and relief.

Blasted PPI, I bet. Although they never hang up...

Kate wants to get back out for the grand fireworks finale, the crescendo to a backdrop of 'Carmina Burana', but 'Withheld number' flashes up again and the phone starts to ring. She stops in her tracks.

One last chance.

'Hello?' Kate says into the mouthpiece as she walks into a quiet classroom so she can hear the caller. Or not hear the caller, if it's another crank call.

'Hello?'

Her mouth sits at an agitated angle.

This is ridiculous.

Suddenly, a mousy voice speaks, just about audible against the sound of 'I Like to Move It' coming from the school hall down the corridor. The DJ has put his Minion costume on and is warming up.

'Hi. Is that Kate Wheeler?'

'Speaking.' Kate's mildly annoyed voice wobbles as she strains to hear the meek voice at the other end of the line.

I'm going to miss the finale. The disco is about to start.

Silence again.

'Look, who is this? Why do you keep calling?'

'My name is Bethany. Bethany Henderson. I was your husband's PA.'

Suddenly, the caller has Kate's full attention.

'Oh. Right. Yes, Bethany, I remember you. How are you?' Even in the strangest of circumstances, Kate's default setting switches to polite. A pause punctuates the classroom with a thousand possibilities. Kate looks up at the handwriting display on the wall in front of her. Iterations of Goldilocks retold by Year 1 children. Her eyes land on a cartoon of a vacuous blonde. 'Why are you calling?'

'It's your husband. He's been cheating on you.'

37

NOVEMBER 2018, TROMSØ, NORWAY

Karin Wiig sits on her low grey sofa drinking a large glass of red.

'Ah, it is so good to be home, darling. If I never see that odious Finn again I will be happy. Shame he's not up for re-election for another three years...'

Cecilie curls into a ball on the sofa next to, but not touching, her mother. Close but distant. Cecilie is dreamy and not that interested in European politics. Her mother can't be doing with the mundane mechanics of the small-town outpost her daughter is anchored to. Tonight is a rare moment of closeness as the two of them sit on the sofa watching *Dirty Dancing*.

'I need to go to Brussels the week before Christmas. I was thinking you might like to come with me, so we can pop to Bruges for some market shopping – how does that sound, darling?'

'Thanks, Mamma, I'm not sure.'

Cecilie doesn't want to go anywhere. It is two weeks since Hector Herrera said he was leaving his wife and coming to Europe and she hasn't heard from him since. That hollow gift. The grand gesture. Nothing. Cecilie knows Hector had read her texts. She knows he ignored her calls. But she can't work out *why* he suddenly shut her out, why he ghosted her, just at the point she was planning a trip; to finally leave the Arctic Circle, for the first time in years, for a romantic rendezvous behind Big Ben or under the Eiffel Tower – and her confusion and dejection is making her not want to go anywhere.

'Why so listless, Cecilie? I'm sure Espen will give you time off work for a trip with me.'

'Yeah, but there's the library and the cafe... I can't just drop everything and go.'

I said I'd drop everything for him.

'Darling, babies will keep gurgling, coffees will still be drunk, and the world won't stop turning just because you're taking a long weekend away. Come on, get out of here for a few days. Andreas was telling me how keen he is to get you to Copenhagen – and it's such a wonderful city. Where's your adventurous spirit, Cecilie?'

Cecilie looks at the fire roaring in the hearth, and her eyes lose focus.

'Which reminds me. Christmas. We need a plan.'

'What do you mean a "plan", Mamma? It'll be the same as ever. Espen and Morten won't want to host in their flat – so we'll do it here. I can cook it again.' Cecilie feels despondent. She had imagined this Christmas being different, but it's going to be the same as all the others.

'You did do a delicious dinner last year. But your uncle and aunt want to join us; they're not going to the US this Christmas, and I'll send for Mormor and Morfar again. Their carer might want to stay, but let's hope not.'

'That's fine, Mamma, I can cook for... nine. Morten is a great sous-chef.'

'What about Andreas? There's room for him at that table.' Karin gestures her wine glass towards the window.

'He'll be with his kids.'

'Invite them!'

Cecilie looks at the crackle of a kamikaze flame, darting out of the fireplace. 'Mamma, we broke up.'

Karin puts her glass down on the oak coffee table and repositions herself.

'Why?' she asks, running her fingers through her sleek silver bob. 'I mean, I know he was married, but he was such a good sort.'

'He was divorced, Mamma, they had divorced. But it wasn't that. He just wasn't the sort for me.'

He's not Hector.

Karin looks at her daughter in bewilderment. 'But he was so... genial. So affable. He had such good potential.'

Cecilie follows the flames in the fire and decides not to respond. She feels too broken to put up a fight.

Karin perches on the edge of the sofa now, her body upright and tense.

'Did you do this because of The Mexican?'

Cecilie doesn't answer and Karin puts a hand to her brow. 'Darling, you're living in a dreamworld. Your brother said The Mexican got married.'

Cecilie thinks of Pilar, her tight dresses and full hair, and feels wretched.

'Me ending things with Andreas has nothing to do with The Mexican... with... with... Hector.' Cecilie struggles to say his name out loud, she's so unaccustomed to it. 'Just because Andreas likes me, and I'm thirty, doesn't mean I'm going to settle down with him, convenient as it might be for you.'

'It's not convenient for me at all!' Karin says, taken aback. 'I just want you to be happy, Cecilie. You're so alone.'

'Well, I wouldn't be happy with Andreas. I don't love Andreas.'

'And you love someone you've never met? Darling, do you know how crazy that sounds? And clearly you're not happy obsessing over a man you've never even met. I've never seen you so miserable. At least Andreas put that beautiful smile back on your face.'

'Don't, Mamma, I can't go through this right now...' Cecilie uncurls from her foetal ball on the sofa and stands. Her heart is going up in flames like the logs on the fire.

'Where are you going?'

'For a walk.'

'It's snowing. It's dark!'

'I don't care. I just need some space before I say something I'll regret...'

Cecilie grabs her snow boots from the shoe caddy by the large front door.

'Something you'll regret? Don't turn on me, young lady,' Karin snaps sternly.

'Young lady? I'm thirty!'

'Then act like it. When I was thirty I was dealing with the shitstorm your father left us in and breaking my back to make a living, to build this. So get real, Cecilie.'

The door slams.

Get real.

Cecilie wraps her coat around her and tramples in the first thick snow of the season. She is drawn by the twinkly lights of the harbour, pulling her to the bridge. Crunch crunch underfoot as Cecilie's eyes fill with each step she takes in the virgin snow. At the quiet junction, she hears the slow hum of the Fjellheisen down the road to her left; organ pipes blow a haunting soundtrack from the white concertina of the Arctic cathedral to her right. She walks towards it.

Why hasn't he called? Where has he gone? Did she take his phone?

A gap peeps through the clouds and Cecilie spies the green whisper waving like a theatrical curtain overhead, ridiculing her from the heavens. She walks up the footpath to the bridge, not knowing where to go or why she's going there, with tears streaming down her cheeks and marches on. She stops at the point she said goodbye to Andreas, the place where her father jumped, and looks over the edge. Suicide railings stop at eye level; Cecilie rises on tiptoes to see what it would look like to jump.

Where was he?
How cold is that water?
What does it feel like to drown?

So many questions Cecilie has pondered every time she walks the bridge, every time she plays her harp. Questions her twin has never bothered his busy brain with.

'It happened, there's nothing we can do about it,' he once said when they were eleven. And Karin thought Espen was the one who questioned everything; that Cecilie was blind.

The Northern Lights above have disappeared and a blanket of thick dark cloud starts shedding another layer of snow.

You said you'd come.

Cecilie punches the metal barrier in front of her with two fists, frantically banging until her knuckles start to bleed.

Through her tears, she can just about see the water beneath her, and in it she sees a familiar face swirling in a pattern of the strait below her. Telling her to go home.

* * *

Cecilie closes the front door and drops her coat and boots on the floor with unusual disregard. The fire in the hearth is reduced to a final smoulder in the dark living room. All but the hall lights are off. She climbs the stairs quietly and looks through the crack in the door to her mother's bedroom. Karin Wiig is in bed but can't sleep. She is fidgeting under her eye mask with her back to the door, which is slightly ajar. Cecilie gently pushes it wider so as not to alarm an already troubled woman and climbs into her bed, for the first time since she was a little girl, hugging her mother from behind.

'I feel like I'm drowning, Mamma,' Cecilie says, sobbing as she holds on tight to her mother's arms, the pads of the fingers on her bloodied hands gripping Karin's shoulders. 'At the library, at the Hjornekafé, in Espen's stupid hotel, every time I look at my phone...'

Karin pushes her eye mask into her hair and rolls over to face her daughter, her silk nightdress twisting slightly out of place. She strokes Cecilie's hair and tucks her sweeping fringe behind a cold red ear.

'He said he would leave her, Mamma. He said he would come to me. He said he was going to come to Europe for Christmas.'

'Shhh, Cecilie,' Karin whispers, taking her daughter in her arms, her tears tumbling onto silk.

'I believed it. I thought he was coming. His face was so sincere, so beautiful... I thought he was coming.' And for the first time in her life, Cecilie lets out a sob that makes her entire body shake as she clings to her mother. She has never felt so broken.

'Oh, my darling Cecilie. Beautiful, beautiful girl.' Karin holds Cecilie to her chest, then lets her go. The heat of their bodies is too much under the fifteen-tog Hungarian goose down. She looks into her daughter's eyes, lit by the light of the open bedroom door bouncing off Karin's dressing-table mirror. Green flashes mottled by tears. 'Don't rely on any man to pull your strings; to make you happy. Not The Mexican, not even Espen. You have to find your own way. Men don't make women happy. You're the only person who can make you happy.'

'But I thought—'

'Hush now, Cecilie. There's nothing you can do about him. There are things you can do to affect your future though. Quit the hotel if it's upsetting you this much. Make choices that will bring you happiness. Come travelling with me. We'll take wonderful trips together.'

The prospect seems all too awful, so Cecilie sobs loudly into her mother's silk nightie, heartbroken and baffled – but blind no more. She is determined not to sit and wait; not to shed another tear, not to dwell on Hector Herrera, for a minute longer.

38

NOVEMBER 2018, LONDON, ENGLAND

Kate swirls her teaspoon into a mug of tepid Earl Grey and wishes she had ordered coffee. She needs to feel alert for the showdown she's about to have. She looks up towards the cafe entrance and tries to remember exactly what Bethany Henderson looks like. All she can remember is that she is young and blonde. And so unlike Kate.

Kate refused to let Bethany's phone call ruin her big night, so she cut the conversation short by arranging to meet her on Monday. She was grateful that the chaos and candy floss and fun and fireworks enabled her to bury the news, for now. Being chair of the PTA was a timely distraction from the phone call from hell. She didn't need to address it, nor even mention it to George until fireworks' night was over and she was finally armed and ready with facts, not suspicions. Besides, this was Kate's moment. It was the PTA's most successful family fireworks party in history – Kate's event raised £6,000 to go towards an outdoor classroom; last year, Melissa Cox had only just scraped four – she was *not* going to let the weekend be ruined by a phone call. Not when, deep down, she'd known something was coming all along.

As Kate collected empty firework cartridges from the school playground the next morning, and had space and fresh air to think, she worked out her strategy. She would keep schtum. Not give George an inkling that she was about to finally rumble him, because that would be showing her hand. She wanted to feel prepared. Ready for anything George might try to come up with this time. She agreed to meet his slut of a secretary on Monday lunchtime and hear her out – to ask why now – and then plan her next course of action. Since she received the phone call on Saturday, that sick feeling Kate felt twenty years ago in a bar in Mexico, when Hector Herrera cheated on her right before her very eyes, came back to wind her like a Catherine wheel doing loops in her stomach. As Kate's muddy hands threw plastic cartridges into carrier bags, she realised that knowing the truth didn't in fact make it better. She thought it would be preferable. At least Hector Herrera had drawn a neat line under their summer of fun – there was no grey area, no element of doubt, no unknown. The unknown had eaten Kate up for the past eight months. But drawing a line under marriage is a different matter, and knowing didn't make it any easier to take.

Now, in a busy coffee shop near Liverpool Street Station, where Kate made the mistake of ordering an Earl Grey instead of a coffee, she twists the scrunchie clasping her low ponytail tight and tries to remember what Bethany Henderson looks like. She remembers the hair on George's scarf; that mass of long blonde hair swishing down her back as she leaned into George that day Kate walked in on them and George said he was in the middle of firing her.

Kate shudders.

A young woman with blonde hair and a circular, passive face walks in. She is wrapped in a white puffer jacket belted at the waist with a white faux-fur-trimmed collar. Not all that dissimilar to Kate's navy parka. Kate remembers her now and is surprised by how plain she is.

Bethany recognises Kate from the awkward family portrait that sat in a thin silver frame on George's desk. She feels guilt rise up inside her under her marshmallow of a coat but powers on, through her nerves, to walk across the cafe.

'Hi,' Bethany says defiantly and pulls out the seat at the little square table.

Kate is so used to being polite, to smiling, to apologising, that it feels so uncomfortable to her that the lines of her mouth are staying straight.

Bethany pulls a bottle of water out of her bag as if to explain why she isn't going to the counter to get a drink. It's obvious she wants to make this as quick and as painless as possible.

'Why did you call me?' Kate asks with a wan expression. 'I was getting used to the idea – you know, "what you don't know doesn't hurt you"? We were getting to a happy place again.' Kate can barely look at Bethany's face, but she does and sees her blue eyes are sad and cold. She looks like the one who's been betrayed.

'I thought you should know.'

'I'm not sure I want to know now.'

'I think you do – that's why you came to the office that day. The day—'

'The day I caught you and my husband at it?'

'*What?*'

'The day I walked in on you... you... going "down" on him, and you made it look like he was firing you. Very clever.' Kate is horrified to have to spell it out, and her voice cracks in the loud cafe.

'The day he *fired* me' – Bethany's passive face suddenly becomes animated, as if there is some substance to her – '*I* didn't do anything wrong. I just told him I thought what *he* was doing was wrong.'

Kate feels rage in her hot face.

The cheek of the woman!

She lowers her voice to an angry hush. 'Let me tell you, whether you're single or not, however despicably George has behaved, you *have* done something wrong. George is a married man. We have *children*. Why would you want to break up a family? My family is everything to me!' Kate's wobbly voice breaks as she looks down at her off-white tea mug and tries to hold herself together. She blinks rapidly, to shoo away the tears, then looks out at the lunchtime bustle, at the worker bees around Bishopsgate, and wonders how George looked as he sauntered through it on his way to work this morning.

Cocksure.

'Look, it's not me he's having an affair with.'

'What?'

'I'm not the one you should be angry with. I'm trying to help you out here.'

Kate is baffled. 'Help me out?'

'It stressed me out so much, I hated covering for them. For their filthy lunches, making lame excuses for him. I told Freya I didn't like it at all.'

'Freya? He's having an affair with Freya?'

Kate thinks back to the girl with the glossy poker-straight hair and pert bottom.

'No! Freya reckoned I should talk to him, let him know I felt uncomfortable with it. Then he fired me and gave Freya my job.'

'So, hang on a minute...'

'But me and Freya are mates and we still meet up. It's not her fault. Poor thing now has to do his dirty work for him...'

Kate can't keep up and is struggling to take it all in.

'So who is it? Who's George having an affair with? And why are you telling me now, when you've known for ages?'

'"Cause Freya hates covering for him as much as I did. She doesn't want to lose her job – but me, I've got nothing to lose now, so I thought, sod it.' Bethany gives a nervous laugh.

'"Sod it" – you're crushing me – breaking my heart and telling me out of spite?' Kate squeezes the handle of her mug of tea.

'Hang on a minute – me and my fiancé had just put an offer on a duplex in Chigwell. We'd been waiting for them to come up for months. We had to pull out when *your* dirty husband fired me unfairly. He's screwing you over, but he screwed me over too.'

Kate looks at Bethany's young joyless face and feels bad for her, for reading her wrong, for reading the situation wrong. 'I'm sorry. Look, this is all a bit hard for me to process. First I thought he was having an affair with you, then he made out that I was going mad, and now this.' Kate shakes two hands with fanned fingers out in despair. 'I'm just a bit all over the shop at the moment.' She tries to compose herself by drinking a sip of tepid tea and inhales a deep breath to steady her nerves. 'I'm sorry for you, I really am.'

Bethany shrugs.

'Have you found another job?'

Chit-chat steers Kate away from the question she really needs answering.

'I had to threaten him for a good reference, said I'd tell you if he didn't help me get another one. He's lucky I didn't make a case for unfair dismissal, but Mick told me it wasn't worth the hassle. Slimy bosses always win.'

Kate feels very uncomfortable with George being referred to as a slimy boss, even though she knows that's exactly what he is.

'So is that why you're telling me, for your reference?'

'No – I got another job in September, so I let it go.'

Bethany gives her rose gold Michael Kors watch a quick glance. 'Actually, I can't be long...'

'So why are you telling me now? Why all these crank calls?'

'Yeah, sorry about the calls – every time you answered I was scared to say it. But I just knew I had to. For Freya. For Mick. For the flat we lost. We can't get on the property ladder now, prices have gone up even more since June... Anyway, it's wrong. He's been mugging you off for over a year, I reckon. Maybe two. I tried to go back over it all last night, but I couldn't access my old work diary.'

'Who is she?' Kate asks before taking a deep breath and holding it.

'He didn't let on for a while – he'd just get me to book hotels and block out lunches.'

'Which hotels?' Kate gasps for air after she says it.

'Sometimes The Rosewood, sometimes The Shard... She likes her luxuries...'

He took me to a dusty old hotel in Bloomsbury for my fortieth.

'He'd get me to block out a couple of hours, once a week, sometimes twice a week. Said to put in the diary that he was having lunch with B. Sometimes Barry.'

'Baz Brocklebank from the Sydney office?'

'No, Barry was her last name.'

Kate suppresses a dry wretch.

Amber Barrie. I saw how he was all over her at the PTA summer social.

'It wasn't until he started getting me to send her flowers that I found out her full name and address. She lives in the same village as you.'

Kate's ashen face falls.

'I know,' she says with a defeated sigh. 'Amber Barrie. She lives at the Manor.'

'I laughed cause Barry Manor sounded like Barry Manilow.'

Kate doesn't laugh.

'But her name isn't Amber. It's Antonia.'

39

NOVEMBER 2018, XALAPA, MEXICO

In a private room on the sixth floor of the Hospital Ángeles, Hector sits in a wooden chair, leaning stiffly on low rectangular armrests. He has sat in this chair for too long now and still can't find a comfortable position. His forearm bends and slightly bulges. On his bicep is the tattoo of a hand with elegant fingers mid click, a flame igniting from the index finger at the top. Hector had the tattoo done years ago, after he stopped working in Jugo's California, to remind him of the brilliant ideas and decisions he is capable of making: choosing the newspaper over shady deliveries; deciding to further his education and go to university; to stay in the back of the car when he'd probably been tempted to sit alongside his mother up front. Now he can add to his mental list: quitting drinking and smoking to be a better husband; sending samples of his drawings to the children's author in Mexico City; shelving his dreams of running away to Europe to answer his phone and rescue Pilar.

Cramped into the low wooden chair for another day, the clicking fingers don't make him feel triumphant; instead, he is empty, void of good ideas. His creative mind feels barren; his body is a tired shell. He pulls his military cap down over his eyes and reads *The Psychopath Test*, hoping to fill in the blanks of his brain, waiting for Pilar to wake from an induced coma. Tubes and wires weave in and out of his wife, connecting her to machines, where monotonous beeps punctuate every line that Hector reads, disturbing him so that all he can think of is death.

Are you coming?

Hector's parents died on the Day of the Dead, a day on which they were out honouring lives lost: Victor's mother Maria, Lupe's grandfather in Monterrey, their friend Ariel, who they had watched unravel to brain cancer in the Hospital Ángeles earlier that autumn. That Day of the Dead was a sombre celebration for Victor and Lupe Herrera, raw from the loss of their friend; excited to be expecting another baby – if it was a boy they would have called him Ariel. They'd taken a basket of *pan de muertos* to the festival in Ariel's home village of Las Vigas, an hour down the road. They ate *tamales* and corn on the cob. Hector remembers tiny flashes of it. A large bottle of fizzy orange pop left with the *pan de muertos* at Ariel's family home. The smell of *tamales*. How a thick rain cloud made night-time come early, and soaked the colourful cut-out *papel picado* hanging across the cobbled streets of the village. The sudden jerk as their Beetle skidded off the bend and tumbled over itself like the drum of a washing machine, down into the ravine.

This year, Day of the Dead came and went while Hector was waiting for Pilar. Alejandro brought him *pozole* in a flask; they drank a tequila shot each to the memory of his parents, of his unborn brother, of Abuela. Pilar didn't die, but she didn't wake up either. Doctors thought she was too weak to wake up for now; she had stopped breathing for a little while, in the time it took Hector to find her, and they didn't know what her brain would be like. So they waited. Still, Hector waits. For his family. For his future.

Every few minutes, tangled in another line of his book, Hector looks up to see if anything has changed. Whether Pilar's mouth moved, or an eyelid flickered. But still she lies, as she has for the past sixteen days and sixteen nights. All the time and all the coffee Alejandro brings Hector, and all the space for reflection doesn't change how he feels in the pit of his hollow stomach: he desperately wants Pilar to wake up. This isn't the girl he fell in love with.

Hector met Pilar more than six years ago, when she walked into the orphanage under the weight of a ring-bound folder and a pile of books. Hector had popped in to see Sister Miriam, Sister Juana, Sister Virginia and the kids during his lunch break from the newspaper, as Sister Miriam had asked him to put up a shelf. Hector was a handy man to have nearby. Many of the past inhabitants of the Villa Infantil never came back to see the women who had brought them up. Benny never bothered to help out, but Hector always loved to drop in, to see the children who were staying. The first thing he noticed about the birdlike girl with the red lips and the pencil skirt was her accent. She wasn't from round here, and Hector was instantly hooked.

Always the foreign girl, always the extranjera.

He could hear Ricky's words. He could see Benny's contemptuous face, but he couldn't help it.

'*Gallega?*' he said, laughing at her Iberian lisp.

'Yes,' Pilar said, trying not to blush as she rolled her eyes at him.

'What are you doing here?'

'I'm here to meet the children who'll be joining us for the new term. Is Sister Miriam available?'

'Not *here* here. What are you doing in Mexico?'

'Why not Mexico?' she said with a sassy smile. She was the sexiest schoolteacher Hector had ever seen, way cuter than the teacher he had when Sister Miriam used to drop him and Benny and the other children at school. There were fewer children at the orphanage back then, and the sisters did the school run themselves. But Pilar was visiting for her first transition meeting, and there were eight children starting *Primaria* that September.

'Ahhhh, you must be Miss Cabrera, do come in,' said Sister Miriam from behind her tiny wire-frame glasses.

'Your caretaker was just letting me in,' Pilar said with a lisp as she looked at Hector's soft muscular arms in his faded T-shirt.

'Hectorcito? He's not the caretaker, he's an old boy, still comes to help us out.'

'I'll get the broom,' Hector said with a playful smile, and Pilar was struck by his face. He was the most handsome man she had seen since arriving in the country two weeks ago.

Soon Hector was sketching cartoons of SupaPila and sending them to school with the children. 'Make sure Miss Cabrera gets this!' he'd say, while giving them a little circular disc of De La Rosa marzipan for their efforts.

A cautious double knock taps the door and Hector turns with a start.

'Come in!'

The door opens unsteadily and Xochitl peers through it. Her face is as round and flat as the moon and her long black eyes are separated by a small straight nose. Her lips are a deep shade of oxblood; her sombre beauty is accentuated by sadness.

Hector stands and removes his cap. 'You took your time.'

Xochitl walks into the room and puts her hands to her face. She's horrified to see her friend, so tiny and lifeless, lying on the bed; tubes going in and coming out of everywhere, so it seems.

She gasps and leans on the bar of Pilar's hospital bed for support, then turns to Hector with solemn eyes.

'Hector, I was scared.'

Hector thinks of how scared he's been feeling. Of Pilar not waking up; of never meeting Cecilie.

'Scared of what?'

'What they'd do to me. What my parents would think.'

Hector gives Xochitl a dismissive glance and turns the corner on the page of his book and shuts it, launching it onto the chair.

He turns back to see the depth of Xochitl's sadness and softens.

'They won't do anything, Xochi, they don't care about you.' He motions to Pilar. 'They don't care about her. They're too busy involved in all their shit to think about this... this... *inconvenience*.'

'Hector, I'm sorry I left her that night, I don't know *what* I was thinking going off like that, that behaviour isn't me. And now... look at her! Is she gonna be OK?'

A soft moon crumples and a tear runs down her face. Hector walks over and holds Xochitl tight. She sobs into the curve of his arm, and the inked flame on his bicep warms her forehead.

'Shhhhh, it's OK,' Hector says, not sure if things ever will be again.

'I'm so, so sorry,' she says, sobbing.

'Shhhhh, don't worry. That shit *isn't* you, Xochi. Get out now while you can. You're better than this.'

'Oh, Hector, I thought you'd be mad at me.' She wipes tears and make-up from under her eyes as she pulls back, leaving snot on Hector's khaki T-shirt.

'I'm not mad at you. I'm not even mad at her any more. I just want her to wake up.'

40

NOVEMBER 2018, LONDON, ENGLAND

Kate marches up the platform at Liverpool Street station, under a crystal and iron roof as breakable and as worn as her beating heart. The platform is almost empty at this time, so she charges freely towards the front of the train because the back won't reach the short village platform of Claresham's nearest station. Steam emanates from the low square heels of her round-toe boots.

Antonia fucking Barrie. I can't believe it. She must be at least ten years older than me!

Suddenly, it all makes sense. The long blonde hair was Antonia's shade of impeccable. The lunches with 'B' were for Barrie, not Baz Brocklebank. The hours spent in the hotel at The Shard weren't long business lunches. The pulsating green spot of Find My iPhone that taunted Kate was actually George pleasuring someone else. Antonia fucking Barrie. How George disabled Find My iPhone around the time Kate was cottoning on, getting closer. His compliance to come to Antonia and Archibald's annual cheese and wine party when he usually eschewed such 'ghastly' events. The ease and comfort with which he opened Antonia's fridge door and helped himself to a beer...

And then there was Antonia's patronising and belittling little looks up and down at Kate's shoes, her clothes, her bakes. Were they out of pity or anger? Did Antonia want George all to herself or was George just a toy boy; a distraction for the cougar? A court jester there to entertain the bored judge's wife?

That day Kate saw Antonia and Amber Barrie on the train as they glided past her with their noses high in the stuffy carriage air; the day he had 'Lunch B' in the diary and Kate interrupted George's firing of Bethany – were they heading into town for a cosy lunch with George? Did Antonia see Kate on the train and tip George off, so he cancelled and decided to sack Bethany in anger?

Perhaps he's fucking the pair of them, the shit.

Kate shivers and starts to feel travel sick as the train snakes out of the station and back to the shards of a shattered idyll.

* * *

'Where to, love?'

Kate slumps into the back seat of a blue Vauxhall taxi and thinks of her cold broken house, its garden grey and threadbare, and wraps herself tightly in her belted parka. There's no one at home. Chloe is at secondary school, and Izzy and Jack won't need picking up for another hour. Home is empty. She could go there, flop on the bed, curl up into a ball and sob until her tear ducts dry up. Or she could go and see Antonia Barrie. Look her in the eye and tell her she knows all about her grubby affair with her husband.

My husband.

'Barrie Manor please,' Kate says, remembering Bethany's amusement at the name, although she still doesn't feel like laughing.

'The judge's house?'

'Yes.'

As the taxi peels out of the quiet station towards the large Italianate house on the edge of Claresham, Kate feels anger overtake fear; incredulousness cancels out British reserve; a need for answers overrules the worry that perhaps no one is at home and this journey will be for nothing. Kate's vision is so tunnelled, her objective so huge, as the car sweeps through the walled front garden of Claresham Hall and up a driveway to an ornate manor house.

'That's £7.60, love. Want me to wait?'

Kate looks at the grand wooden double door, flanked by two immaculately trimmed green orbs. A red and silver Christmas wreath hangs, even though it's not yet mid-November.

Kate presents the driver with a crisp ten-pound note from her shaky hands and then remembers the school run.

'Actually yes, yes please.'

'Right you are,' says the driver, turning off his engine and reaching for the rolled-up newspaper on the dashboard.

Kate gets out of the car like a shot, before she can talk herself out of it, and walks across the circular driveway at the top of the grand approach. She raises a heavy brass ring before banging it down as loudly as she can. The thud thud thud of the knocker beats as loudly as her heart. Kate can hear someone vacuuming on the other side of the door and knows it won't be Antonia.

The vacuum is turned off and the door opens. A small woman with short blonde hair that's black at the roots peers around it. More staff.

'Yes?'

'Is Antonia in?'

'Yes, who shall I say—'

'Kate Wheeler.'

Kate says her name boldly and confidently without a single hint of a wobble in her voice, and the lion inside her roars. She feels proud of herself.

I can do this.

The maid doesn't say anything but indicates that she's just going to look for the lady of the manor.

Kate inhales the dreary grey day and waits to be invited in. Even braced for a showdown, she could never storm into someone's home; she'd have to be invited in first.

Antonia arrives clutching a golden Christmas bauble, and her face has an icy curiosity about it, but before she can even say hello, she knows why Kate is at her door. She flashes white teeth.

'Would you like a cup of tea?' she asks. Ever the impeccable hostess.

'How long? How long have you been shagging my husband?' Kate demands.

'Oh, let's not do this on the doorstep,' scoffs Antonia. 'Do come in.'

Kate wants to raise her arms like the decrepit windmill she can see from the Barries' vast garden and wheel them in a rage towards Antonia. Wipe the smug look off her face. But she curbs it, for now, and follows Antonia inside to the kitchen.

The maid closes the heavy front door behind them. 'Don't worry, Marta, I can get these, if you can carry on untangling the lights... I got into a terrible pickle with the red and gold ones.' Antonia smiles and nods Marta away before sashaying into the kitchen, towards the kettle on the Aga. Even for a day of sorting out Christmas decorations, Antonia looks elegant and crisp in a white shirt and jeans as blue as her eyes.

'Don't bother with the tea and the pleasantries, Antonia. I already know what a slut you are.'

Antonia's face drops.

'I just want to know, how long has my husband been lying to me for?'

Antonia looks taken aback, stunned to be insulted in her own home, but runs her fingers through her bouncy blonde hair casually, defiantly, and fills the kettle with water from the sink on the island anyway.

'Oh, I don't know, a year perhaps.'

A year?

Kate swallows her disgust so she is able to speak.

'How did it start?'

'Well, you know, badminton is such a passionate sport...'

'How can you be so breezy about this? Can't you see what you've done to my family? To me?'

'Oh, come on, Kate, grow up. These things happen all the time.'

'*These things happen?* My husband has been sleeping with... with... *you* and you expect me not to take umbrage?'

'Archie knows. In fact, he's been rather accepting...' Antonia raises an audacious eyebrow. 'I mean, he doesn't exactly want to start playing golf with George, but I think he'd rather I were happy. Archie always was a bit of a teddy bear really.' Antonia looks wistfully out onto the fields beyond the kitchen windows, to the old ruined windmill in the village beyond.

Kate is floored. 'Your husband knows about this?'

'Yes,' Antonia replies with a surprised smile, as if it were perfectly obvious he would know, and be accepting, of his wife having an affair with a man twenty years younger than he. 'Amber too. She and George get on spectacularly actually. Clarissa less so, and the boys are still a bit young, but give them time...'

Her daughters know.

Antonia puts the lid on the kettle and cranks up the heat.

'Time?' Kate stands like a dishevelled cat, her big brown eyes wide and shocked, her mouth hanging open in disbelief.

'Yes, time. For them to get used to the idea.'

'Used to the idea?'

'Of course. Have you not even talked to George about this? Am I really your first port of call?' Antonia gives a smile and shakes her head in disbelief. 'George wants to move in. Archie is working on a deal, an exit strategy if you will. For them both.'

'An exit strategy?' Kate is astonished how businesslike Antonia is being. How devoid she is of any human emotion.

'Well, Archie's far too old for the commute; for rough and tumble with Alistair and Bertie. He's wiped out after a day in court. He can't keep coming back here. He's moving into the apartment on Chancery Lane – George is moving in here. Did he not mention that?'

For the first time ever, Kate sees a flash of insecurity and doubt glide across Antonia Barrie's self-assured smug face. Polished lines crack just a little. But it doesn't offer Kate any comfort. The water in the stovetop kettle starts to bubble and the steam erupts through a hole, sending a whistle and a hiss screaming into Kate's brain. She looks at the ivory and silver sparkles of the granite worktop and her vision starts to blur.

'I think I'm going to be sick.'

Heat inflames her cheeks as bile rises in her throat. Kate slams her hand against her mouth and runs to the front door with the charge of the kettle whistle. She pulls the heavy door, opens it and is hit by an afternoon chill as she vomits all over the pruned green sphere to her right. She looks to the taxi driver, embarrassed, but is relieved to see he's fallen asleep, leaning back like a bear in winter, mouth rattling as he snores, newspaper draped over the steering wheel in front of him.

Kate takes a second to clean the corners of her mouth with an anti-bac wipe and opens the taxi door with deliberate noise.

The driver wakes with a start.

'Oops. You got me there, love. Where to?' he says, not looking into the mirror to see Kate's pale and pasty horror.

'The Finches,' she says meekly.

Home. I just want to get home.

41

'Where are the kids? It's eerily quiet,' says George, pausing by the front door to peer into the dark living room. A swirl of soggy brown leaves settle on the doormat before he can close the door; sideways November rain lashes on the bay window. The TV isn't on. Tinny music doesn't pour out onto the upstairs landing. Jack isn't playing Crossy Road on the iPad at the breakfast bar. The girls and their mates aren't upstairs. George walks into the kitchen. There isn't any sign of leftovers for him to nibble on while he waits for Kate to finish preparing their meal. In fact, George is starving, and he can't even smell the usual wafts of Bolognese, chicken pie or quiche that usually greet him when he comes home. 'What's going on?'

Kate leans solitarily against the cluttered island, clutching a hot cup of tea. Her face is still white, her hair bedraggled as if she's been pulling it out. George opens the fridge door and leans in, looking for a morsel, which reminds Kate how comfortable he looked helping himself to a beer from the enormous fridge in the kitchen at Barrie Manor.

'Why so quiet?' George says, taking a cold cooked chicken leg out of the fridge and gnawing on it clumsily.

He doesn't know.

'The girls are staying at the Coxes', Jack is having a sleepover at Herbie's.'

'On a Monday?' George gives Kate a disparaging look.

She hasn't told him.

'On a Monday,' Kate whispers.

'What's wrong, Kate? You look awful.'

Kate widens her eyes to offer a silent and sarcastic thanks. George puts his manbag on the breakfast bar stool and unwinds his stripy scarf in three shades of blue from around his neck. *That* scarf.

Kate grips her cup tighter. Her knuckles look as ashen as her face as she stares into space in the middle of the room. Family photos on the fridge look down on her with pity: Chloe playing Nala in the Year 6 performance of *The Lion King*. George teaching Izzy how to fish off Southwold pier. Jack holding his rugby under-8s player of the week trophy in the sunny autumn sunshine from a year ago. Kate pinned them all up there. The photos showing triumphs, achievement, pride and love. There are no photos of her up there. No one is proud of her.

'When were you going to tell me you were moving in with her? *After* you'd gone?'

George gives a nervous laugh with chicken still in the corners of his mouth.

Shit.

He's not sure how much Kate knows but he's got good at acting, so he smiles his best bumbling smile.

'What?' he asks, blinking rapidly.

'That old... old... *BITCH!*' Kate rages.

George looks alarmed.

'In her mansion! When were you going to tell me? In fact, when were you going to tell the kids? Hers know all right.' Kate's wobbly voice quietens, as if she's worried the children might hear her from across the village.

All the blood drains from George's grey face. 'Kate...' he says, walking towards her.

She bats him down.

'Don't "Kate" me, George,' she says with a quiet tremble. 'It's not a misunderstanding; I'm not being paranoid. You utter bastard, you can't make me look mad any more. I was right all along.'

'Kate, please...'

'She told me herself! How the dodgy old judge is even in on it. And her daughter! I knew it!' Kate clutches her face in despair.

'Just listen...'

'What will Chloe and Izzy make of you choosing her daughters over your own? How will you explain it to Jack? His teacher's *mother*?' The thought is too much, and Kate puts her tea towel to her mouth and sobs into it as George walks to her and pulls her into his coat.

'I'm so, so sorry. I'll end it, I promise. I've been trying to end it for ages...'

Kate pulls away, her eyes and nose streaming, a hurt face in despair.

'When did it start?'

'I can't remember exactly.'

'Yes, you *can*!' she pleads.

Kate knows no one ever forgets the time of year when new sparks ignite; the way the air feels, the seasonal punctuations that witness a new flush of excitement. She herself remembers the balmy mountain heat of her summer fling with Hector Herrera. The sticky thunderstorm the night she turned to him in the bar and saw him kissing another girl. How it was Independence Day – mid-September – she was due to go back to England in a few weeks, to start her graduate trainee job at Digby Global Investors in London, but she changed her flight so she could leave the very next day. The autumn chill in the air when she and George first started eating their sandwiches together on a bench in Elder Gardens. 'You don't forget those things,' she adds with a measured whisper.

George removes his coat in defeat. 'Last summer. It was last summer.'

Kate looks at him with pure hatred. '*Last* summer?' Every second Kate thinks it can't get any worse, it does. She'd at least hoped it was this spring, around the time the text came in as she stood in the kitchen at the exact same spot.

'After we got back from France. She joined badminton. Said it was a shame we missed their cheese and wine party – it was a shame *I* had missed their cheese and wine party.'

'Bitch. She went after you.'

'One thing led to another. It just went from there. It didn't mean anything.'

Kate's blotchy face crumples as she imagines George and Antonia entwined. She takes a big sip of tea to give herself a momentary shield.

'I'll end it tonight, Kate. I promise. I don't love her. I want to be here, I do *not* want to leave this house...'

Kate studies George's small eyes, not knowing whether to believe him.

'Not even for Barrie Manor and all Antonia's millions?'

'What are you talking about? You and the kids are my world. *They're* so dysfunctional! It was just a bit of fun – call it a mid-life crisis or whatnot, I've not been myself recently – but she told her bloody husband and then—'

'Just a bit of fun? You'd ruin your family and hurt me like this – make me think I was going mad or being paranoid – for just a bit of fun?'

George looks flustered, and ever-so-slightly annoyed. 'I didn't mean that. I meant I don't *love* her, Kate...'

Kate shakes her head in her hands, angry that she's meant to feel relieved about this; disappointed in herself that she does.

'But she went and bloody told Archie – and he saw his way out. He invited me for a drink at the Red Hart, was giving me advice on how to handle her, as if she was one of his vintage cars, wishing me the best of luck – it's a nightmare, Kate...'

'Oh, boo-fucking-hoo, George.' Kate wobbles between two octaves, her volume rising.

'I've been trying to get out of it since. I'm so bloody sorry. I was trying to be discreet.'

George doesn't look all that sorry to Kate. She wonders if he's just sorry he was caught.

'Discreet? *Discreet?*' Kate slams her empty mug onto the kitchen worktop. 'Cosy drinks with her husband in the Red Hart? Civilised lunches with Antonia and Amber in London? Shagging for hours up The Shard? Who else knows? I bet the whole village knows! All those *bitches* at the WI must have been laughing at me behind my back.'

Kate pulls at her low ponytail in despair and looks at the mug on the cluttered island. She wants to pick it up again. This time she wants to throw it at George's lying face, but knows it will be her cleaning up the tea stains and shattered ceramics, so she holds back.

George puts his scarf back on and winds it around his neck, trying desperately to save his family from unravelling in front of him.

'I'll go there now. I'll end it, I'll speak to Archie if he's there too. You and the kids are my life, Kate,' he says, his eyes piercing into her from where he stands at the kitchen door. Despite all the treachery, despite the fact that, while he protested that he didn't love Antonia, he forgot to tell his wife he loved her, Kate can't help feel the small relief of a hollow triumph as she watches George leave in panic.

At least I know. At least he's choosing us.

42

NOVEMBER 2018, XALAPA, MEXICO

At his art desk at *La Voz*, Hector tries to sketch but is lost for inspiration. He's meant to be drawing a cartoon for tomorrow's paper but can't think of anything funny to say about the twenty-five million pesos found in a suitcase on the governor's private jet. He's all out of ideas. He puts on his headphones to switch off from the background noise of fingers hammering on keyboards; telephones ringing; discussions between editors.

Play.

Depeche Mode's 'Poison Heart' comes on shuffle. Hector flips to the back of his sketchbook, to the drawings of wolves baying for each other's blood, drool hanging from their teeth. He starts to work on one while he waits for inspiration, adding detail to a snarling and sweaty canine nose.

I can't end it and walk away.

As he shades the darkness of a wet nostril, Hector feels a finger tapping the fingertip igniting a flame on his arm and looks around suddenly. His art director Oscar is standing over him with a sympathetic face. Everyone's been looking at Hector like this lately. Their heads slightly cocked to one side while they talk to him.

Hector slides his headphones down and around his neck. 'How's tomorrow coming along, Hector?'

'Nearly there,' he lies. 'I'll file it by 4 p.m.'

'I'd like to see it first,' Oscar says with a kindly smile, his white shirt tinged cream under the armpits.

'Sure thing, *jefe*. Give me two hours.' Hector looks up and Oscar is reassured by his wide brown eyes. He smiles and walks away down the corridor. Hector's never failed to deliver.

He replaces his headphones and scrolls through his phone to find a different song. A beep rings in his ear. A quick pulse of hope. Hector thinks of Cecilie, then pushes the image of her love heart-shaped face in a circle to the back of his mind.

Not now.

As desperate as he is to talk to her, to see her, to *feel* her, Hector can't face Cecilie right now. How can he explain his anguish to her? How can he ask her to wait when he doesn't know how long for? Until Pilar wakes up from her coma, his plan – his treacherous plan – has to be buried, and he doesn't know how to say it. He can't leave his wife dying in the hospital.

As much as he hopes the message is from Cecilie, he's relieved to see it isn't.

It's from Abuelo, and a smile appears on the corner of Hector's lips. He already knows how long old thumbs spent typing a simple twelve-character message.

> She woke up.

* * *

Pilar's weak smile strengthens when Hector walks into the room.

'Hey,' says a frail and husky voice.

'Hey, you. How are you feeling?' Hector walks over to the bed and sits by her knees. He rubs Pilar's shoulder tenderly and then withdraws. He thinks of how he found her covered in vomit, shit and semen, and walks around to the low wooden chair on the other side of the bed. *His* chair, although Pilar doesn't know how well Hector knows the view from it. He sits down and studies Pilar's pale and haughty face as she tries not to make eye contact, guilt driving her to look at the plate on the little table in front of her. Propped up in a hospital gown, without a jot of make-up on, she looks like a fragile lamb. Black hair and white skin. Frail, meek and sheepish.

She nibbles on some corn from her plate. 'Did you tell my parents?'

'No.'

Hector doesn't tell Pilar how close she came to dying. If she had died from choking on her own vomit that night, her parents wouldn't have made it to Mexico in time anyway. There was a time for calling them, and it wasn't then. They would have died with shame had they known what their respectable Catholic daughter was capable of. In the days after, as Pilar lay in a coma, Hector battled with his conscience, but knew she would rather Mari-Carmen and Leonel Cabrera didn't know at all. It's not like they missed Pilar's calls; she'd been communicating less and less, since she was too ashamed to let them know she'd been fired.

'How long have I been under? The doctor said it was, like, three weeks.'

'Twenty-two days.'

Pilar looks shocked, as if she thought the doctors were playing a trick on her.

'Your mother did call, once. Left a message on the apartment phone to see if you wanted to go home for Los Reyes. They said they'd pay for your flights. I didn't call them back.'

Hector doesn't say that Mari-Carmen hadn't mentioned him in their family Christmas plan.

'Well, they don't need to know now. The doctor said I'm going to be OK.' Pilar's cheeks are so sunken, her olive Moorish skin so pale, that her teeth look large and yellow.

Hector circles his mouth with his thumb and forefinger while he considers his words.

'I just spoke to Dr Fuentes outside...' His brow furrows, and his eyes look troubled. 'You ought to make a full recovery, but your liver is weak. You've had hepatitis and jaundice, as well as the overdose... You have to change your life, you understand?'

'He already spoke to me, Hector.' He can hear the graveness in Pilar's gravelly voice. 'He said I was seconds from death, that I'm lucky not to have brain damage. He said your quick thinking saved me. *You* saved me.'

'You're my wife, Pilar, what else was I going to do?'

Pilar's eyes well up and she looks at her plate on the thin table and nods. Hector sees shame in her face for the first time.

'I guess I'm just not as strong as you, Hector. My privileged life made me soft, my indulgence made me weak.'

'Don't be silly, baby...'

'It's true. You could see what was happening and I couldn't. I'm weak and I'm toxic.'

'No, you're not. We can clean all this up. If I managed it, you can.'

'I am toxic. You don't know the depths of my dark thoughts. You have experienced so much more hardship than I have and you rose above every shit thing thrown your way. I am wretched, and I don't deserve you. I'm weak.'

'You're strong enough, Pilar.'

'You think I'm strong enough to change? I want to change.'

'I'll help you.'

Hector rubs his frail wife's shoulder and smiles.

'I want to go home,' Pilar says.

'I'll take you home, as soon as Dr Fuentes says you're ready. I suspect you'll need a few more days here, but I'll get you out and I'll get you any help you need to recover fully, to live clean.'

'No, I want to go *home* home. To Spain. I can't be here any more. I'm too ashamed.'

Hector looks at Pilar, tiny and remorseful, although she still can't bring herself to say the word sorry to him.

'Come with me, Hector. Come with me to Spain. We'll start afresh.'

43

JANUARY 2018, DAY 1,661

'Happy New Year!' Cecilie giggled as she slumped onto the swing chair of her mother's veranda. The tumble of snow from the sky had stopped and a chink in the clouds revealed a green beam arcing over the mountain behind the Wiig residence. The light of her mother's en suite bathroom was suddenly switched off, making an illuminated rectangle disappear on the white lawn in front of her. Stars peeped through to brighten the inky sky, before retreating gallantly to let the aurora have her moment.

Cecilie narrowed her eyes and peered into her screen. Perhaps her vision was blurred but Hector didn't look ready to party. His military cap was lowered and almost covered his eyes. 'What does 2018 look like?' Hector asked with a forced smile.

Cecilie turned her phone to face the dark snowscape of the front garden. Hector could just about make out the lights on the bridge, twinkles in the town beyond it on the other side of the harbour.

'That's what it looks like!'
'Looks cold.'
'I feel warm.'

Cecilie's Aperol-infused cheeks were so warm she didn't feel the bite of the Arctic blast as it whipped across the Barents Sea and onto the veranda, where it started to push her swing. She had spent the evening at a private party at the Iskrembar. Abdi took over the kitchen and made a big vat of lamb stew served with lentils and *muufo* flatbreads. He created a special coconut and cardamom ice cream that was so tasty Grethe insisted it become a regular on the Iskrembar offering. Espen was working, but Morten popped in to say hi, and as midnight struck, Grethe whispered her secret to Cecilie and pressed both their hands to her stomach.

Hector was silent. He didn't seem chatty, or excited about another New Year's Eve of hedonism ahead of him.

'The lights are on show,' Cecilie said with pride as she turned her phone to the sky.

'Oh, I can't see them.'

Hector seemed polite and functional, his manner unusually brusque. There was no sign of his sparkle or his playful soul, which hadn't ever had problems crossing two seas, a gulf and an ocean to get to her before.

'Everything OK?' Cecilie asked as she curled her legs underneath her on the swing chair. The breeze made it rock gently. *Everything OK?* was usually code for *Are you alone?* or *Can we talk?* but Hector didn't *have* to answer her FaceTime call if he hadn't wanted to talk. Cecilie started to feel frustrated.

'Yeah, sure. Pilar's out getting her hair done for the party.'

Cecilie's heart sank and she put one boot on the decking to stop the swinging motion; it was starting to make her feel nauseous.

'Where's the party at tonight?'

'Elias's house. It's gonna be a big one.'

Saying it made Hector feel bad, so he looked out the window, away from the screen.

Double celebration.

Cecilie was thrown by the awkwardness and changed the subject.

'Hey, I had some good news tonight. Grethe is pregnant!'

'Wow,' Hector replied flatly. 'Great news.'

'Not due until the summer, very early days, but gosh, I can't believe I'm going to be an auntie. Well, of sorts...'

'Congratulations.' Hector removed his cap, ruffled his hair, then replaced it low, almost over his eyes again. 'Hey, *mira*, I have news too.'

Cecilie suddenly sobered up. She pulled her knees in to her chest on the swing and pulled the phone closer in. Her vision didn't seem blurred any more. She could see everything in Hector's faraway face.

'What is it, Hector? What's wrong?' She wished she could rise up out of the swing chair, float over the fjord, to half a world away so she could see him, touch his arm, look into his eyes.

'I'm, erm...'

A shipping container tooted its horn on the harbour, wishing revellers a happy new year while drowning out Hector's big announcement.

Cecilie laughed at the timing of it. She knew something terrible was about to happen, that her world was about to turn upside down. She almost appreciated the captain's censorship.

'What did you say?'

'I'm, erm... I'm getting married.'

What?

'We decided yesterday and we saw the priest this morning. We've booked the church. For March.'

Double celebration.

By the glare of the screen under the light of the aurora, Cecilie's glassy green eyes filled and her pretty face crumpled. She turned the phone up to the sky so she could stifle and silence her cry. Tears tumbled, but no sound came out of her open mouth. She took a deep breath and looked back to her phone, at Hector's warm brown skin, his sad cinnamon-flecked eyes, finally looking right back at her, lovingly, apologetically, pleadingly, cruelly.

And with that, Cecilie realised Hector didn't have to see her cry, so she hung up.

44

DECEMBER 2018, SUFFOLK, ENGLAND

'Urgh, Mum, I so don't want to come in. I'm, like, ten. Surely you can leave me in the car?'

Kate turns off the engine of the S-Max and the windscreen wipers stop mid-swipe. Heavy drops pummel the glass and Kate's vision becomes increasingly obscured.

'Izzy, love...' Kate negotiates nervously. 'It's cold and it's dark and it's raining, and look, it's packed in there.' She gestures towards the tinsel and tension inside the bustling supermarket. Checkout queues trail towards the back half of the store. The customer service desk has a line of disgruntled click and collectors, clutching phones and order numbers, backing up to the flowers gondola and preventing people from getting to the fruit and veg. And Kate doesn't even know that there's a separate queue for the turkey collection point, lurking at the back of the store.

Kate looks at her daughter in the front seat, while the phat headphones Izzy got for her birthday almost drown her mother out.

'Come on,' Kate says, lifting one ear. 'I'll buy you one of those giant Florentines you like.'

Izzy smiles in defeat and unclicks her seat belt. 'Okayyyy,' she says, and they open the car doors, ready to make a run for it.

Izzy's never been that keen on spending time with her mother. She's such a daddy's girl. Even when she was a baby, she rarely sat on Kate's lap; unlike Chloe or Jack, she didn't turn to her for one of Mummy's Magic Kisses if she fell and hurt her knee. And as her teenage years approach, Izzy seems increasingly repulsed by her mother. Often running to Daddy if Kate won't let her play on the iPad, or complaining to George that Mum is such an ogre. But still, Kate plugs away. Trying to win Izzy over, with warmth, with patience, with Florentines. And Kate has never once implied that, actually, her father came very close to breaking her little heart recently. Kate's done very well to bite her tongue, as much as it hurts. They walk through the automatic doors and shuffle through the queue at customer services, Kate apologising left, right and centre.

'Right. The turkey, star anise, figs, goose fat. It's all I need. We'll be as quick as we can, poppet,' Kate says as she strokes Izzy's chestnut hair from her crown to her back, and she flinches. 'Turkey collection point turkey collection point turkey collection point...'

'Mum, what's wrong with you? You sound deranged.'

Kate gives a harangued smile. 'Can't believe I forgot the goose fat last week. Doesn't matter...' she whispers under her breath. 'Ooh, sorry. Turkey, star anise, figs, goose fat... oh, and cream. I need more double cream. Oh, excuse me please, sorry, where's the turkey collection point? It's not back at customer services, is it?'

A young man in a green tie gives a big smile. He clearly loves Christmas.

'Back of the store, madam, there's a special stand, wait there and one of our partners will go and find your turkey for you. Do you have your order number with you today?'

Kate waves her phone and smiles before hurrying Izzy along with an arm around her daughter's shoulder. Izzy slinks away to the seasonal aisle.

'Stay with me, poppet, it's too busy and I have to get the turkey.'

Izzy ignores the instruction and walks off. 'I'm just looking at the tins.'

'Turkey collection point turkey collection point turkey collection point. Ah. Here you are, sorry...' Kate is flapping, but excitedly. She's always quite liked Christmas, but this year will be a good opportunity to draw a line under the year they've had, to batten down the hatches and get her family back together. Strangely, Kate hasn't looked forward to a Christmas this much since their first Christmas with Chloe. This one means so much.

Kate joins the back of the queue and waits, level with a little table. On it sits a box of own-brand chocolates to sample. She leans to take one wrapped in purple foil and feels her thighs rub together as she reaches in enthusiastically.

Three bored-looking customers stand in front of Kate with slumped, accepting shoulders. They all look at their phones, at lists, recipes, texts. A chill runs down Kate's spine when she realises who the shopper is in front of her.

Maybe I'll get the star anise first...

The customer in front is irked by the rustling of the chocolate wrapper and turns before Kate can leave.

'Oh, it's you,' says a face filled with disdain.

Kate feels like she's had the Christmas cheer and stuffing knocked out of her.

'Hello, Antonia,' she says, picturing Antonia's naked body

stretched out underneath George's. Anger washes over her. She thinks of Izzy across the store, and the lioness inside her roars.

'Doing your own errands today?'

Antonia stands tall in her long red woollen coat with a black fur collar. 'Quite the little comedian I see, Kate.' Antonia smiles, eyeing Kate's dark blue winter duffel coat with icy pity.

Kate smooths down the rain-fuelled frizz all the way from her fringe to her ponytail.

I will not walk away. I won this.

Antonia turns her back to Kate, stands tall, and returns to the sanctuary of her phone. Kate sucks on the hazelnut until the caramel is all gone and imagines the texts George and Antonia must have exchanged over the 'year and a bit' they were shagging. Were the messages dirty? Were they functional? Were they full of yearning and mischief? Were they full of passion and love?

She's not texting him now, is she?

'Mum, can I get this?' says Izzy sullenly, clutching a bumper tin of Quality Street with a snowy reindeer scene on the lid, knowing Kate is going to say no.

'Yes, poppet, you can, it looks lovely.'

'Really? Wow.' Izzy raises her eyebrows and wonders who kidnapped her mum and replaced her with someone who's even more of a pushover.

Antonia waits for her order.

A woman as wide as she is tall comes out clutching a box. 'Goose for Lady Barrie?'

'Here!' Antonia nods as she slings her Gucci bag onto the crease in her elbow so she can take the bird in the box. Her red coat sweeps around and her thin frame looks resolute. Down but not out.

Antonia gives Izzy a loaded smile and leans in to whisper in

Kate's ear. 'He's. Still. Miserable,' she says, and glides away to the checkout at the front of the store.

Kate stands, stuck to the spot, frozen in time. Her eyes well up. She doesn't hear Izzy.

'Mum? Mum? Are you OK, Mum?'

Kate blinks and a tear falls down her mottled cheek and onto the grey square tile of the floor.

'Yes, darling, fine,' she says, nodding reassuringly, voice wavering, relieved that between Izzy's Bose headphones and her tweenage agenda, she didn't seem to hear.

45

CHRISTMAS DAY 2018

Hey beautiful,

I hope you're doing OK.

Long time no speak, I know, and I'm so sorry, for... well, everything. But I have to let you know, whatever you think of me, I'm coming to Europe and I need to see you. I must see you! I need to make amends for everything, and I hope you can forgive me. I arrive in Paris on New Year's Day – it would be super cool if you could meet me, if it's not too difficult for you to get there. I think about you a lot and want to make things right.

Besos,

Hector

x

Kate closes the lid on her laptop. She was only looking for her go-to cranachan trifle recipe, just to check how much whisky to put into the cream, and there it sat, a timebomb waiting to explode in her messages list.

She unscrews the lid off the Glenlivet, inhales the bitter

blend of malt and wood, and a flame ignites in Kate's stomach. Hector Herrera is coming to Europe.

Whatever for?

She shakily pours whisky onto a tablespoon six times, spilling it clumsily into the cream, where it dances dizzily under the Kenwood whisk.

How did he find me on Facebook? And why now? After all this time.

Kate thinks back to that summer, and the scents of mango, corn and motorbike exhaust fumes fill her with an excitement she hasn't known for a long time.

A beep emanates from the kitchen island, pulling Kate away from the summer she graduated. It's George's phone. Face up.

Spatula in hand, Kate leaves the Kenwood to mix alone while she tries to read the message, but the reflection of the bulb in the pendant light above the island bounces off it and obscures the screen.

George walks in, wearing his Christmas Day jumper, and heads straight to his phone. Kate pretends she hadn't noticed the beep and turns off the motor of the mixer.

'Well, the Xbox is going down well,' George says as he punches in a code only he knows and goes to read the message. 'Ahhh. Mum and Dad. "Happy Christmas from the Jurassic coast! Love to Kate and the kids." That's nice.'

Kate nods compliantly, quietly, as she scrapes silky folds of cream onto raspberries.

I didn't ask him who it was from.

46

DECEMBER 2018, MEXICO CITY, MEXICO

At the Iberia check-in desk in the bustling departures hall of Benito Juárez International Airport, Hector heaves Pilar's case onto the scales – 38kg. It must weigh almost as much as her. She looks like skin and bones in the blush-pink tracksuit that hangs off her frame. Her cheeks have a little more colour in them than they did when she left hospital a month ago, and her whip of black hair has been coiffed back to give her frame more stature. But her face, free of make-up but for thick black eyeliner, looks hollow. For once, Hector is worried about what Mari-Carmen will think when she's reunited with her daughter in Madrid.

'There will be a charge for this, *Señora*,' says a woman with a Castilian lisp. A red and gold hat sits primly on her head at a jaunty angle.

'Obviously,' says Pilar, flatly.

'But how many bags are you checking in today? If *Señor* is under 23kg you can have some of his allowance. It will bring the charge down at least.'

Hector wonders why the woman in the hat is trying to be helpful when Pilar is responding so brusquely.

'Just me,' Pilar says soberly as Hector rubs the small of her back. 'I'll pay whatever.'

* * *

'So, this is it,' Hector says with a faux melancholy as he places Pilar's carry-on holdall on the floor between their feet. They face each other and Hector takes her hands in his. She looks up at him with wide eyes.

Despite knowing that this is what Pilar wants, this is what she's chosen, Hector can't help feeling guilty about the sensation of overwhelming relief in his tummy, and he feels terrible when he looks in the eyes of the fragile bird standing in front of him. Despite what she did. He checked out long before she reached the check-in desk; the toil and the chaos and the shouting was just too much, even though Hector knows he played his part.

And then she says it.

'I'm sorry, Hector. I'm truly sorry.'

Pilar clutches her travel pillow to her stomach as she falls onto Hector's chest.

He wraps his arms around her.

'Hey, it's OK, we're gonna be OK. *You're* gonna be OK. The whole of Spain is waiting for SupaPila to return, to educate them in the art of *molé*; the alchemy of the perfect *salsa*; what a *totopo* should actually taste like...'

Pilar laughs, then her face drops again.

'I'll always love you,' she states in a husky, low voice. Hector doesn't know what to say. His mouth stays closed as passengers stream past them in their tense misshapen bubble.

'I'll always love Xalapa. I did have lots of good years there.'

'I know you did. *We* did. It won't be the same without you,' Hector says, releasing Pilar from his arms.

'*Vuelve*. Go back and do wonderful things, Hector.'

Hector puts a hand on each of her shoulders before lowering his head so he's level with Pilar. 'And you in Spain, yes?'

'Yes.'

'So you need to promise me something, Pilar. If you promise me this, then there's no need to dwell on the past and be sorry.'

'What is it?'

'Slow down, baby. *Cál-ma-te*. You have a lot of happy times ahead of you, I know it. Just *cálmate*. Go easy on yourself.'

Pilar's hooded eyes well up and she plants an accepting kiss on Hector's closed mouth before she picks up her holdall, hugs her pillow even tighter and snakes off through security without looking back.

Hector puts his hands in his pockets and watches as Pilar doesn't turn around; as she puts her belongings into a black plastic tray, as she walks through an archway, as she disappears around a corner, clutching her pillow to her stomach again. Then he lets out a sigh. He didn't tell Pilar that he's not going back to Xalapa tonight. Instead, he will wonder around the Zócalo, go for a cold Negra Modelo in his favourite bar on Calle Tacuba. He'll catch up with Efrain's brother Raymundo and his girlfriend to see their new baby, then Hector and Raymundo will wander to the market at Coyoacán to grab them all tortas before Hector beds down on Raymundo's couch. In the morning, he will return to Benito Juárez International Airport. Tomorrow, Hector will fly to Paris.

47

DECEMBER 2018, SUFFOLK, ENGLAND

'So, here's a funny thing,' Kate says as she sits on the sofa, leaning into one arm of it with a glass of red wine in her hand. Her legs curl underneath her, a little plumper than they were a week ago from turkey, trimmings and the hangover of leftovers. Her slippers hang off her feet, hot in the warm living room. George sits in the middle of the sofa, his arms wide on the back of it, bottle of beer in one hand, legs stretched out in front of him on a pouffe. Casual, relaxed, little regard for his companion in her corner as he watches James Bond on the telly. 'I'm thinking of a little jaunt to Paris in a few days. Eurostar has some excellent fares...'

'Paris? Why Paris?' George says dismissively as James Bond deftly weaves his way through a street parade somewhere far away.

'Well, an old friend is going to be there; a friend from that summer I spent in Mexico, just for a few days... I don't think he's ever been to Europe before, so given it's not far for us, I thought we could go and say hello. Welcome him to the continent sort of thing,' Kate says, sounding flustered. When she feels nervous about something, she talks too much and witters. 'It must have been about twenty years since I saw my friend...' Kate knows it was exactly twenty and a half years since she last saw Hector Herrera, and her wittering makes George suspicious.

'Which friend? I don't know about any friends from Mexico.'

'Oh, you know, my friend from the orphanage that summer I was volunteering.'

'What, the boyfriend?'

'Well... he wasn't exactly my boyfriend.'

'You said he broke your heart,' George says, laughing. 'That's why you were so wary of me when we met. Bloody Mexican, I thought, getting in the way of me getting to first base.'

'First base? George, is that what you thought?' Kate lets out a surprised laugh, her voice wobbling up and down an octave, although it's nice to think that George might ever have been jealous. 'Well, it didn't seem to do you any harm in the end,' she says cheekily. The wine is turning Kate's lips a deep shade of Rembrandt red, giving her some Dutch courage along the way.

'Why would you want to see an old Mexican boyfriend? They don't age well – look at these guys,' he jokes, pointing to the skeletons in a Day of the Dead parade, pleased with himself and his quip. Kate doesn't laugh. 'I didn't know you were in contact.' George sounds blasé. It's not a cover for jealousy, he's just surprised.

'Oh, well, we're not really. I get news via Sister Miriam every Christmas. The occasional birthday greeting. I think he's married now.'

'Good, well, so are you, so why do you want to drag us all to Paris? It'll be January, nobody goes anywhere in January unless it's St Bart's. And we can't afford St Bart's.'

Kate thinks of Antonia Barrie and wonders if she's in St

Bart's. Is that why St Bart's sprang to George's mind? She feels a slosh of anger.

'It's hardly dragging! We could go to Disney, have a mini-break before the kids go back to school.'

'Disneyland Paris? Sounds vile.'

'OK, I'll go on my own when the kids start back. He's there for a few days,' Kate says, trying to call George's bluff.

George shrugs and takes another slug from his bottle of beer.

An irritation runs up Kate's blotchy neck that makes her feel invisible, like she can't breathe and no one cares, but she speaks up again, boldness fuelled by Bordeaux.

'I thought we were going to make more of an effort, George.'

She looks along the sofa, pleadingly. George glances back but his gaze stops at the Christmas tree in the window.

'Make an effort?' George returns to the TV and talks at it as if he's talking to Bond. 'Well, Paris seems a bit extreme. Why don't I book a babysitter? We can go to Corky's one evening...'

Great.

'Or I'll get Freya to sort dinner and a show in London. There are always cheap pre-theatre deals to get people out in January.'

You took her to the Shangri-La at The Shard.

Kate takes a large sip to finish her vessel of wine and George carries on talking to Daniel Craig.

'But really, Kate, I don't think going to Paris for a cosy reunion with the man who broke your heart is really making an effort for "us", is it?'

'He wasn't the only one who broke my heart.'

George tips his head back as he blows an exasperated zephyr towards the ceiling. The faux crystals on the Homebase chandelier tinkle.

'I thought we'd moved on?' he groans, even though this is the first time Kate has referred to George's affair since she confronted him about it; since he chose to stay with her; since they decided to make a go of their marriage.

Kate's trying, she really is, but a message out of the blue from Hector Herrera has put the wind in her sails, and she's all in a pickle.

'Well, maybe I'll take the girls shopping. Paris is meant to have some lovely department stores. We could just meet up with my friend for a coffee between shops.'

'If you want,' says George, giving Kate a sideways glance, wondering what's got into her, knowing fully well she won't be going to Paris.

48

MARCH 2018, DAY 1,725

> Hola.

> Hei.

> Where are you?

> Does it matter?

> I like to picture where you are if I can't see you.

Cecilie hovered a thumb over her phone, and the green gem in her silver ring shone. But she didn't reply.

> Can we FaceTime then?

> No, it won't help.

> Won't help what?

> You know, Hector.

There was a pause. Hector didn't respond.

> I just wanted to say goodbye.

> Good luck with the wedding, I hope it all works out for you, I really do.

Cecilie *did* want Hector to be happy, but it made her feel sick that it couldn't be with her.

> That's it?

> Yes, that's it. It's not fair on your... on Pilar. It's secretive and sly. It's not fair on her. And it's not fair on me.

Hector felt wretched to the core.

> I didn't mean to hurt you.

> I know you didn't. What I meant was, I'm not being fair on me, living each waking moment around you; or allowing you into my dreams at night; or thinking about what time it is somewhere I'll never go; or wondering whether I'm going to talk to you today; or judging my mood based on how well our last conversation went; or my unwillingness to meet anyone in 'real' life while you move forward with yours. It's not fair. I need to be more present. I need to stop being blind to what's in front of me. My life here. My family. The children here in the library...

She's at work.

Hector didn't say anything. He couldn't believe that this was the last time they were going to talk. He didn't want to say anything heartfelt or final, because he didn't want this conversation to be more significant than any other. So Cecilie carried on.

> And you're getting married. Give your marriage a chance. Embrace it! My mother always says I should get out of my dreamland and embrace reality, so I'm going to embrace what's in front of me – and you should too. And I think the best way for us to give our lives the best shot is if we make this our last conversation.

Hector broke.

> I don't want that.

Parents and their toddlers started to gather in the basement of the library, untangling themselves from coats, scarves and papooses. On the top floor, ensconced between two rows of white bookshelves, a tear rolled down Cecilie's cheek as she looked at her phone and typed furiously in silence. She didn't want that either.

> Well I'm afraid you don't have the choice now.

> But we're friends.

> You might think that, Hector, but my heart breaks every time I think of her stroking your face; that I can't...

> But you told me you can, how your daydreams take you to me, that you can see me and touch me. Well I can too now. You taught me how.

Cecilie's shaky hands struggled to type as she wavered, but she carried on, knowing this was for the best. That she had to be brave and steel herself once more.

> You're getting married, Hector. You say we're friends but this isn't how friends talk. We must stop talking. It'll free us both. I'm sure you want me to be free.

As Hector lay in the dark, his schoolteacher fiancée snoring next to him, her wedding dress hanging on the wardrobe door like a ghost watching over them, he pictured Cecilie's eyes and wondered what shade of green they were at that moment; what the light was like under Candela's curved roof.

> Please, mi amor...

> Farvel, Hector.

> Te quiero, Cecilie.

And with that, Cecilie swiped right to switch the power off her phone, shut down the conversation, and ran down three flights of stairs to the library basement, ready to rouse the little ones with *So, ro, lillemann...*

'*No mames...*' Hector cursed quietly, looking at his screen in the darkened room. Pilar rolled over in her sleep. The dress on the wardrobe fluttered eerily in the breeze of an open window.

49

JANUARY 2019, TROMSØ, NORWAY

'Remember our party last year?' says Grethe with a smile, sitting a bouncy Ahyana on her knee at the end table in the empty Hjornekafé, marvelling at her daughter.

Cecilie stands wistfully over them. Her strongest memory of last New Year was of Hector breaking her heart. For the first time. And a wash of sadness sprinkles over her like the snow in the dark daytime of the street outside. But she knows what Grethe is referring to.

'Of course, you told me the stork was bringing this little miss,' Cecilie says, bending down to stroke Ahyana's creamy brown cheek.

'Amazing, huh?' Grethe's long blonde hair is flattened under the bow of a colourful headscarf. She doesn't take her eyes off Ahyana as she picks up her coffee cup.

'Can't believe it,' says Cecilie, smiling. She's so in love with her best friend's baby. Some people feel distanced when a friend becomes a mother first; unable to understand the sleep deprivation, the jargon, or frustrated by the fact that friends can no longer finish a conversation, but Cecilie doesn't mind. She's so besotted with edible Ahyana, she doesn't mind the chaotic conversations that bounce from one subject to the next. 'Look at her, sitting up! Clever girl.'

'Abdi's coconut and cardamom is our bestseller now...' says Grethe with a wry smile, referring to its debut last New Year's Eve, as if they'd been talking about ice cream the whole time.

'Do you want another coffee?' asks Cecilie, looking around the empty cafe. 'Or a hot chocolate? I'm going to make myself one.'

Cecilie walks back around the counter. It's New Year's Day. The library is closed and Henrik is visiting his family over the border in Kiruna, so Cecilie was happy to work, to take her mind off the noise in her head.

'Not sure why my mother told you to open up,' says Grethe as Ahyana starts to fidget on her lap.

Cecilie takes the biggest cup she can find.

'It might get busy later. I saw loads of lights chasers heading out last night. They'll wake up soon. They better had or you and I are eating cloudberry cake all afternoon! Did you want one?' Cecilie lifts a cup, gesturing to Grethe.

'Ooh, yes please, I'd better have a hot chocolate. Milk milk milk, help production for this little Milkychops, huh?' Grethe coos and Ahyana fidgets some more. 'Actually, I'd better feed her,' she says, lifting Ahyana up under her cheesecloth top. Grethe finds a comfortable position and leans back. A few minutes' peace. 'So, how are you doing?' she asks candidly.

'How do you mean?'

'I know Christmas has been rough for you.'

'It wasn't rough. It was fine. Uncle Hakon and Aunt Tove were here. They're always a laugh – I think Svalbard turned them crazy.'

'Oh yes, I remember them...'

'And Morten was the best sous-chef and always kept everyone's glasses topped up.'

'Of course...'

Cecilie wonders why Grethe is looking at her expectantly, but she keeps talking all the same.

'And Espen was his usual self – always had one eye on the i-Scand even though it was his day off. And Mamma, well you know Mamma...'

'Well, that's great, but I didn't mean Karin or Aunt Tove. Or Morten. Or Espen. I meant how are *you*? What's going on with The Mexican?'

'Oh.'

Cecilie puts a metal jug to the stainless-steel spout and turns cold milk into comforting warm foam. She inhales the sweet scent to galvanise herself.

'What's going on?' asks Grethe as she repositions and reattaches Ahyana. 'You said he was leaving his wife.'

'*He* said he was leaving his wife. But then he didn't. So I blocked him. And then unblocked him. Oh, it's all a mess, Grethe.' Cecilie pours the milk into syrupy chocolate sitting at the bottom of two large mismatched teacups. Grethe's blue eyes look sad.

'Oh no! But is it all doomed? Can you salvage it? He must have had the intention of leaving her. Maybe something happened?'

Cecilie seems conflicted, like she's holding something back. She thinks of the message Hector sent her this morning, pleading her to meet him under the Eiffel Tower, saying he'll wait for her forever, and decides to confess.

'He's flying to Paris. He wants to meet me.'

'Wow! He's coming to see you?'

'I don't know about that. He might be going to Spain. His

wife is Spanish. I don't even know whether he left her or not. Paris could be en route to Madrid... I think he's a man of grand gestures but not much else.'

'Did you ask what happened with the wife?'

Cecilie carries the tray from behind the bar to the table at the end of the empty cafe and sits on the wooden chair facing her friend.

'Look at me, Grethe! I'm thirty. I've spent more than five years wasting my time on him. Look at how your life has progressed. I can't drag my heels waiting for something that isn't going to happen. Not any more.'

'But aren't I the poster girl for overcoming those hurdles? Look at Abdi! He's a refugee. "Too brown" for our country. "Probably a criminal in his homeland." Remember my mum's reaction?'

Cecilie remembers. And laughs. Grethe's mother Mette is not as progressive as Karin. When she first met Abdi, she inspected his faraway face as if he were an alien. For the first time in weeks, a beautiful burst of laughter lights up Cecilie's face.

'Abdi crossed continents to make a life here, with me, despite the hurdles we had to jump. It *can* work. And look at the fruits of it!' she says, patting her feeding baby on her swaddled bottom. 'The Mexican – Hector – is coming to Europe and he wants to meet you?'

'Yes. Tomorrow. Apparently. It could be bullshit.'

'It could be amazing, Cecilie. Go to Paris. Meet him.'

Cecilie feels hot and terrified at the prospect of an impromptu trip to another country. She's spent thirty contented years in Norway; her imagination has always provided her with escapades and adventures. The thought of going on one in real life makes her freeze at the table and her eyes glaze over.

'Cecilie? Cecilie?'

The bell above the door rings as a tourist couple enter, bringing Cecilie back into the room. Grethe feels relieved.

'At least meet him, so you can look into his eyes. Touch him. Hear him out.'

The thin fair hairs on Cecilie's arms stand on end.

Cecilie nods, then takes a big sip from her cup of hot chocolate and rolls down her sleeves.

'But if he's coming tomorrow, you must hurry – you have to get a connection in Oslo. You'd need to move fast.'

Cecilie stands slowly and looks at the couple at the door. 'Table for two?'

50

2 JANUARY 2019, PARIS, FRANCE

Lines snake around the four bronze legs of the Eiffel Tower. Excited faces from far away shuffle and smile. Hector Herrera stands next to the *pilier nord*. He chose that corner as it was the least crowded and had the shortest queue. Not that he's planning on going up it today; he just wanted a comfortable vantage point, so he could see the spot in the middle, which is surprisingly empty but for a few photographers peeping up the tower's iron girdle.

Hector stands on his own, leaning, surveying the throng of people around him who are looking at maps or taking selfies or sipping hot coffee in a queue or huddling together in the bleak and bitter cold of a grey day they will never forget. He inhales the sweet and earthy scent of chestnuts roasting in a metal pan nearby and pulls his revolutionary's cap down low over his eyes. He rubs his gloves together as if he's standing at a campfire. He observes.

Midday, under the Eiffel Tower, in the middle.

Hector pulls up the cuffed sleeve of his fleece-lined military jacket. He had to borrow it from Ricky because Ricky had been to the Rockies a few years ago; Hector didn't even own a coat. He looks at his watch and feels like a child in fancy dress; a boy on an adventure, like the cover of *TinTin Au Tibet* he picked up yesterday from a vendor on the Rive Gauche.

12.30 p.m.
I'll wait.
She's not there.

51

3 JANUARY 2019, PARIS, FRANCE

Lines snake around the four bronze legs of the Eiffel Tower. Excited faces from far away shuffle and smile. Hector stands at the *pilier est*, just in case the *pilier nord* was unlucky. He waited for five hours there yesterday. At first, he was wide-eyed and vigilant, looking up at every lone woman who crossed the centre circle under the Eiffel Tower, weighed down by hope and expectation as beautiful and as heavy as the wrought-iron latticework in the sky above his shoulders. As the hours passed, Hector started to recognise people exiting their aerial adventure, having seen them when they joined the back of the queue what seemed an age earlier, and he became more cavalier in his watch. More accepting that she wasn't going to come. So he lost himself in Hergé's *ligne claire* and hoped that, on the tiny off chance she would turn up, she would seek him out, sitting on the floor, leaning against a concrete pillar, reading about adventures in an even colder world than this.

The view from the east pillar looks slightly different and he can't smell the chestnuts from here, or perhaps the *marrons* man isn't out yet. But at midday, Hector looks at his watch, removes and replaces his cap, and leans. Waiting. Observing.

A family from the New World, carrying balloons and backpacks, stand under the empty vacuum of the tower's skirt and laugh before their balloons pass, and Hector sees a woman in the middle, with bewildered eyes, and gets up off the floor.

It's her.

Brown hair tied into a low ponytail, a fringe now, but her round eyes look as nervous as they did more than twenty years ago.

'*Güera!*' Hector shouts, straightening the strap of his hessian messenger bag as he walks across to greet her. He opens his strong arms wide, and Kate blushes and laughs.

He's even more handsome than she remembered.

Not the *flaco* skinny boy she first met in the orphanage that summer they painted the whole thing over. The kids were staying in Coatepec while Kate and the local boy, former inhabitant of the Villa Infantil De Nuestra Señora, Hector Herrera, were charged with painting the walls varying shades of white and terracotta. Hector was studying fine arts at the university campus across town, and painted frescoes and murals to lift the décor. Kate remembers how much of the summer she spent gazing up at him, watching as he straddled a wooden plank between two ladders, tongue poking out from the corner of his mouth as he concentrated on his art. How she gazed up at him as he straddled her in her accommodation – but only when her kindly hosts were away by the coast.

The skinny shoulders of a younger boy are now broad. That warm earthy-brown skin looks a little tired and pallid under a bitter Parisian sky. But he is unmistakably Hector. His face is so handsome; his cinnamon-flecked eyes are as impassioned and as playful as Kate remembers. A youthful brown curl peeps out from under his cap at his temple, reminding Kate that he is four years her junior as she smooths down her home-dyed hair. Ricky's fleece-lined army-surplus jacket is buttoned up to the neck and Hector looks *cold*. Kate lowers her reddening face into the neck of her dark blue duffel coat as he approaches, her nose knocking the top brown toggle, and even though Hector can't see Kate's mouth, he can tell she is smiling.

'Hello, you,' Kate says, falling into his arms. They hug tightly and she loses her breath in his jacket, his chest, his heart. As Hector squeezes Kate tight, she feels self-consciously thicker set. She knows she's curvier than when Hector last saw her, when she fled Mexico a week early, heartbroken but braced and ready to start her graduate job at Digby Global Investors. Her hips have since borne three children, and as Hector releases Kate from his embrace, she tugs at the waistband of her polyester trousers, and then looks up.

Their eyes lock. The apples of Kate's ruddy English cheeks rise as she feels nothing but warmth for the man who broke her heart.

'It's good to see you, Hector,' she says, intrigued as to why Hector Herrera wanted to see her now, on a bleak January day, after so many years.

Why now?

'*Ay que friiiiiiiio!*' Hector laughs, shivering in this borrowed coat.

'Oh, I've forgotten all my Spanish!' Kate apologises.

'That's OK, I learned English,' Hector says, startling Kate with the ease at which he speaks it. 'Come on, let's get outta here, so crowded, *malditas turistas*.' Hector rolls his eyes and Kate laughs. She'd forgotten how easy he was to be around, a feeling she hasn't felt with anyone in so long.

'How are you? What are you doing in Paris?' Kate asks.

Hector puts his arm around Kate's shoulder and leads her away without answering. There's too much to cover; they can start somewhere warmer.

'Where are we going?' Kate giggles giddily, her wobbly voice warbling.

'I found a good *creperie* in the park down there, you hungry?'

'Not really...' Kate was too nervous to eat this morning as she got the first train to Liverpool Street and crossed to St Pancras to catch the Eurostar. She didn't even buy an almond croissant at Pret A Manger, an old favourite from her Digby days, her stomach was in such knots. 'But I'm sure I will be shortly. Crepes sound delicious.'

'*Vamos*,' Hector says, playfully pulling in Kate as they walk side by side. Her temple brushes against his chin. Kate leans in and is surprised by how comfortable she feels, how the bubbling anger, humiliation and heartache that simmered inside her for so long have gone. They snake through the crowds like careless lovers again, heading to the Champ de Mars.

52

Lines snake around the four bronze legs of the Eiffel Tower. A woman with shiny black skin jingles miniature Eiffel Towers from a large copper ring. A family of five, all with similar high cheekbones and long quilted coats, appear in the centre of the tower like Matryoshka dolls popping out of each other. A man drops to one knee and makes his sweetheart smile with a ring. Cecilie Wiig stands between four bronze feet and looks across at a gap in the crowd, her mouth wide open. She arrived a day late without telling him. To see if he really would wait forever. His beauty is breathtaking. And now she's watching him walk away, a jubilant arm slung around another woman's shoulder.

* * *

'So, let's start with the most important stuff. You have kids, right?'
'Yes! Three of them.'
'Wow, congratulations.'
Hector now walks with his hands in his pockets, happy to be reunited with his first lover; sheepish because he knows he broke

her heart. Feeling empty because Cecilie didn't come to him, but trying to put a brave face on it, as Hector always does. Kate clutches her floral bag under her shoulder because she's worried someone will snatch it. She'd heard pickpockets are rife in Paris, but she's managing to relax as they amble slowly along a dusty track within the park, the Eiffel Tower shrinking behind threadbare trees in their wake.

'Two girls and a boy. I wanted to bring them to Paris, they don't go back to school until tomorrow... but not one of them wanted to come.'

'Really? Wow.' Hector is baffled.

Kate isn't sure if Hector is surprised that she has three children or that none of them wanted to come to Paris, which makes her realise she doesn't actually know him very well. But she witters along to fill any confusion.

'I know, mad, hey? My girls are almost teenagers. And my boy wasn't interested unless I took him to see PST or something play.'

'PSG,' Hector says, correcting her.

'Pardon?'

'It's PSG. Paris Saint-*Germain*.'

Hector laughs a fond laugh. The sort of laugh that shows he's really tickled by something. That old familiar life-and-soul laugh reminds Kate that she *does* know him. It's like that laugh never went away, but as it recedes, Hector swallows hard and realises he hasn't laughed out loud in weeks.

'Do you have kids?'

'Negative.'

'I'll show you a photo of mine over lunch.'

* * *

Hector and Kate sit on green wrought-iron chairs under the striped awning of an open-sided creperie. A waitress with yellow hair and fuchsia lipstick puts two cans of Coke on the table with a thud.

'So I was surprised to get your message. You wanted to... to "make things right",' says Kate as she rips the white paper case from her straw and fumbles to insert it into the can. Hector's earthy eyes widen with humility. 'It's OK, Hector, as you can see, I did manage to get over you.' Kate's cheeks flush a shade of flirty and she surprises herself.

Hector softens the tension with a joke. 'You didn't call your son Hector?'

'No, sorry. He's Jack.'

'Jack...' Hector ponders how it sounds. 'I like it. Like *Samurai Jack*?'

Kate doesn't get it so she just agrees with him as she sips in brown bubbles that dance in her mouth. She didn't realise how thirsty she was. Her face becomes more serious, her eyes earnest.

'I met George, my husband, well, at the end of that summer I suppose.'

'Did you get my letters?'

'Yes, but I didn't know what to say.'

'Well, there was nothing to say I guess. I was a dick. Which is why I wanted to apologise for being a dick. Turns out I carried on being a bit of a dick for quite a long time, but I'm trying to put all that right. I finally grew up.'

'I'm sure you haven't been a dick,' says Kate with kind eyes. 'Very good use of English by the way.'

'Thanks. I watch a lot of English TV. "Sits com", I think you call them.'

'*Sit*coms.'

'OK, sitcoms.' Hector smiles, finding the comedy of the situation he's in quite heartening; it's helping him to forget the pain of Cecilie's silence, her absence.

Kate is tickled and the lines around her eyes crease. 'Which sitcoms?' she asks. She can't imagine Hyacinth Bucket or Margot Leadbetter using the word dick.

'Oh, you know... *The Young Ones. Bottom. Blackadder*. I learned from the best. I can now call you a twat, a tosser, a codswalloping imbecile. And a bellend. But I won't,' he says, chuckling.

'Thanks!' Kate laughs. 'Perhaps you didn't grow up!' She lowers her face back into the neck of her duffel coat. It's too cold and the creperie is too open to the elements to get comfy, but she hopes melting ham and cheese will soon warm her up. 'I always get a Christmas card from Sister Miriam – she said you got married last year.'

Hector's sweep of thick lashes look downcast towards his can. 'Yes, I got married.'

Kate can't help but feel a pang of disappointment, which she knows is ridiculous.

'So where's your wife?'

'She's in Spain.'

'Gosh, a European tour for *Los Herrera*.'

'Very good,' Hector says. 'You didn't forget *all* your Spanish...' The waitress with the yellow hair places two plates on the table with a clatter. Kate looks around for cutlery. 'But no. No grand tour. Pilar's Spanish. And she's kinda my ex-wife, so she's staying in Spain. She went back to her family.'

'Golly. Sister Miriam didn't say anything about that.'

'I guess not!'

'I'm sorry.'

'It's OK, it's for the best. Here, let me get *cubiertos*...'

Hector stands, solid and strapping, looking for the waitress, who's disappeared, so he can sort out the cutlery situation. He calls out to the back of the open kitchen and the waitress reappears begrudgingly, already knowing what she's being summoned for, with two sets of knives and forks each wrapped in a thin white serviette.

'*Merci*,' Hector says with a roll of a Mexican tongue as he sits back down. With one tiny gesture, Hector has managed to make Kate feel protected in a way George never has. Butterflies rise in her stomach. She smiles and unravels her cutlery from its napkin. She feels like a teenager on a date, then remembers these most curious of circumstances.

'So... your ex-wife is in Spain and you're in Paris. What are you doing here? I'm sure you didn't come all this way to meet me, just to say sorry for being a "dick", a "tosser" or a "codswalloping whatever-it-was", about that one night twenty-something years ago.'

'Imbecile,' Hector says soberly.

'I barely even remember what happened,' Kate lies. 'Until I got your message anyway. It was so out of the blue.'

Kate will never forget how it felt to be publicly humiliated by the teenage boy she had resisted falling for because she suspected he might be the type to break a girl's heart. She will never forget how proud she felt to stroll under the arches of the Palacio de Gobierno with Hector Herrera's arm around her. How it felt to be stopped in the street by everyone Hector knew, all pleased to meet his English *güera*. She'll never forget that feeling of being taken for a fool. The girls laughing at her in the reflection of a ladies' bathroom mirror; making her run out of a bar, out of a town, out of a country, because Hector was kissing their friend Dani and not the *gringa güera*, wherever *she* came from.

'So why now? Why here?' Kate takes another bite of her crepe.

'I came for love.'

Kate stops. Hot cheese melts in her mouth. She was about to put down her cutlery and get the family photo out of her wallet and show it to Hector. The pride in her daughters. The cuteness of Jack. But now a bombshell. Hector Herrera has come to Europe to tell her that after all these years, he's in love with her. Kate Wheeler. She swallows hard, knowing she can't eat any more. Her stomach is flipping.

All this time.

'Gosh, Hector. I don't know what to—'

'I know, right? I've fallen in love with a girl I've never met before.'

To her surprise, Kate's heart sinks like a stone from her ribcage to her belly.

'I came to Europe to meet her, but she doesn't want to meet me. She didn't turn up.' Hector's strong shoulders droop.

'Oh, how ghastly. I'm sorry.' There are a million reasons Kate feels sorry, but she can't quite put her finger on any of them. Mostly she's sorry for Hector. 'So am I your plan B?' she asks, trying to lift the mood, her eyes involuntarily filling with water. She picks up her Coke, discarding the straw on the table, so she can use the can to obscure her face.

The past forty-eight hours have totally exhausted Kate. Two nights ago, she stood at the ironing board while George sat on the sofa, again, legs stretched out on the pouffe in front of him, again, beer in one hand, again. As Kate ironed George's work shirts and the kids' uniforms ready for their return to school, he kept looking at his phone as he watched *Horizon*. Then she plucked up the courage to tell him.

'I'm thinking I might go to Paris myself, on Thursday perhaps. Just for the day...'

'You've still got this silly little Paris idea in your head?' scoffed George as a text beeped on his phone. Water bubbled furiously beyond a clear window in the iron and steam burst through limescale-clogged holes in its base.

'Well, the kids don't want to go, you don't want to go... so if you don't mind entertaining them for the day. I'll be leaving on the first train to Liverpool Street. My Eurostar is at 7.55 a.m.' Something in Kate felt triumphant about being so bold. The iron stopped fizzing.

George let go of his phone and it fell onto the leather cushion next to his thigh.

'You've actually booked it then? Have you gone completely mad?'

Kate finished the sleeve of George's pale blue shirt with force and stood firm.

'I should get back into St Pancras just before nine; home by eleven or twelve. There are pizzas in the freezer...' she said as she walked out of the front room with George's shirt hanging on her finger, ready to be hung up on his side of the mirrored wardrobe.

Now she's here, in Paris, feeling second best again: to a woman Hector Herrera's never even met, to his ex-wife in Spain, to George's phone, to Antonia Barrie...

'No! I wanted to see *you*, Kate. I wanted to see you both, it just hasn't gone completely to plan...' Hector removes and replaces his cap ready for a candid confession. 'I know I blew it with you, but you were the first. You were the girl who taught me to broaden my horizons a little. That there was this exciting world beyond the ceiling of the Villa Infantil, beyond Xalapa. The art, the music from another world. You were my first lover...'

'I was your *first*?'

But everyone loved Hector, and Hector so loved to be surrounded by friends, by women. Kate had assumed the twinkle of his eye and the agility of his body came from experience.

'Yes. You changed the course of my life – and I was just an asshole to you. So, all these years later, here I am, saying sorry to you for being such a... a... codswalloping imbecile.'

Kate giggles.

'And that I hope you can find it in your sweet heart to forgive me.'

Kate's mouth purses and she looks flattered.

'I forgive you, Hector,' Kate says with fondness. How could she not? He'd travelled halfway across the world and sought her out just so he could say sorry. 'And doesn't every encounter we have change the course of our life? Big or small, every relationship can have a profound effect.' Kate thinks back to the autumn she got together with George: the aftermath of her humiliation and heartbreak; leaving the shame behind across an ocean; a nice reliable English boy on the graduate trainee programme; his very beige family in the West Country; a wedding and three children without stopping to question if that's what they actually wanted...

She looks from her empty can up to Hector and feels a familiar tingle of excitement, unleashing a wash of clarity as she realises something: she never felt the butterflies or excitement in half a lifetime spent with George as those she felt in a few short weeks decorating the orphanage with Hector Herrera.

'Thank you,' he replies, with brooding brown eyes. 'I felt so terrible for so many years, when really I wanted to say sorry, and thank you – I have nothing but gratitude to you, and I guess I wanted to tell you that.'

'OK, well, you're welcome. Thanks for toughening me up in the ways of men!' Kate counters with a self-conscious laugh. She doesn't feel entirely grateful but knows that without Hector, there wouldn't be Chloe, Izzy or Jack.

All these confessions make Kate feel a bit uncomfortable.

George would never tell her how he was *actually* feeling. This is all so strange. So Kate goes into mother mode, to help herself as much as Hector.

'So. Where is the girl you fell in love with and why didn't she come to meet you? I made the effort to come all the way from England! I hope you appreciate that.'

'I do,' Hector says, laughing. 'But she lives in the Arctic Circle.'

Kate laughs, thinking it's a joke, then realises it isn't. 'Gosh. That beats England. Where in the Arctic Circle?'

'Norway.'

'Arctic Norway isn't very near Paris, you know that, right?'

'*Sí*, I know! We had spoken about meeting in Paris before. She once said that if I ever made it to Europe, she would come find me. Meet me halfway, so to speak. *Entendido?*'

Kate, sitting in a creperie cafe on the Champs de Mars, understands.

'So *why* didn't she come? Does she not feel the same way?' Kate asks nervously.

'I thought she did... but I let her down, so she's pissed at me. Sorry, pissed *off*.'

'Hector!' Kate groans.

Hector knows his story is going to take a while, so he orders two beers from the waitress and over the course of an hour, he tells Kate about Pilar. How their marriage crumbled. How he fell in love with someone he's never met before. And his eyes are so full of love and passion and conviction and warmth that Kate forgets she's in another country with a man she doesn't truly know. She forgets how out of character it was of her to go to Paris on a whim, to drink beer at two in the afternoon. She gets lost in his story, his eyes. Kate's never heard a man talk more openly and purely about love, or anything else for that matter.

Hector shows Kate a photo of Cecilie on his phone. She is struck by her beauty and hit by a feeling of inadequacy.

'Goodness, Hector, she's beautiful.'

'I know.'

'Right then,' she says, warmed by the beer, taking off her duffel coat and rolling up the sleeves of her jumper. 'What's your plan?'

'I don't know, I don't have one. I sent her message after message, telling her I'd be under the Eiffel Tower yesterday. She got them, but she didn't reply. And she didn't come. I blew it. I don't know what to do. What can I do?'

Kate studies the despair on Hector's face. It's so different from the youthful confidence he exuded when they were together in Mexico, it doesn't feel right. She is compelled to find a solution, and she finds one quickly.

'Hector, it's so obvious.'

'What?'

'Go to Norway.'

'What?'

'Go to Norway. Go find her.'

'But clearly she doesn't want to see me. She won't answer my messages, my calls... She might not even be there,' he says, knowing that this is unlikely.

'Go see her. I'll help you book a flight or do whatever it takes. I've *been* her, Hector. The truth is, if you would have come to me, explained that you were foolish, looked at me with the same conviction in your eyes as you just showed then, I would have embraced you. All our lives might have been different.'

'I couldn't come to England, I had no money.'

'Hector, you didn't come to England because you didn't feel like this about me. That's fine! What I'm saying is, go to her. Turn up. If she feels half what I felt about you, she will look in your eyes and it will all be OK. I promise.' Kate's cheeks turn red and blotchy like a cox's orange pippin.

Hector's eyes widen. 'You think?'

'I know. You've come this far. Don't blow it now.' Hector shivers and wraps his arms around his ribcage. 'Get your phone out again. Find an airline. Arctic Norway, you say? What's the town called?'

'Tromsø.'

Kate taps furiously into her own phone. 'T-r-o...?'

'M-s-o. *Sí*, Tromsø.'

'Right, it has an airport. Look, Norwegian fly there, via Oslo. Book yourself one of those. And then let's get you some thermals. You think Paris is cold...'

53

Kate's doughy bottom sinks and splays onto a small cubed seat in the departures lounge at Gare Du Nord. A quiet couple wearing his-and-hers Karrimor coats look at her disgruntledly while she doesn't notice. She places a plastic bag from the gift shop on the floor between her tired feet and checks the boxes are sitting horizontally within. Eight Fauchon macarons for each daughter, a weighty Paris Saint-Germain keyring for Jack.

I hope they like them.

She smiles to herself, but her smile soon fades. The black pleather cubes remind Kate of where her children sit in the shop where they try on school shoes, and she remembers the drudgery of the week ahead: back to school, back to the routine, back to the PTA and the WI.

I never want to see her again.

She thinks how different this one day in her life has been.

What a day.

This morning, Kate breathed a nervous but invigorated sigh as she left the house and got into a taxi even before George woke up. He'd taken two whole weeks off work over Christmas, as some kind of marriage-saving, dedicated-dad gesture, although Kate found his skulking about the house, watching Bond films or looking at football results or whatever it was he was looking at on his phone, actually more of a hindrance than a help to their marriage. Christmas felt like forced fun, and she'd so been looking forward to it. But when the day came, and the table was laid with all the trimmings, Kate realised that the most exciting thing about Christmas was the message she had received out of the blue from Hector Herrera. The kids weren't grateful for their presents. George wasn't even interested in the idea of an impromptu trip to Paris.

Kate takes the copy of *Hello!* magazine from her handbag and looks at the beauty guru's Swiss chalet retreat, but all she can think of is Hector Herrera. His warmth. His forlorn face. How protective his arm felt around her. What a day they had had. After crepes, Cokes and beers in the Champ de Mars, Hector and Kate walked along the Seine and crossed over a bridge so they could marvel at the wrap of water lilies in the Musée de l'Orangerie. Then they ambled to Galeries Lafayette to buy long johns (a new English phrase for Hector, which tickled him) and eat steak frites in the cramped cafe before Hector saw Kate off in the chaos of the train terminal. 'Go find her,' Kate said as she clasped the artist's soft hands.

Hector nodded and planted a kiss on Kate's left cheek before wrapping his arms around her.

Kate can feel Hector's kiss lingering as she looks up at the departures board and doesn't touch her face. Such a perfect day. She feels a burst of pride. For being the adventurous girl she once was again. For coming all the way to Paris on her own. For meeting Hector. For finding her own strength and power. For telling Hector what to do, and how, in turn, Hector made her realise what she had to do.

As Kate looked deep into Hector's impassioned eyes in the creperie, and saw how much he loved a woman he'd never met, she realised the power of love, and that empowered her. She closes the magazine on a TV actress's winter wonderland wedding and gathers her shopping bags ready to board. She takes a deep breath and exhales with a peculiar smile. The couple in the Karrimor coats look irked because they have to let her pass again. She senses their frustration, but for once she doesn't apologise. It doesn't bother her. She is so focused on what she needs to do she doesn't care. She knows that she will get off at St Pancras and get the Circle Line to Liverpool Street. She'll make the last train home to Claresham. She will put her keys in the bowl on the telephone table and she will climb the stairs in the silent house and get ready for bed. As she closes her eyes, she knows it will be the last time she looks at George's white, moley back and spindly spine, and she will fall asleep. Tired but resolute. In the morning, she will ask George to move out, and, as she rises to board the train, she knows she will be OK.

54
JANUARY 2019, PARIS, FRANCE

Cecilie stares at a black curved rectangle floating above a red curved rectangle, framed in oil the shade of heartache. Her grey feather-down coat is slung over her bag in the warmth of the gallery, her jumper sleeves rolled up. She feels as solemn and as tragic as the artist must have intended. The room is crowded, but people come and go, buzzing and blurring around static Cecilie as if they're in fast motion. Still she stares, seeing depths of black and red emerge from the wall in front of her. Jumping out and screaming at her. The painting is a thing of frightening beauty and she can't take her eyes off it. She stands anchored, fixated, waiting to see what else emerges from the picture. Surprised that it hasn't taken her away to another place. Wondering if perhaps she has lost the ability to.

A schoolgirl knocks into Cecilie and doesn't say sorry as she rushes past the picture to catch up with her friends. Cecilie's left knee bends and jerks with force and she has to straighten herself sharply to prevent herself falling over. The painting's spell is broken.

Cecilie looks into her bag obscured by her slung coat and fumbles for her Paris guidebook.

Where next?

She ponders the map and decides to walk through the 2nd and 9th arrondissements to the Basilica of Sacré-Coeur, to really earn the baguette she hopes to find in a Bohemian cafe there. The air will do her good after three hours in the Pompidou.

I can't feel any lonelier than I already do.

As Cecilie slowly and gently makes her way out of Salle 29, she doesn't see Hector Herrera enter the room from the opposite corner behind her, ready to be struck by the painting Cecilie was just mesmerised by.

Hector doesn't notice the girl with the short white-blonde hair swept across her sad face, leaving the room. Just like he didn't see her at the top of the escalator when he was at the bottom, gazing through the Perspex tunnel out to the rising vista of Paris, wondering how on earth he could convince Cecilie Wiig to hear him out; whether he should take a chance on Arctic Norway, or stop being crazy and just get his flight back to Mexico.

55

JANUARY 2019, TROMSØ, NORWAY

A woman resembling a woollen Womble ambles into the Hjornekafé, blinded by snow and steam. She is followed by her faithful and abiding husband.

'Uff!' announces Gjertrud with a chuckle as she starts to unravel the layers that reveal her ruddy face. 'That wind is biting!'

Cecilie looks to the door and smiles as she tucks her pen behind her ear, pinning her hair into place as she does. She looks back at the family of four from Norway, but not from this way, and tells them that their soup will take just a minute.

The mother at the table nods and smiles and remembers to ask for more bread for her ravenous teenage son.

'Sure,' says Cecilie, smiling. 'Anyone else want extra bread? Or we have these tasty cheesy pinwheels on the counter you might like. They go brilliantly with the broccoli soup.'

The mother cranes her neck and widens her eyes.

'I'm OK,' says the husband, not looking up from his guidebook.

'I'll have one, please,' says the excited teen daughter.

'Just bread,' grunts her brother.

'Two pinwheels,' says the mother as she smiles at her daughter opposite and licks her lips.

'Of course.'

The family wouldn't know it from her serene face, but Cecilie is somewhat flummoxed inside. All holiday season it's been hard to predict whether the Hjornekafé would be heaving, or whether it would be empty. Some days Cecilie was able to sit down and chat for hours to Grethe while bouncing baby Ahyana on her knee; others, she was rushed off her feet with tourists spending their Christmas in search of the Northern Lights. Luckily, Cecilie was able to call upon Stine to cover her for that ridiculous little jaunt to Paris, and Henrik is back from spending the New Year in Swedish Lapland and is in the kitchen, keeping an eye on the soup. Cecilie is busy juggling bowls, plates, cups and menus, but it's all a welcome distraction.

She nods towards Gjertrud and Ole's usual table at the end, to indicate to take a seat, even though they were already shuffling towards it. A man in a suit eats fish pie at a small table against the smaller window that looks out onto to the side street that leads down to the port; honeymooners from Australia lace their fingers together at the table along from him.

Ole takes off his woolly hat but doesn't fluff up his matted hair. He has a twinkle in his currant-sized eyes.

'How was Paris?' asks Gjertrud excitedly as she peels off each layer from her round frame and places it on the wooden chair next to hers in the corner. It's an elaborate performance.

They knew I went?

'Let me just take that couple's order, I'll be one second,' says Cecilie, grateful to buy herself some time.

She goes over to the Australians. They want what the man in the suit is having.

'Fish pie?' says Cecilie. Her smile makes her cheekbones rise, but it doesn't reach her eyes.

'Yes, two of those, please, and two cups of coffee,' says the husband, twisting his new wedding ring around his finger proudly, awkwardly, not yet used to wearing it.

'And two glasses of tap water,' says his wife, without taking her eyes off her husband.

'Won't be long,' says Cecilie, nodding and walking back to the kitchen to give Henrik the order. She returns to the front and wipes down Gjertrud and Ole's table, aware that their expectant eyes are following her every move. 'Oh, Paris was OK,' Cecilie says, shrugging as she pushes the last of the cake crumbs onto the floor.

'Just OK?' a shocked Ole says. 'Paris is the greatest city in the world!'

Paris didn't feel like the greatest city in the world to Cecilie, but she doesn't want to disappoint such nice people. She stops wiping the table and looks up, reassurance pouring from sad green eyes.

'It was beautiful. I had a wonderful time. I walked and walked.'

'Well, if those boots didn't have holes in before...' says Gjertrud, laughing, looking down at Cecilie's DMs with more affection than Karin has for them.

'Luckily, they're sturdy. Got me around all the galleries I wanted to see.'

'And your friend?' asks Ole, expectantly, tiny eyes widening.

Gjertrud hits Ole with her glove and calls him a silly man under her breath, but it's Cecilie who feels winded.

She knows.

'I had a wonderful time,' Cecilie repeats with a wan smile. 'I'll be right back to take your order.'

One pot of tea. One coffee. One slice of cake. Two forks.

And another slice of cake in ten minutes' time.

'I'm just going to help Henrik...'

Henrik walks out of the kitchen with the bread and pinwheels for the family, ruining Cecilie's excuse for taking cover.

Gjertrud changes the subject. 'Ah...' She laughs, looking up at the chalkboard next to the counter. 'Broccoli today, Henrik?'

'*Ja*, broccoli.' He nods while he places the extra bread and warmed cheesy pinwheels in front of the family.

On the other side of the glass façade, in the biting wind and sideways snow, Grethe walks along the path, past the length of the window as she approaches the cafe, Ahyana strapped to her chest. In each hand she carries boxes of cakes made by her mother, carefully balanced as if her baby is the centre of the scales; the centre of her universe. Grethe looks down at black eyelashes, downcast over sleeping eyes but still peeping out from under a knitted hat, and she smiles at her daughter, whose arms jolt as Grethe brushes into the arm of a man on the pavement.

'I'm so sorry,' says a voice from a faraway land. Yet another tourist who was looking up at the sky and not where he was going. The man steps into the road to let Grethe past.

'*Tak*,' she says forgivingly and nods. His eyes are comfortingly familiar.

'You want help with those?' The man gestures to the boxes. Grethe does look weighed down, by the boxes, by her baby, by the swathes of fabric under her multi-coloured woollen coat.

'No, I'm fine, thanks, this is me.' She gestures to the other side of the glass. The man walks off and Grethe lets another flurry of snow and wind into the cafe as she walks in.

Henrik rushes to help take the weight of the boxes off her hands.

'Ah!' says Gjertrud with glee, her purple cheeks sprouting. 'Baby girl, let me near you!'

Grethe hands Henrik the box in her right hand and puts the others on the counter. She looks down proudly at Ahyana, who was woken by the collision outside, and starts to unwrap her colourful woollen cocoon to show her off to Gjertrud and Ole, although Ole is more interested in the fresh delivery of cakes.

'What have you got there, Grethe?' Ole asks.

My daughter, obviously.

Grethe has to think for a second. 'Oh, the cake! Well...'

Before Grethe has a chance to unwrap the cloth of her papoose, Gjertrud has lifted Ahyana out and is enchanting her awakening eyes with jolly cheeks of a colour Ahyana hasn't seen before. They're not like her mother's cheeks, and they're definitely not like her father's, so she looks up at Gjertrud in wonder, her immense dark brown eyes and light brown ringlets poking out from under her hat.

'Not so little now, are you?' Gjertrud coos. 'Gosh, it must have been a couple of months since I saw her. Your mother says she's on solids already, Grethe? Although, in our day, we waited a bit longer...'

'Yes, she's taken well to it. Pureed carrot is a winner so far.'

Ole looks expectantly at Grethe, waiting for his answer. 'Oh, sorry, Ole, yes... There's spiced cloudberry, elderberry, chocolate... oh, and a new one – lemon, pistachio and polenta. Is Cecilie here?'

'Yes, she's in the kitchen,' says Gjertrud authoritatively. She makes it her place to know all of the goings on in the Hjornekafé.

'Well, I need to tell her about that one. Mamma said it

reminded her of Cecilie when she made it – all yellow and green.'

Henrik laughs gently as he gets two coffees and two glasses of tap water for the couple by the side window.

'I bet it's as tasty as Cecilie too,' says Ole appreciatively. Gjertrud can't hit her husband with Ahyana on her lap, but she scowls at him all the same.

Grethe is keen to see her friend, so she walks out the back into the kitchen.

A lone tourist walks through the door, stomping snow off his new hiking boots onto the coarse mat.

Henrik looks up and smiles.

'Wherever you like.' He points to the three remaining tables. The man takes the smallest, by the door, at the start of the large window façade.

'Hey,' says Grethe, taking the cake boxes with her into the kitchen, where Cecilie stirs soup melancholically. Grethe puts the boxes on top of the fridge. 'Mamma's latest creation.'

'Looks yummy,' Cecilie says, without looking up.

'It's lemon, pistachio and polenta. Mamma says it's inspired by you because it's so beautiful, all kinds of Cecilie colours...'

Cecilie tries to smile. She's grateful for the kindness, but there's a sadness stopping her.

Grethe feels terrible. Terrible for her friend, terrible that she encouraged her to go.

'You OK?' she asks, empty sling still strapped to her chest, her head tilting to one side.

Green eyes flash up, filled with water as Cecilie ladles broccoli soup into four bowls.

'I'll be OK,' she says with a blink that sends a tear tumbling. 'I feel terrible.'

'Don't! You did what a good friend should. You told me to

fight for something. To be adventurous. You said the right thing – I *did* the right thing by listening to you, by going to Paris.' Cecilie puts the bowls onto a tray while Grethe watches. 'And it wasn't all shit. Just that... minor part.' Cecilie can't get the image of Hector walking off with another woman out of her head, but she tries to raise a smile.

Grethe nods. 'Here, I'll take those out front for you...'

'Thanks, I'll put the cakes in the fridge and on display. They look scrummy,' Cecilie replies, trying harder.

Grethe takes the tray with four bowls and four spoons out to the front of the cafe to the family at the table in the middle of the window while Cecilie lifts the plastic lids on the cake boxes and marvels at the creations within. Spicy, zingy Arctic cloudberry oozes wholesome golden zestiness; the purple bubbles of the elderberries almost sparkle in situ, and the bright green burst of the pistachio against lemon yellow sponge really do reflect the colours of Cecilie's face.

The Norwegian family tuck into the broccoli soup, bread and pinwheels, Grethe joins Gjertrud and Ole to check on Ahyana, and Henrik goes over to the man in snow boots sitting by the door. Henrik can tell that, like most of their customers, he's not from round these parts.

'What can I get you?' Henrik asks, pushing his circular glasses back up his nose. 'We have a fresh delivery of Miss Mette's finest home-baked cakes...' he says, uncharacteristically talkative but in his usual quiet tone.

'Hmm, whichever cake you recommend, man, and I'll have a coffee to warm me up,' says the tourist, rubbing his hands together as if to ignite a fire.

'OK, Arctic cloudberry is our signature cake. I'll be right back.'

Henrik takes the menu from the man and puts it back in the

wooden menu holder at the end of the bar, then calls out to Cecilie.

'A slice of cloudberry for table number one.'

'Sure,' comes a voice from the kitchen.

Gjertrud lowers her voice to a conspiratorial whisper. 'Terrible news about Paris... Our cleaner works in housekeeping at the i-Scand and Espen told her...'

Grethe frowns and internally curses Espen. 'Some things aren't meant to be,' Grethe says with a shrug.

'I always thought Cecilie was a lesbian,' says Ole, holding his palms up in submission.

'Oh shush, Ole!' hisses Gjertrud, even more purple with embarrassment. She rocks Ahyana a bit faster in her arms. 'Don't be ridiculous!'

'Well, you said it too!'

Gjertrud laughs nervously and shakes her head. 'Is she sleeping through the night yet...?'

In the kitchen, Cecilie methodically slices up the cakes into squares, rectangles and triangles, depending on Mette's *way*. A neat square for cloudberry, an elegant rectangle for elderberry, a triangular wedge for chocolate, and she's not sure about the new lemon and pistachio one, so she cuts it into rectangles for now. A jigsaw of cake shapes on the stainless-steel counter of the kitchen remind Cecilie of the map of Paris she clutched to her heart for three days solid as she walked and walked. How her heart crumpled like the creased map when she saw Hector Herrera walking off with his arm around another woman, only seconds after seeing how beautiful he was in the flesh. Crumpled, sunken, embarrassed. Cake arrondissements remind Cecilie of how awful it felt there and how awful it feels now – and how mortifying it is when she has to tell people that her impromptu trip to Paris wasn't the success she'd hoped for.

As Cecilie ambled along boulevards, heartbroken and alone, she dreamed up scenarios she might be able to tell people back home, so as not to disappoint them. Not lies as such, just *imaginings*, that kept her whimsical mind company and enabled her a little escapism from her dismal reality.

There was the scenario where Hector had swept her off her feet under the Eiffel Tower, leaning Cecilie back for a sweeping kiss, before he took her off to a downbeat but oh-so Bohemian artist's apartment in the Marais to make love to her before whisking her back to Mexico.

There was the scenario where Hector didn't turn up at all, but it didn't matter because Cecilie had already fallen in love at first sight with a mime artist in the Tuileries, just on eye contact and hand signals alone.

And then there was the scenario where Cecilie had got to Paris, but decided *not* to go to the Eiffel Tower. She would tell people she didn't want her happiness and her existence to be quantified by a man, so she *chose* not to meet Hector. She was a strong independent woman who loved her own company thankyouverymuch, so she busied herself walking through the galleries, along the Seine, across its bridges. Trouble is, as dreamy as Cecilie is, she always snaps back to reality. Her eyes might glaze over and her mind wanders off, but her heart is anchored in truth. She couldn't lie, even if she wanted to.

At least Cecilie only told a few people she was going to Paris; that's a consolation. There was Grethe, of course. Then Stine and Mette at the cafe while Henrik was away, Fredrik at the library, and her mother, Espen and Morten. She didn't really have anyone else to tell, so it's probably best Cecilie doesn't know that the cleaners and the housekeepers of Tromsø know that her trip has ended in heartache; that her fantasy boyfriend ran off with someone else.

But it wasn't all misery. After seeing Hector Herrera walk away into the crowd, Cecilie embraced her fledgling, independent woman and blocked Hector from her phone. Again. For good this time. She had made the bravest, boldest move of her life, to go to another country, by herself, and had been made a mockery of. So she had to make the best of it and throw herself into Rothko, Braque and Picasso at the Pompidou; croissants and coffee in the cafes of Montmartre. It was a beautiful place in which to cry.

Cecilie hears Henrik battling it out with Gjertrud and Ole over one and a half slices of cake and almost raises a smile to herself as she cuts through colours of bright orange, soothing cream and flecks of warm brown spice. She puts a square onto a vintage floral plate sitting on a tray and opens the freezer door to take out a tub of Grethe's blackcurrant ice cream. Absent-mindedly, Cecilie curls a quenelle to accompany the cake, before taking it through to the front. She picks up the coffee Henrik has made on the bar and places it on the tray.

A man sits by himself at the table by the door, leaning into the window as he scrolls through pictures on his phone. Cecilie sees the man's phone and wonders what he's looking at as his thumb caresses the screen.

'Here you go...' Cecilie says, placing the plate and the coffee down on the table in front of the gentleman.

'*Gracias, querida,*' the man says as he removes his military cap and looks up with molten eyes.

Cecilie gasps. 'It's you.'

'It's me.'

Cecilie's heart starts pounding out of her chest; her pale cheeks flush pink. Hector stands. He is taller than he looked under the Eiffel Tower. His shoulders, which had seemed smaller and less proud than Cecilie had imagined, are now wide and strong as he stands in front of her wearing his friend's coat, not warm enough for the Arctic blast outside.

Cecilie puts her hands to her mouth and looks into Hector's eyes. They are so familiar even though they have never met, that she sees *home* in the dots of cinnamon and spice. The beat of her heart regulates; she takes a deep breath and lowers her hands. Hector touches them as she does and Cecilie gives a nervous laugh that's something between a whisper and an aria.

Gjertrud hits Ole, who hits Grethe, who hits Henrik, and they watch in silence across the Hjornekafé.

'I understand why you didn't come,' he says, sparks shooting from his hands to hers. 'I know what you must think of me. Please let me explain.'

Hector looks serious as he searches Cecilie's face for a good outcome, but he's blinded by panic and can't find his words.

Cecilie's brow furrows in confusion and she releases her hands a little.

She did go. She went all that way from the Arctic Circle to Paris. He said he'd wait forever, but he didn't even wait twenty-four hours before walking off with another woman. A woman who wasn't even Hector's wife.

Hector holds on, not letting go of Cecilie's hands.

'I was there. I was in Paris,' she says quietly. But looking at Hector's eyes, without barriers or screens or lenses, she feels calm. She knows there is an explanation.

'You were there? *No, mames...*' Hector releases Cecilie's fingers and lets out a defeated sigh.

'Yes, I came, silly. A day later...' Cecilie's amused eyes seek to comfort Hector, who lifts one hand to touch the apple of her now-pink cheek, but he flinches and withdraws it to rub at his temple.

The enthusiastic soup slurps and chatter of the Norwegian

family at the next table drown out what Grethe, Gjertrud, Ole and Henrik are aching to hear. They know he is The Mexican. Grethe recognises him as the man she bumped into outside.

'I was there. Under the Eiffel Tower. I saw you walking away with someone else.'

Hector shakes his head. He looks more serious than Cecilie imagined he would. Hector, the life and soul of Mexico, who Cecilie always thought she might be a little overwhelmed by, is standing in front of her in *her* hometown, and she just wants to comfort him and tell him it's OK.

'Kate. Kate is my friend from England. I was meeting her too. I wanted to be with *you* when I met her...'

Cecilie can tell by looking into Hector's eyes that he's speaking the truth, and that's all she needs to hear. She puts her index finger to his mouth to silence him. 'Shhhh, I was there. I've always been there; always been with you. But now you're here. It's all OK. I know it's all going to be OK. I'm not blind, I see everything so clearly.'

Her finger moves from his lip to his cheek and she touches him, marvels at his brown face. He looks into her green eyes and feels the weight of four thousand watermelons rise from his shoulders again.

Hector and Cecilie wrap their arms around each other and hide their faces in the curve of each other's neck, their bodies entwined like the graceful roots of two cherimoya trees bursting together. They inhale each other's smell and Cecilie breaks to whisper into Hector's ear.

'I see you. I *feel* you. And it's the most wonderful feeling in the world.'

Hector turns his head so his lips meet Cecilie's at her whisper, and they kiss.

'*Olé!*' shouts Ole as he leads a raucous clap. Gjertrud cheers with Ahyana on her lap, and happy tears run down Grethe's cheeks. The family of four, the businessman and the newlyweds glance up and see their waitress locked in an embrace and join in with Ole's clap.

Hector and Cecilie, oblivious to the world around them, enjoy the silence within the cocoon of their first kiss.

EPILOGUE
JUNE 2019, TULUM, MEXICO

Cecilie reclines against a smooth wall of artfully swishy concrete and looks through a crack in the white voile that hangs around her four-poster bed. She is still. She gazes out through the open cabana door to a beach beyond the path lined with bougainvillea and leafy shrubs. Palms sway gently in the soft breeze as loved ones gather on the light powdery sand, sparkling bright against the clear turquoise sea.

Alejandro stands under a cream canopy, anchored to four tall bamboo poles, billowing in the breeze. His hands sit in his pockets as he looks at the sand and listens to the chatter of women. Karin embraces Sister Miriam – they've been getting on like a house on fire since they met at dinner last night. Cecilie wishes she could lip-read as she looks at their animated faces. Grethe, blissful in her haute hippie habitat, hands Ahyana to Morten so she can lift her hair for Abdi to adjust the halter straps on her stripy multi-coloured dress. Cecilie smiles as she watches Espen fuss between the officiator and a Mariachi ensemble, and then her vision focuses on her deep-red painted toes outstretched in front of her, the same shade as the mariachis' silk ties. She doesn't think she's ever felt more relaxed in her life as the sound of distant conversation and rolling waves wash over her.

The silhouette of a figure obscures her view. Hector approaches up the path in an oatmeal suit, his white shirt unbuttoned at his chest. He walks barefoot into the cabana, sand still trickling through his toes.

He looks at Cecilie lying on the bed, sighs, and puts his hand to his chest. He feels like the luckiest man in the universe.

'*Mi amor.*'

Cecilie smiles as Hector opens the voile curtain and falls onto her in submission, breaking his fall with his elbows on either side of her.

'Careful,' she says, laughing.

Hector stops at Cecilie's belly and puts his cheek to it with a smile.

'Are we all ready?' he says, rubbing the curve of her stomach.

'They're excited, they haven't stopped dancing.'

'I'm excited... Come on, let's go,' Hector says as he puts his hands around Cecilie's to pull her up from the bed. She stands proud in an off-white dress with sheer long sleeves and a cascade of lace appliqué flowers that tumble down over her stomach into swathes at her feet. A single full peony as pale as Cecilie's hair sits at her ear, fastening her fringe into place. She looks at Hector with an impish grin and he falls to his knees, again kissing her stomach. He knows his parents would be proud of him today.

'Shall we go?' he asks, standing, looking through the open door to their family and friends, now sitting on wooden benches facing the sea.

'Yes. Let's,' Cecilie answers as she lifts a bouquet of tied peonies with one hand and Hector leads her out by the other as they walk down the path towards the shore.

Nine thousand six hundred and fifty-one kilometres away, a library door closes shut and the lights in the bright summer sky remain out of sight until winter.

* * *

MORE FROM ZOË FOLBIGG

Another book from Zoë Folbigg, *Five Days*, is available to order now here:
https://mybook.to/FiveDaysBackAd

ACKNOWLEDGEMENTS

Thank you so much for reading *Under One Sky* – I hope you loved Cecilie and Hector as much as I loved writing them. This book was first released as *The Distance* in 2018 and I was so proud of it then, as I am now. It is still an honour to travel from Arctic Norway to balmy Mexico without leaving my writing room as I reread and revisit two beautiful worlds.

Thank you readers old and new. I absolutely love hearing from you and appreciate every book read, every kind word sent to me, every gorgeous review and every Instagram story or post of support. You're the best!

Thank you to Rebecca Ritchie: best agent in the world (fact) and enormous thanks to my editor Sarah Ritherdon, warrior and queen, for everything you have done for me. We three will forever be the Axis of Awesomeness and I trust and respect you women more than you know.

Thank you to the wider team at brilliant Boldwood: Amanda Ridout you are a hero. Hayley Russell for managing this redux. Niamh Wallace, Claire Fenby, Marcela Torres, Jenna Houston and Rachel Odendaal (marketing team extraordinaire), and Jennifer Davies for the eagle eyes. And thank you Jane Dixon-Smith for the beautiful cover – my most romantic yet for sure.

To my author friends, my non-writer friends who are always such champions, and my family – thank you. You are the glue that binds and the gifs that make me giggle.

Finally, thank you to Mark, Felix, Max and Margot. You are my world.

You can follow me @zoefolbigg on all social media platforms.

Lots of love, Zoë x

ABOUT THE AUTHOR

Zoë Folbigg is the bestselling author of many novels including *The Note*. She had a broad career in journalism writing for magazines and newspapers from Cosmopolitan to The Guardian. She married Train Man (star of *The Note*) and lives with him and their children in Hertfordshire.

Sign up to Zoë Folbigg's newsletter to read the EXCLUSIVE true story of the meet-cute that led to her marriage!

Visit Zoë Folbigg's website: www.zoefolbigg.com

Follow Zoë on social media:

- X x.com/zoefolbigg
- f facebook.com/zoefolbiggauthor
- instagram.com/zoefolbigg
- BB bookbub.com/authors/zoe-folbigg
- tiktok.com/@zoefolbigg

ALSO BY ZOË FOLBIGG

The Three Loves of Sebastian Cooper

Fairytale of New York

Five Days

Under One Sky

BECOME A MEMBER OF
THE SHELF CARE CLUB

The home of Boldwood's book club reads.

Find uplifting reads, sunny escapes, cosy romances, family dramas and more!

Sign up to the newsletter
https://bit.ly/theshelfcareclub

Boldwood

Boldwood Books is an award-winning fiction publishing company seeking out the best stories from around the world.

Find out more at www.boldwoodbooks.com

Join our reader community for brilliant books, competitions and offers!

Follow us
@BoldwoodBooks
@TheBoldBookClub

Sign up to our weekly deals newsletter

https://bit.ly/BoldwoodBNewsletter